Token of Remorse

A STREETER MYSTERY

Michael Stone

WASHOE COUNTY LIBRARY
RENO, NEVADA

VIKING
Published by the Penguin Group
Penguin Putnam Inc., 375 Hudson Street
New York, New York 10014, U.S.A.
Penguin Books Ltd, 27 Wrights Lane, London W8 5TZ, England
Penguin Books Australia Ltd, Ringwood, Victoria, Australia
Penguin Books Canada Ltd, 10 Alcorn Avenue,
Toronto, Ontario, Canada M4V 3B2
Penguin Books (N.Z.) Ltd, 182–190 Wairau Road,
Auckland 10, New Zealand

Penguin Books Ltd, Registered Offices:
Harmondsworth, Middlesex, England

First published in 1998 by Viking Penguin,
a member of Penguin Putnam Inc.

1 2 3 4 5 6 7 8 9 10

Copyright © Michael Stone, 1998
All rights reserved

Publisher's Note
This is a work of fiction. Names, characters, places, and incidents either are the product of the author's imagination or are used fictitiously, and any resemblance to actual persons—living or dead—events, or locales is entirely coincidental.

LIBRARY OF CONGRESS CATALOGING IN PUBLICATION DATA
Stone, Michael.
Token of remorse: a Streeter mystery/Michael Stone.
p. cm—(Viking mystery suspense)
ISBN 0-670-87774-3
I. Title.
PS3569.T64144T65 1998 97-22193
813'.54—dc21

This book is printed on acid-free paper.
∞

Printed in the United States of America
Set in Minion

Without limiting the rights under copyright reserved above, no part of this publication may be reproduced, stored in, or introduced into a retrieval system, or transmitted, in any form or by any means (electronic, mechanical, photocopying, recording, or otherwise), without the prior written permission of both the copyright owner and the above publisher of this book.

Token of Remorse

OTHER STREETER MYSTERIES
BY MICHAEL STONE

The Low End of Nowhere
A Long Reach

To Carolyn Carlson,
a terrific friend and a great editor

The author would like to thank and acknowledge
my special best friend Lynda Ferguson,
Donald Knight, Harry McLean, Greg Rawlings,
Craig Skinner, Diane Balken and Bill Wise,
along with Brett Favre, Reggie White,
and Mike Holmgren and company.

Token of Remorse

1

When Dexter walked out the back of the Manhandler massage parlor, Richie Moats panicked and almost blew his own leg off with the .357 he was holding. Great, he thought. Why him tonight? Dexter Calley is pure mean crazy and damned near bulletproof. Part Arapahoe, part black, and just up from Nogales. Big and quick enough to play pro football in Canada for two seasons. Vicious enough to serve thirty-eight months in Oklahoma on a manslaughter beef. Luckily, they'd only met a couple of times, so he probably wouldn't recognize Richie behind his mask. Dexter glided slow and easy, a cornerback's poise in a prison-yard strut. Shoulders wide as a dashboard. He studied the alley and casually sniffed at the air. His black hair was in a luxurious long ponytail that Cindy Crawford would have envied. Although the late-March Colorado night was cool, he wore only a T-shirt and charcoal pleated dress slacks. Suddenly, he turned back to the door and nodded.

If seeing Dexter made him nervous, Richie almost had a seizure at what came next. Out into the alley strolled all five feet, five inches of Sid Wahl. Richie swallowed hard. Not that he was intimidated by Sid. But the two men had talked to each other a dozen times or more and the little man might make him, eye mask or not. What then? Killing people was definitely not in Richie's repertoire. Relax, he told himself. Like Tina had said just that morning, "If armed robbery was easy, everyone'd be doing it."

"Let's get a move on," Sid said as he adjusted the leather briefcase in his hand. "I told him we'd be back by eight."

Dexter grunted and they both turned to head toward the car. Before they could take two steps, Richie moved from behind the Dumpster. Standing firm, he waved the huge .357 blue barrel between the two. "Hold it right there!" He was relieved that his voice was deep and steady.

They stopped, although Dexter swayed a bit. Even standing still he seemed to be in motion. Richie leaned back a tad and aimed his gun squarely at the big man. "I said stop!" he yelled. Glancing at Sid, he added. "And you, drop that briefcase!"

"You got any idea who you're fucking around with out here?" Dexter asked, clearly pissed, but calm. He sized up the masked man standing about four feet away with the cannon aimed at his chest. Could he lunge and grab the barrel before the guy fired? Probably not.

"I'm sure he does or he wouldn't be here." Sid's voice was flat and he broke into quick grin. A flesh-colored Band-Aid was wrapped around the nose bridge of his horn-rimmed glasses and he squinted hard at the mask. Not much those eyes missed. "Ain't that right, Zorro?"

Richie glanced down at himself. He *was* wearing all black: shoes, sweatshirt, pants, eye mask, and fedora pulled low over his forehead. "Drop it, asshole," he said, looking up again. "And keep your hands where I can see them. Both of you." He forced his voice deeper, but Sid was boring in. Damned smile, Richie thought. Sid knows he knows me, even if he can't come up with a name yet.

Sid held his gaze for another moment before tossing the case to the ground in front of him. The alley was quiet as a coffin and the thick smell of Chinese cooking from the restaurant next to the Manhandler made it feel cramped and stale. Szechuan and garlic. On both sides, ancient brick walls the color of dried ketchup appeared to lean inward. A bare bulb over the doorway Sid had just left was the only illumination. To Richie, there was a stark, almost comical contrast between the two men standing in the dirty light. Dexter's tight physique and dark features next to Sid's squat, lumpy body stuffed into a plaid cloth coat like so much ripe produce.

"What now, hard guy?" Sid asked. He let out a soft hiccup. Whenever he got mad or anxious, that happened. Standing there with his hands raised to his shoulders, he was both. Furious with the man holding him up and nervous about the bitter fallout that would roll his way later. "Is this where we're supposed to beg you not to kill us?" His head hopped as he finished another hiccup.

"You got a big mouth for being such a little pecker," Richie said. "Whoever's got the car keys, toss them down."

Dexter Calley let out a long sigh like the whole deal was getting too tedious for words. Richie took a short step toward him and stopped. With both thumbs, he pulled back the gun's hammer, making a loud, clicking noise. "I'd hate for this thing to go off, me being so buggy and all," he said.

His voice was deliberately lifeless and it had the desired effect. Dexter reached into his pants pocket and pulled out the keys to the Lincoln. Without looking, he tossed them onto the ground next to the briefcase. Richie Moats drew them toward him with his foot. Then he squatted and grabbed them, all the while keeping the .357 on Dexter. "Let's go," he barked as he straightened up.

No one budged and Richie frowned behind his mask. "If I have to shoot you two jerk-offs every time I give an order, it's gonna start hurting after a while." Slowly, Dexter and Sid started toward the big white vehicle parked about fifteen feet in front of them. Richie stepped aside and then followed them. When they got there, the pair stopped and looked back, their faces betraying nothing.

"Move over," Richie ordered. As they did, he walked forward

and opened the trunk with the third key that he tried on the chain. Then he stepped back and motioned toward the car. "Get in!"

"What the fuck?!" Dexter shouted.

Richie raised the gun with both hands. "I'll tell you 'what the fuck,' Geronimo. Get in the trunk or you're dead. That's what."

Dexter looked at Sid, who just shrugged, so the the big man crawled into the trunk, keeping tight eye contact with Richie as he did. Sid moved forward and stopped. "Don't you want our wallets?" he asked. His head bobbed again in the tiny spasm of a hiccup. A hint of a smile was back on his face. "This *here's* a robbery, ain't it?"

Richie didn't say anything. He released the hammer on his weapon, but kept it trained on them.

"A real coincidence, us walking out with that particular briefcase just now and you being right here," Sid continued as he lowered himself next to Dexter. The two were now spooned together in scrunched-up, interlocking positions. "Yes sir. With what's in there you sure don't need our wallets."

It was Sid's way of saying he knew this was an inside job. He and Dexter were making the rounds of sex shops and massage parlors like the Manhandler, picking up a week's cash gross. Had to be at least four hundred thousand dollars stuffed into the huge briefcase. The masked man knew that the massage parlor, just off Colfax Avenue on Denver's West Side, was their last stop. He had to know: a total inside job.

Richie ignored Sid and grabbed the trunk top, about to close it.

"You're gonna regret this, pal," Sid hissed from below him. "That's a promise. You're gonna regret it like the plague."

Richie bent in closer, glared at Sid, and then pulled back. As he did, his black fedora hit the edge of the lid and slid off his head. In one harsh motion, he reached for it with his left hand. His fingers brushed hard against his temple, causing the cheap elastic string on his party mask to snap. The mask tumbled after the hat into the trunk. His mouth dropped as Dexter and Sid stared up at him. He frowned, confused and terrified, and his legs felt weak. Then he swallowed and took a step back. The best he could do was utter "Holy shit," barely above a whisper.

Sid's face flickered with anger, but his mouth quickly turned up again in a smile. "My, oh my. If it isn't little Richie-what's-his-name. Tina's friend. That's one very slick disguise. You got any idea what kind a deep shit you just stepped into, Richie boy? Any idea whose money's in that case?"

Richie was suddenly nauseated and his mouth was so dry he began moving his tongue around furiously to work up some saliva. But his voice stayed even. "Well, seeing as how I'm the one with the gun, I guess it's mine." His eyes bulged with stress. "Organ-grinder, Dago eyes," his uncle used to tease him when he was a kid. Large, intense, and almost black. Same color as his mustache and the mop of curly hair that now dangled freely around his face.

"Clever boy," Sid shot back. "Too bad dead men don't get to spend their money. You might as well kiss your sorry ass goodbye right now, Richie." He paused. "Jesus, who'd a thought you had the stones to pull a move like this? I always pegged you for a queer or something like that."

Richie put his left hand on the trunk top, his body swaying for a moment. His stomach twitched in violent nausea and he squinted to focus. He could feel the sweat forming over his eyes and he quickly ran the back of his gun hand across his forehead. What the hell was his move now? The gun seemed to weigh about a hundred pounds and it almost fell from his hand. Say something, do something. But what? Sid and Dexter were glaring hard at him and he knew they were thinking of lunging out. Richie pulled his head back and managed to steady his .357, moving it slowly and evenly between the two men. His mouth was so dry by now he wasn't sure he could say another word. He glanced down at the party mask and hat resting on Sid's legs and just that quick motion of his head caused the nausea to flare.

Suddenly he spoke, his words sounding thick and tentative. "We'll see who's the queer." Then, before he even realized it was happening, Richie's body shuddered wildly and he vomited straight out his mouth and nose, all over the two men. They jolted upright screaming, with Dexter crashing his head on the trunk frame. Then they fell back to their original positions, both swearing so broadly that Richie couldn't make out what they were saying. With his left hand, he jerked the trunk lid closed.

As he took a step back, wiping at his mouth with his free hand, he could hear the two men groaning loudly and banging into the sides and top of the trunk. Almost against his will, he smiled as he thought of that extra helping of pasta in white wine and clam sauce he'd had for dinner. "Enjoy," he said toward the car, his grin widening.

When he got back to his Chevy Blazer, he jumped in and quickly drove east. It would probably take Sid and Dexter hours to get free and they wouldn't be thinking all that clear once they were out. Still, Richie had to get Tina fast. Their contingency plan in case something went wrong was for them to leave Colorado. Right now. They each had a suitcase packed full of clothes in the back of the Blazer. As he drove, he picked up his cell phone and called her at work.

"Get out of there," he told her when she answered. "Grab whatever we need and get the hell moving. I'll pick you up in fifteen minutes in front of Currigan."

"What happened?" Her voice stayed calm.

"Sid Wahl happened, is what. He made me. I thought you said he never did pickups."

"He was there? He doesn't . . . I mean not usually. From what I heard, he's only done that maybe twice."

"Well, make that three times," he responded. "And he was working with that psychotic Indian, or whatever he is. Calley. I 'bout wet my pants when those two came out the door."

"*Dexter?* He never makes pickups either. Almost never, anyhow. Are you sure they knew it was you?"

Richie said nothing at first. "It's a long story but Wahl ended up calling me 'Richie boy, Tina's friend.' I'd say that's a pretty good indication they made me."

"Damn," she said. "Rudy's going to want us dead for sure."

"He has to find us first. Plus, Sid and Dexter are furious. We had a little accident that's not sitting too well with them right about now. Grab that stuff and get going."

Tina looked at the phone for a long time after she hung up. Running her hand down the front of her skirt, she shook her head. They'd planned for the worst but she'd never really thought it would happen. Other than cops stumbling into the alley, Richie being recognized was about the only thing that could go wrong. Now Rudy would know for sure that she was involved. Two and two always equals four, even to an utter bozo like Rudy Fontana.

And he'd be doubly furious because she'd had a position of trust. Although only twenty-nine, Tina Gillis had worked for him for nearly four years. First as a topless dancer at one of his strip joints and later as full manager of his three massage parlors. Finally as his Gal Friday. But she never turned tricks. Didn't have to. When she was stripping, she'd make an easy twenty-five hundred a week just for shaking it up a few hours a night. All smiles and flying red hair, moving around the stage like a jungle cat, Tina seemed to just magically pull the fives and tens out of their pockets from across the room.

In her current job, she helped with the overall operation of Rudy's incredibly lucrative sex-for-sale empire scattered throughout Denver. She ran personal errands, advised him on hirings and firings, kept his appointments straight and his office organized, and was a part-time confidante. He didn't tell her everything, but she knew plenty. Like when and where the cash pickups were made.

For his part, Rudy liked Tina from the first day he met her. Oddly, the attraction was never sexual. She was much sharper than the rest of his girls: dependable and with a work ethic that would make a Japanese CEO blink. He trusted her completely. She knew that, which is what made her think she'd be above suspicion for the robbery. But all that changed when Sid recognized Richie.

Tina walked to her file cabinet in Rudy's outer office and opened the bottom drawer. Muffled downtown traffic noise from Champa Street outside the window was the only other sound. She grabbed the two fat file folders she'd been assembling over the past few months. The Denver Vice Bureau would give up doughnuts forever just to get their hands on them. They contained names, numbers, code words, addresses, and dates, along with cryptic ledgers. Also, they held a couple of dozen photos of naked middle-aged men frolicking with Rudy's girls, doing things that a Doberman in heat probably wouldn't even consider. Tina recognized several of the johns from local television and newspaper stories. These were important men. Although she didn't understand all the material, she was pretty sure that she had enough goodies to put Mr. Fontana behind bars for all eternity, plus ten. Her and Richie's life insurance policy. She stuffed the folders into her large purse and glanced around the room one final time.

"So long, Rudy," she whispered. "Thanks for the severance package." With that she walked out and headed to the nearby Currigan Exhibition Hall to meet Richie.

2

Streeter just knew that the dipshit in the fancy Saab was going to plow into his Buick. Driving slowly past the parking-lot entrance, he'd noticed that the driver, instead of looking ahead, was perched up on his Yuppie butt, one hand on the wheel, and studying his reflection in the rearview mirror. Combing his hair with his right hand as his new convertible rolled forward. Immediately after they collided, Streeter pulled over. This would really mess up the rush-hour crunch on First Avenue. He got out and glanced at his right rear quarter panel. Not much of a collision. He wouldn't even bother repairing a fifteen-year-old tank like the Buick. Just tell the Saab moron to be careful and then head on home.

"I had the right-of-way," the other driver said as he walked to the front of his car. He nodded toward the traffic light, which was now in his favor. "Look." His voice was high and whiny. "It only comes in one shade of green. That one! Yours was red."

He was maybe thirty, tanned, and well dressed. And there was a pinched-up arrogance about him that said he wasn't about to take the fall for some lumbering jerk in an *American* car. A brown one, no less.

"Those lights change color from time to time," Streeter said firmly. "You don't have to be a Supreme Court justice to figure this one out. I had the green light, and besides, you've got front-end damage and that usually means you're at fault. Which planet did you learn to drive on?"

The young man raised his shoulders in indignation and

pointed at the Buick. "The same one where you got that piece of shit."

Streeter glanced at the clogged, late-afternoon traffic. They were in front of Denver's posh Cherry Creek Shopping Mall. He shook his head. "Look, there's not much damage for either of us. Let's just forget it. Life's too short to deal with insurance claims adjusters."

The Saab guy wasn't buying any of that. He went back to his car to get paper on which to write Streeter's name and license number. He was gone a couple of minutes, and just as he returned, a Denver motorcycle cop pulled up behind the Buick and parked. The officer got off and approached them, studying the damage. "Back up into the lot," he finally said. "Both of you."

They did as ordered. Streeter was hesitant about giving the cop his license. As a bounty hunter and part-time PI, he valued his privacy so much that he didn't even have a license in his own name. When an old friend of his who looked like him had died a few years earlier, Streeter had sort of inherited his driver's license. By now, it had been renewed, with Streeter's photo. The cop silently read it: Sex: M; Height: 6′2″; Weight: 220 lb.; Birth Date: 4/22/53; Eyes: Brown; Hair: Brown. He noted the address, which used to be the friend's. When he finished, he took the Saab driver's license and clipped it to his ticket pad. Then he started writing him a citation, no questions asked.

"You *have got* to be joking," the Yuppie said. "I had the right-of-way. This clown even suggested that we leave. That must mean something."

The cop stopped writing. "It means you should have listened to him. The one with the front-end damage most always gets the ticket, pal."

When Streeter got home, he looked for his partner, Frank Dazzler. The two men lived and worked in a converted church on the fringes of Denver's booming Lower Downtown: about a mile northeast of Coors Field, where the Rockies played, and two miles due north of the downtown financial district. The old warehouse/liquor store area had been deteriorating for years. Then, in the early nineties, the new baseball field and a sharp upturn in urban real-estate values changed all that. On all sides of the ballpark, ancient brick buildings were converted to lofts, brew pubs, and restaurants, or leveled for parking lots. Those improvements hadn't reached Dazzler's Bail Bonds yet, but the down-and-dirty mood of the area around the church was shifting.

Streeter headed back to Frank's first-floor office. An ex-sheriff's deputy, Dazzler lived in the rear of the church and had a work area in the old rectory. When Streeter got there, his partner was lying on the couch across from a stained-glass window on the west wall. Frank was wearing a red sweatshirt, black running shorts, white Nikes, and plaid socks that came up almost to his knees. There was a gray towel over his face and he was asleep. A few years earlier, in his late fifties, Frank had taken up racewalking to keep his expanding waistline in check. "I'm starting to look like a duck with an eating disorder," he had told Streeter back then. "Guy my age can't let too many things go south."

Streeter wasn't surprised when Frank took up exercising for the first time in his life. Frank had been a widower since just before he moved into the church in the mid-seventies. He tended to give people long-winded lectures on the building's varied history. Built shortly after the turn of the century, the church had gone through several incarnations under different exotic Christian denominations. The two men took actual ownership of the place in the mid-eighties, when the previous owner put it up for a surety bond for his son, who subsequently fled to Mexico. Frank loved the place and planned to live there forever. He even had jumped into a romantic relationship with the owner of a feminist aerobics studio that he rented space to on the first floor. Coincidentally, that's when he started exercising. For such a tough-looking man, Frank was highly conscious of his appearance. He usually wore linen suits in summer, spring, and fall, while favoring navy and charcoal sport coats in winter. With a quick smile, thick hair, and deep blue eyes, he still cut a hell of a figure.

The bounty hunter stared at the bondsman. Frank's stomach moved up and down, regular as an iron lung. The two men had been partners for eleven years and Streeter thought of Frank as a father figure. He reached down and gently shook his shoulder. "Hey, old guy," he said. His voice was low and calm as he lifted the towel. "Wake up. It's almost time for your afternoon feeding."

Frank's head moved from side to side in confusion, his eyes remaining closed. His mouth made a smacking sound and finally he looked up. "Wha'? Feeding?" Focusing on the man bending over him, he added, "It's you. I just been out walking for over an hour. Passed everything on two legs like they were made out of cement. Go ahead with the wisecracks, but I'm probably in better shape than you are, Street." He sat up.

"I'm sure of it." Unlikely, as Streeter was a former college football player who worked out almost daily with weights in the church's basement. "You're a regular poster boy for the *Lawrence Welk Show*."

Streeter stepped back to let him get up. Frank moved to the middle of the room and, yawning, arched his back. Then he went behind the huge desk in front of the window and dropped into a swivel chair. He stared at Streeter, who was now seated on the other side of the desk. Soft pastels from the setting sun filtered through the colored window and made the room feel like Christmas.

"Stick around for a while, okay?" Frank asked. "I got a call today from an old pal. Martin Moats. We've known each other for at least a couple of centuries now. Marty's a real character from out in the middle of nowhere. A little farm town on the Western Slope. A self-made millionaire, but money or not, the guy still acts like a hick with an attitude. You can take the boy out of the country, but you can't shake the hayseeds out of Marty. God knows, his wife's tried to give him some class, but he's from the old school all the way. Usually pretty tight with a buck, too." Frank paused, pondering that. "He's coming by in a minute and he wants to talk to us. He asked that you be here."

Martin "Marty" Moats was the self-proclaimed Waterbed King of Colorado's Front Range. He owned thirty-four stores stretching from Fort Collins in the north all the way south to Pueblo. "For Sleep That Floats, See Marty Moats." The slogan jangled relentlessly over the radio and television. As his own spokesman, Moats was better known than the governor.

"What does the waterbed guy want with me?" Streeter asked.

Frank shrugged. "He didn't go into any details, but it seems he wants you to find someone. Wanted to know if you still do skip tracing." He glanced toward the door. "Ask him yourself. I think that's him now."

They could hear the church's front door open and close, followed by footsteps approaching down the hall. "Frank, what the hell kind of place is this?" Marty Moats's familiar baritone rumbled into the office. "Looks like the damned headquarters of the German High Command."

Frank rolled his eyes at Streeter and stood up. "That's our Marty. The man never had an opinion that he didn't immediately let the whole world in on." Then he glanced at the door and yelled, "In here, you old farmer."

Martin Moats had a way of taking over a room immediately. He looked slightly older and larger than on TV. More impressive, too. Barely an inch shorter than Streeter, he carried himself stiff as a surfboard and his dark gray eyes honed in on whomever he met. Although he was smiling, those eyes were serious, almost sad. He squinted into the darkening office. "Jesus, you running a gay bar in here, Frank? Colored windows and no lights. Very romantic."

Frank leaned over his desk and switched on his reading

lamp. "That any better, Marty? You been here less than a minute and already you called me a Nazi and a bunny rabbit. How does Marlene put up with you?"

Marty stiffened even more but his face and voice both softened. "I don't know, Frank. But I'm just glad she does. We celebrated our forty-sixth anniversary last week, if you can believe that."

"I can't." Frank smiled back. He took a step forward and the two men hugged. "Give her my regards, huh?" the bondsman said as he backed off.

Streeter now stood and faced the visitor. Marty glanced at him over Frank's shoulder and his smile instinctively widened. "Is this your linebacker?" he asked as Frank stepped aside and he moved in Streeter's direction. Seeing the bulk and cut-up muscles under Streeter's gray T-shirt, he added, "Looks like the Broncos could use you."

"Those days are over," the bounty hunter said as he stuck out his hand. "I'm just Frank's partner now. Streeter."

Marty nodded and grabbed his hand, shaking it with a strength surprising for a man of seventy. "I'm Marty Moats and I sell waterbeds. Exactly what do you sleep on, son?"

Streeter felt a pinch of annoyance at the sales question. "Mostly my side, but sometimes on my stomach. Frank tells me you're looking for someone."

The Waterbed King read his mood and appropriately shifted gears. "You got that right." He sat in a chair in front of the desk, pulling a thin Corona cigar and a lighter from his pants pocket as he did. His matching salt-and-pepper hair and mustache looked old-fashioned but distinguished. The mustache was trimmed tight as a worm, and it gave him the look of a Waspy Cesar Romero. He smelled of faded cologne and his stomach bubbled over his belt when he settled in. But he sat as proud as he stood. "My nephew. No one's seen him for a week or so. Not that I give much of a rip, myself. To be perfectly honest, the boy's a flake and he's not the brightest thing in long pants, either. Move the toilet over a foot or so and he'd piss on the floor. But Marlene, now, she thinks the sun rises and sets on Richie's ass."

"Is that unusual? You not hearing from him for that long?" Streeter asked as he sat in the chair next to him.

Marty fired up his cigar and studied the burning end. Then he stuck the red Bic back into his pocket and looked at Streeter. "Not really. Like I said, the kid's a flake. He usually doesn't shine around unless he wants something. But this is different." He glanced at his cigar again. "He's really in trouble this time."

He seemed lost in thought and didn't say anything for a while, so Frank spoke. "Mind telling us what makes you think that?"

Marty's eyebrows shot up for a second as he refocused on the conversation. "This morning Marlene got a call from the State Department, of all things." He exhaled smoke as he talked. "Seems they found Richie's Blazer down in Mexico, about an hour or so inland from Mazatlán. Abandoned." His voice broke for an instant. "There was blood on the side and Richie was nowhere around. They told Marlene that the damned thing'd been in the area for several days, but no one saw any gringos. It's an isolated town called San Ignacio. Americans come through there about as regular as comets." He looked hard at Frank. "And I'm sure the locals would've remembered a boob like Richie wandering around." Pausing again, he added softly, "It was the boy's blood type on the car, too."

Streeter shifted in his seat. "Did your nephew have any business that would have taken him down there?"

Marty shook his head. "Not that I know of. He's never been to Mexico before, either. But hell, even if he went down there for a vacation, that town's so far off the beaten path it wouldn't make sense that he'd end up there."

"What did they mean when they said the Blazer'd been around for a few days?" Streeter pressed.

"Now that's a hot one," Marty said, getting visibly angry.

"Seems the mayor had been squiring his mistress around town in the Chevy for a while. Looks like those greaseballs fucked up Richie and then used his car to get some trim. You believe that?"

Frank stepped in now. "Jesus, Marty. Age and prosperity sure didn't do much to soften you up. It's plain to see why you never got an appointment to the United Nations."

"Marlene comments on the same thing." Marty shrugged. "But I never saw any point in soft-coating things, even though I do try to tone down the rougher edges now and then."

Streeter spoke up. "They didn't find a body?"

"No. Nothing but the Blazer and a little blood." Marty's voice shifted back to polished and assured, like the Waterbed King's from television. "They told Marlene that the State Department is doing all it can. Now that'll make you sleep a whole chunk better at night. We called our congressman's office but I won't be holding my breath on that one, either. Pat Schroeder. She's got her own agenda. Let some lady flier get grabbed at Tailhook and Schroeder's your man. But a lost male constituent, hell, she probably won't even lift a finger."

Frank spoke. "I take it you want Streeter, here, to see if he can get a line on Richie."

Slowly, Marty tapped his cigar on the edge of an ashtray on the desk. He stared at the bounty hunter. "I want you to get down to Mazatlán and ride herd on everything for me. We're dealing with the United States government and a bunch of Mexican cops here. Between the two, they couldn't find horse-shit at a rodeo. Marlene and me want to do what we can for the boy. That means getting someone down there who knows his ass from his elbow. That means you, Streeter."

Leaning over to one side, Marty reached into his pants pocket and pulled out a roll of hundreds the size of his fist. He tossed it on the desk. "There's about five grand there, give or take. That'll get you going. There's a flight for Mazatlán leaving DIA in a couple of hours and I've already booked you a room at the El Cid. It's a luxury hotel right on the beach, but don't bother taking any tanning lotion. You'll be inland, mostly. The American consul knows you're coming. He'll set you up with an interpreter. Then get out to that damned town and squeeze the hell out of anyone who knows anything. That sound like something you can handle, son?"

Streeter liked the way the cigar smoke smelled. It gave the room a warm, homey feel. He stared at the cash and then back at Moats. "I've worked in Mexico before. If it's the local police doing the search, you might as forget you ever had a nephew. They tend to be corrupt and incompetent. State and federal cops are better but you're still talking about just a notch or two above Barney Fife. And U.S. law agencies can't do much with Mexican permission, which I'm sure they won't get."

"That's exactly why I want you down there," Marty said. He reached into his back pocket and pulled out his wallet. Taking a photo from it, he handed the picture to Streeter. "That's Richie, my brother's boy. His folks died about the time he got out of high school. Richie's thirty-two now, give or take. It'd mean a lot to Marlene if you'd spend a few days looking for him. If you need more money, just let me know. Nose around and call me every night. Collect."

"The way business has been around here lately, Street, it's not like you can turn your nose up at that kind of money," Frank said. "Plus, Marlene's one fine lady." He threw Moats a glance. "Too good for this old fart." Looking back at his partner, he added, "All those ex-wives of yours, I know at least a couple of them get alimony."

Streeter knew that between his regular expenses, his credit cards, and the stipend he paid two of his four former wives, there was no way he could turn down five thousand dollars. He studied the photo. Richie's curly charcoal hair and mustache stood out. Eyes large and intense. He wasn't bad-looking and he had the same I-want-to-get-in-your-pants grin that his uncle used on television. The bounty hunter looked up at Marty.

"We'll take it day by day. First thing tomorrow, call the consulate and let them know that as far as they're concerned, I *am* the Moats family. They shouldn't hold anything back from me. And give me all the numbers where I can reach you day and night."

"Thank you, son." Marty paused. "There is one other thing."

"What's that?"

"Richie's probably not traveling alone. He's got a girlfriend and he's convinced she burps perfume and pees champagne. The guy can barely get through the day without seeing her. No way he'd take a trip like this and leave Tina behind. She works in what you might call an exotic field. Some sort of local porno operation. Used to be a stripper, too. But I'll tell you one thing, you see Tina Gillis, you'll understand why he wants to be with her night and day."

"Anything else I should know?"

Marty shook his head. "This'll get you going. And don't worry about expenses. Just do what you have to do, son. Whatever it takes."

"Look, Marty," Streeter said, "if your nephew's alive and if he has any brains and common sense at all, he'll probably turn up at the consulate pretty soon."

Moats studied him for a moment. "Yeah, and if my aunt had balls, she'd be my uncle. You follow my drift, son?"

Streeter shook his head slowly. "I'm not sure I want to."

"It don't matter. Just get down there and find out what's going on."

3

“The trouble with Mexico,” Streeter’s father had told him years ago, “is that the Germans didn’t stay long enough.”

He’d explained to his son that in the early nineteenth century, German explorers had settled parts of Mexico but then left within a few years. In Harold’s mind that was bad news for the locals. “Those Krauts should’ve stayed longer. Laid down some of their famous order and discipline. The Mexicans themselves are good people, but nothing works the way it should down there. Nothing’s on time and nobody seems to know what they’re doing. Don’t seem to give much of a darn, either.”

The bounty hunter thought of that as he drove through the darkness from the Mazatlán airport to El Cid. He felt queasy. Streeter didn’t like to fly. It wasn’t being in the air that he minded, it’s just that he hated being a passenger. Not that he knew how to fly, but he felt best when he was steering whatever it was that was moving him. Also, he’d had three stiff Johnnie Walker Reds en route. Four, if you counted the one at the Denver International Airport bar. His stomach sure as hell was counting it as his rented Volkswagen Jetta bounced over the empty, pitted streets heading west to the beach just before midnight. All he wanted in the world was to go to sleep.

But that wasn’t about to happen quickly. When he got to his room and crawled into bed, the Scotch-induced queasiness kept him awake. After about a half hour of lying there in his boxer shorts, he got up and walked out onto the small balcony facing the kidney-shaped swimming pool. The night air felt sensuously thick and warm, and the moon seemed close enough that you could hit it with a solid five-iron shot. Oil lamps on tall metal stands flickered around the pool. As Streeter leaned into the railing he felt alone. Suddenly he heard a woman laughing down below. On one of the huge lounge chairs close to the pool, a man and a woman lay curled together, cuddling. The woman had long, dark hair and wore a red dress. Streeter couldn't see her face but her tanned, shapely legs were obvious. The man wore light slacks and a deep-blue shirt. Both appeared to be young and they were kissing and giggling. Now Streeter felt really alone.

It was a feeling he had been wrestling with more and more lately, and traveling by himself intensified it. He had a growing, gnawing sense of loss at all the time he was spending alone, without a special woman in his life. Thinking of his failed marriages and the countless flings he'd had over the years didn't help. And those flings were getting further apart and, more important, less and less satisfying. His this-pilot-flies-solo attitude had been fun and free in his twenties, but merely okay in his thirties. By now, it was getting hollow and sometimes painful.

A couple of months earlier, he had broken up with his latest girlfriend, a Denver police psychologist. That was one he thought might lead to something permanent. But she'd taken a job at a California clinic and their clunky attempt at a long-distance relationship had ended fast. Standing on his balcony now, watching the couple below, Streeter wondered if maybe he should have tried harder with her. Too late. The last time he'd talked to Linda she had sounded uninterested and even alluded to a man she was dating in Los Angeles. Neither of them had called the other since. He glanced back into his suite. Another empty bed in another strange room. No one back home waiting for him, hoping he's all right: safe, happy, sleeping well. No one to give a shit. No one but Frank and that didn't exactly count. Not in the way he needed it to count this late at night in the quiet hotel on the hazy magical beach at Mazatlán.

And there was no one on the horizon either. In Streeter's line of work, he didn't meet many keepers. Mostly just hyper girl-women with too many problems and too little time. The few quality ones he met usually worked in law offices and seemed to have husbands, fiancés, or boyfriends. Or they weren't interested. Or he wasn't.

He glanced back at the couple. They were getting up from the lounge chair now. They hugged one more time and then walked toward the rooms holding hands. Streeter stood back from the railing. Maybe a cigar would help calm him. Smelling Moats's Corona that afternoon had put him in the mood. He got dressed and went to the lobby to buy one. When he got back to his room he started pacing and smoking. To keep his mind occupied, he ran through the possibilities of what might have happened to Richie and Tina.

He knew little about Richie Moats, and less about his girlfriend. Marty had said his nephew had no police record other than for shoplifting right after high school and a D.U.I. in his mid-twenties. Richie and a friend named Eddy Spangler had run a boiler-room telemarketing operation for the past two years selling "Premium Investment Programs" that were little more than glorified coupon packages. They made a nice profit, but as Uncle Marty had put it, "Richie thinks sticking money in the bank is about the same as sticking it into a shredder. He's never saved a dime."

Like his uncle, Richie was born to sell. Brash and outgoing, he considered the truth to be something you trotted out only if it helped you close a sale. But behind all the flash and trash, Marty had said, when Streeter walked him out of the church earlier that day, he was "jumpy, and he tries too hard. It's like he's always scared or trying to prove something. All that fast talking won't fool you for long." As for Tina, the old man knew little other than that she was a knockout. Streeter figured it was unlikely that they had come here to pull something illegal. Unlikely, but not impossible. Anything was possible with a scammer like Richie. As he finally dozed off, Streeter realized he had no idea what he'd be getting into when he hit San Ignacio.

Walking to his car the next morning, he felt the Mexican humidity clinging tightly to him. Coming from Colorado, where there's so little moisture in the air, he experienced any humidity as unbearable. The drive from the hotel to the consulate was two miles on a main road along the oceanfront. Located on the south side of Mazatlán, the U.S. consulate was a few short blocks off the beach. It was a stucco building overgrown with dense, trimmed vines and shaded by large trees, and tucked away in a residential area. When Streeter arrived a few minutes before nine, there already was a line of about fifty people waiting for it to open. Most of them had come to get entry visas for the United States.

Streeter told the guard at the entrance that he had an appointment with Ben Howell, the vice consul assigned to the Moats case. He was steered inside, where the cool red floor tiles, freshly painted white walls, and faint odor of disinfectant reminded him of a clinic. Within minutes Howell appeared at his office door behind the huge front counter. He nodded for Streeter to join him.

"Mr. Moats called me last night and told me you might be by this morning," he said as he let Streeter into his office and closed the door. "Did you have a good flight?"

Streeter nodded. The room had the same tight clarity as the reception area. Ben, however, did not. He was round, soft, and bearded, and wore rectangular wire-rimmed glasses. In his flowered cotton shirt, he looked like a young Santa Claus vacationing in the tropics. Despite that, he had hard eyes and a manner that was anything but warm and fuzzy.

"I've got some news for you, but I don't think it'll make Mr. Moats very happy," he continued. "I've been on the phone with the chief of the San Ignacio police for the past hour and it seems that late last night they made a couple of arrests. Two local guys with bad reputations. The police haven't found Richard's body yet, but the chief says that the men confessed and they're going to show them where he's buried."

Streeter sat up. "Confessed to what? From what I was told, this was being treated as a missing persons."

"Until last night." Ben swiveled slightly in his chair and his eyes narrowed. "We had hoped that Richard had just gotten separated from his car and was lost. But since the police tracked down these two, we have a homicide. I know it's going to be rough on the family, but once we have the body, there won't be any doubt."

Streeter considered that for a moment. "You say you haven't called Mr. Moats yet?"

Howell shook his head.

"Let me do it. I want to get up to San Ignacio right away and see what's going on for myself. I'd hate to get the family all worked up if this is a false alarm. We can call Denver when I get back."

"I don't know. They should hear this as soon as possible." Ben leaned forward and put his elbows on his desk. "Hell, I guess a few more hours won't hurt. After all, Mr. Moats did say that I was to treat you like family. Maybe they'll have found a body by then. I'll wait until you get back but make it here by three."

"Thanks. One other thing. Martin Moats told me you'd arrange for an interpreter."

"Rafael should be here by nine-thirty. He's a good man. Reliable and knows the area." Ben sat back again. "He owns a little T-shirt shop in town and he's got some free time. Speaks perfect English and won't charge you much." Howell thought for a moment. "Look, I don't know what you think you can accomplish up there, but the chief seemed pretty sure of what happened and that they've got the killers."

"That might be, but I was sent here to get a firsthand look."

Howell stood up. "I've got a call to make. Would you mind waiting outside?"

"No problem."

Streeter went back to the reception area, which was now filled with the people who'd been outside. Most of them sat in a long row of lacquered wooden benches waiting their turn with the woman at the front counter. He took a seat along one wall. Suddenly a young woman with short red hair wearing blue jeans and a white blouse, and a bearded man carrying a small television camera blew into the room. She appeared to be flustered and hot. He just looked hot. She looked around and glanced at Streeter without reacting. He stared back and tried to remember where he'd seen her before. It came to him as she walked toward the counter. Lise-something-or-other from one of the Denver television news shows. He never could keep straight which station had which reporter. Lise had just started in Denver, and Streeter placed her at about twenty-five. He liked watching her on television, even though she wasn't particularly professional. Not yet, anyhow. On camera she always seemed sincere, if uncertain of herself at times. He pegged her for hardworking, trying to prove herself in a new market. She was fairly plain-looking by TV standards, but she had a nice smile. A small, upturned nose added to her youthful appearance. Abbott, that's it, he remembered. Lise Abbott. In person she was shorter and thinner than she appeared to be on the screen, but she had the same earnest quality.

It figures that the media would pick up on Richie, Streeter thought. Blood on the car and a connection to the Waterbed King of Colorado. The receptionist said something to Lise and she and her partner lifted the half door in the front counter and marched toward Ben's office. Then they opened his door and went inside.

A few minutes later, a man looking to be in his mid-thirties, thin but with a confident open face, walked into the reception area. Wearing a plain white T-shirt and khaki shorts, he glanced around for a moment before going to the front counter. He spoke to the woman for a couple of minutes, the two of them laughing and talking as if they knew each other well. Then he turned toward Streeter as the receptionist pointed to the bounty hunter and said something. Streeter figured the guy must be Rafael, so he stood up. The man walked over to the large gringo and extended his hand.

"Mr. Streeter? I'm Rafael López, your interpreter."

Streeter nodded. "Good to meet you." They shook hands. "Listen, I don't want to rush things, but we have to get up to San Ignacio right now. I told Ben that we'd be back by mid-afternoon. If it's okay with you, we can talk about your fee on the way."

"Fine."

The trip took just over an hour. Even the main highways had only two lanes, but there was little traffic and Streeter pushed the Jetta hard. The temperature was easily eighty-five but because the car's air-conditioning was broken they left the windows open. With Rafael's easy charm and the beauty of the countryside, Streeter enjoyed the trip. On their right, the mountains were dramatic and thick with trees, something he didn't see often in the Rockies. On their left the Pacific Ocean rolled quietly forever to the west. As they drove, they settled on an hourly rate for Rafael and the American filled him in on what Howell had told him about the arrests.

"I tell you, Rafael, I've done business with local Mexican cops north of here and it wasn't what you'd call a peak experience," Streeter said as he wound the car along the highway. "They like to clear cases fast and the truth can get lost in the shuffle. We've got a situation here where town officials used the Blazer for a little fun after the owner disappeared. Then, magically, right after they hear the guy's family is sending someone to investigate, they turn up two killers."

"I'm sure they want to get you off their backs," Rafael

responded. He'd mastered English as an undergrad at the University of Iowa and had barely a trace of an accent. "The police here hate outside interference."

They turned off the ocean highway onto a narrow, aging asphalt road that was nothing more than one wide lane and wound into the mountains for about twenty-five miles to San Ignacio. The scenery changed dramatically as they moved through a long, broad mountain valley that looked to Streeter like a desert. Every few miles they'd pass a few run-down houses with a small store or two that Rafael said were towns. Finally they could see their destination. From a distance, San Ignacio was as idyllic as a movie set. Its red-tiled roofs and white buildings offset some of the dull browns and tans of the hills around them. Vegetation was scarce and consisted mostly of low, mean-looking cacti and shrubs. The mud-and-brick buildings sat on a plateau flat as pool table, across a deep valley. It was accessible only by the longest, narrowest bridge Streeter had ever seen. Although the setting was picturesque, up close the town itself was disappointing. They drove slowly down a main road that looked as though it doubled as a hand-grenade range.

"The police station's usually in the town square," Rafael said, pointing straight ahead.

Streeter took a left at the square. Halfway into the first block, four armed men lounged in front of a white brick building. They didn't wear uniforms or smiles and appeared monumentally unimpressed with the approaching Jetta. "Nice-looking crew," Streeter remarked to Rafael as they parked.

"This is a labor-intensive country," the interpreter said. "There's probably one officer for every thirty people in a place like this. Chances are, most of them were just given badges and guns and about all they do is run errands for the chief."

They got out of the Jetta and approached the cops. Rafael spoke to them for a couple of minutes, nodding toward Streeter once as he did. One of them pointed slowly to the front door of the police station, which was also the town hall, municipal court, and mayor's office. Rafael thanked him and then headed for the door with Streeter right behind.

"The chief 's name is Omar Ruiz and the mayor is Daniel Hernández," Rafael explained once they were inside. "Hernández is out of town on 'big business.' "

"I'll just bet he is," Streeter said. "When the shit hits the fan, there's always big business somewhere else. Same as back home."

They walked down a tiled hall to a huge oak desk in front of double wooden doors. A drop-dead gorgeous young woman in a flowered sundress sat behind the desk reading a magazine. Rafael told her who they were and that they wanted to see Chief Ruiz. He explained that Streeter was a representative of the Moats family. The woman appeared as bored as the officers outside, but she finally stood up and went through the double doors. A couple of minutes later she came out again. Leaving one of the doors open, she motioned for them to enter.

Ruiz's office was dark, smoky, and made frigid by a huge window air conditioner. The chief was pretty dark and smoky himself. With a thick neck and mustache, and lifeless features, he looked like Stalin. He didn't get up when the two men entered, but, rather, just sat back, puffing thoughtfully on a long, unfiltered Mexican cigarette and glaring. No invitations for anyone to sit down were offered. Undaunted, Rafael stepped to the desk and started speaking. The chief 's face showed no reaction. At one point, Rafael turned to Streeter and pointed while mentioning "Señor Moats."

When he'd finished, it was Ruiz's turn. Although his voice was high for such a stocky man, the words came out slowly, like he had cough syrup instead of coffee in the cup on his desk. Streeter studied him as he spoke. The cop's words were flat and the slow confidence of his voice indicated that Ruiz basically didn't give a shit about his visitors or Richie's case.

Rafael translated for Streeter. "He says that the suspects and his men are at the burial site right now. We should go there and see for ourselves. The chief *deeply* regrets that such a horrible thing happened here, but the two men they arrested are capable of such a thing." Rafael spoke without emotion, letting Streeter know that he wasn't impressed with Ruiz's story. "He says that when they confessed, they admitted that they robbed Señor Moats and then killed him to keep him silent."

"That'll do the trick, I guess," Streeter said. "Ask him when the mayor'll be back and also where the Blazer is. Get directions to this burial site, too."

Rafael turned back to the chief and they spoke for a couple of minutes more. Then Rafael looked at Streeter. "He says he believes the mayor will be gone for at least three weeks. He also says that the Blazer has been thoroughly cleaned and taken back to Mazatlán, where a driver will be hired to return it to Colorado."

Streeter thought about that as he watched Ruiz light another cigarette. "Ask him if the two killers mentioned anything about a woman with Mr. Moats." Ruiz glared back and then took a whack at a smile. His lips curled up but the rest of his face didn't go along. The result was that he looked even more hostile.

Again, the two Mexicans spoke together. At one point, Ruiz looked at Streeter and seemed shaken, but quickly regained his stony attitude.

"The chief says there was no mention from the killers of a female companion," Rafael said. "His men are looking for just one body."

Streeter tucked that away. "Let's go, Raffie. I want to see these two 'killers.' We can come back here tomorrow if I have more questions."

The chief's receptionist ignored them as they left, as did the armed cops in front of the building. "It's nice to feel welcome," Streeter said as they drove out of the town square toward the bridge out of town. "I wonder if Ruiz ever leaves his office. What's your read on him, Rafael?"

The interpreter said nothing at first, but, rather, just looked out his side window at the one-story buildings they drove past. "Who knows? Maybe these two guys actually killed your friend."

"I wouldn't be surprised if they got encouragement with their confession," the bounty hunter responded. "I'd confess to killing Richie if it kept me out of Ruiz's office."

When they got back on the bridge, a black Ford Bronco approached in the other lane. As it shot past them, Streeter saw Lise Abbott in the front passenger's seat. She was talking and gesturing to the cameraman who was driving. Another man was in the back.

It took them almost half an hour to get to the alleged burial site. They drove about ten miles southwest, back toward Mazatlán, on the paved road before turning off onto a dirt path heading east. In the deep ruts, the Jetta hopped like a cricket. Luckily, the digging was being done only two miles from the paved road. As they approached a clump of low trees, Streeter couldn't believe what he saw. Several cars and a pickup truck were parked in a circle in the middle of a flat field. About half a dozen men leaned on the vehicles and faced a man in immaculate white clothes. The lounging men were all heavily armed, with at least two of them holding automatic rifles. The man in the white suit was standing about twenty feet from the others, facing off into the open field. He was holding a golf club and stood next to a small bag on the ground with golf balls spilling out of it. He was taking practice swings and every so often would glance back over his shoulder at the others and say something. It looked to Streeter as though he was giving them a lesson.

"Don't tell me that Greg Norman over there is one of Ruiz's men," Streeter said as he pulled over and parked.

"It might be Sergeant Rivera." Rafael smiled. "He's in charge."

"What the hell?" Streeter said as he shut off the engine.

They waited for the thick plume of road dust they'd kicked

up to settle before getting out. The golfer turned to face them and leaned on his club, which appeared to be a driver. Rafael got out and walked toward him. He was already talking to the man, who indeed turned out to be Rivera, by the time Streeter got there. Rivera was the flip side of Ruiz. Although short and stocky, and with same thick mustache the chief wore, the sergeant was handsome, with a broad, friendly face, and he spoke English as well as Rafael. He was wearing a white-on-white disco suit that would have done John Travolta proud. When the bounty hunter got within a couple of feet, Rivera straightened up and extended his hand to be shaken.

"Señor Streeter," he said as he grinned vastly. "It's nice to meet you. I'm Sergeant Rivera." He shot a glance at the cherry head of his three-wood. "Do you play this evil game, sir?"

Streeter frowned in confusion as he looked at the club. Then, turning back to Rivera, he answered, "I used to. Not very well."

Rivera narrowed his dark eyes and continued to smile. "Then we have something in common. Golf is more of a curse than a pastime. It's already practically ruined my marriage, but still I come back for more."

"Sergeant, I don't want to interrupt your stroke here," Streeter said, "but we were told that this was Richard Moats's burial site. Your chief said you had two suspects in Mr. Moats's killing and you were looking for the body."

"This is true." Rivera nodded earnestly. "Mr. Ruiz informed me this morning about the confession. He then told me to get out here and supervise the digging for Mr. Moats." He rolled his eyes quickly, confidentially, as if he and Streeter were sharing a joke. "We've been out here for over three hours now. I always do what Mr. Ruiz instructs me to do."

"If you always do what he says, how come you boys aren't digging for the body?" Streeter asked.

Rivera nodded, his smile still in place. "We're policemen, not grave diggers." He pointed over Streeter's shoulder toward the vehicles. "The digging continues even as we speak."

Streeter turned around to face the cars. A couple of the men lounging against them perked up and glanced toward the middle. There, almost in the center of the circle, a lone worker with a shovel chopped casually at ground damned near as hard as poured concrete. In over three hours, he'd opened a hole almost big enough to bury a dachshund. A very small dachshund.

The bounty hunter took a couple of steps toward the cars and studied the worker. Then he turned to Rivera. "You're kidding."

Sergeant Rivera hunched his shoulders into a quizzical shrug and shook his head. "I am not. This is what the chief wants, and in my opinion, this is the effort it deserves." Then he nodded again with that shared-secret grin back on his face. "Wouldn't you say I'm right?"

Streeter agreed. He moved back to Rivera and lowered his voice. "That's exactly what I'd say." He paused. "But if you know this is nonsense, why bother with it at all?"

Rivera shifted his weight and grabbed the golf club with both hands in front of him, studying the head again. Then he looked up. "I have my orders. They came from the chief, who probably was instructed by the mayor. Someday, when I'm chief, things might be different. But for now, as I said, I have my orders." He smiled broadly once more. "Tell me, which part of this game gave you the most pain? For me it is the tee shots."

Streeter shrugged, considering what the sergeant had just said. "Me, too." He glanced back at the other officers before returning to Rivera with another question. "And the suspects? We were told they'd be here."

Rivera turned around, with his back to Streeter and facing the rough fairway he had been hitting balls onto when the visitors arrived. He curled his lower lip and let out a wolf whistle loud enough to stop a train. About fifty yards down the field, two young men stepped out from under a large tree. One of them waved his hand wildly and Streeter could see that he was smiling. He couldn't see much else of the boys at that distance, but they both seemed to be smoking cigarettes.

"Those are the two desperadoes? The chief said they have criminal records. They're supposed to be a couple of tough guys."

Rivera turned back and grinned, but this time there was little humor in it. "I wouldn't know about criminal records, but they're both excellent shag boys. I haven't lost a ball all morning and it's not because I hit them straight."

Streeter shook his head and smiled himself. "Aren't you afraid they'll run off?"

"To where? It's a long walk back to San Ignacio and it's pretty warm out here. Those two are cousins. The Durán boys. I've known them their whole lives. They won't run anywhere."

"This is one hell of an investigation." Streeter looked around for a moment. "Let me ask you something, Sergeant. What do *you* think happened to Richie Moats?"

The golfer shrugged slightly. "I haven't given it much thought."

"Did you personally see a young American around here lately? He'd probably be traveling with a beautiful woman."

Rivera shook his head. "I'm certain I would have heard about the woman."

Streeter liked Rivera but he knew that he wouldn't be getting anything more of value from the man. "Goodbye, Sergeant. Thanks for leveling with me." He paused. "And keep your head down and your body silent. Let the club do the work."

Rivera's grin widened. "I try to, Señor Streeter. It's not always easy."

When Streeter turned to leave, Rafael, who had been standing quietly off to the side during the conversation, joined him and they walked back to the Jetta. Once inside, Streeter started the engine, backed up, and quickly turned the car around. It wasn't until they got back to the paved road that the bounty hunter spoke. "No point hanging around here. Those guys'll find Jimmy Hoffa before they get to Richie."

4

"So you're telling me this whole murder thing's nothing but a crock of refried horseshit," Marty said. His voice sounded tinny and distant on the consulate phone.

Streeter glanced at Howell, who was on the extension. "I can't say that for sure, Marty. Richie may have been murdered. It's just that based on what I saw today, if you want to find out what really happened, you won't get it from the San Ignacio police. Certainly not the chief. He'll say anything to get rid of us and protect the mayor. If I'm going to get you solid information, I'll have to spend some quality time with the locals. Find out if any of them saw Richie and Tina."

Marty considered that. "What do you say, Ben? You think the cops are full of it?"

Howell sat up slightly in his chair. "I have no substantive reason to doubt what they say, sir. Unless we receive solid evidence to the contrary, I have to believe that the San Ignacio police are on the right track."

"But Mr. Streeter there says they're out scraping at the dirt in the middle of a field and playing golf or some damned thing. Sounds like a bad dog-and-pony show to keep the gringos off their backs. And what about the mayor leaving town? Hell, the guy was laying pipe in my nephew's car. Wouldn't that make him a suspect? Not to mention there's no contents left from Richie's Blazer. They don't have squat."

Howell's eyes narrowed slightly. "Well, there certainly seem to be a number of holes in their investigation, but as an official of the U.S. government, I can't interfere. We have to believe they're making a good-faith effort at finding the truth."

"That sounds like a lot of bureaucratic manure, son." Clearly, Marty was losing his patience. "Just between us girls, what do *you* make of it?"

Howell cleared his throat. "I don't see how Richard could still be alive unless he's a survivalist. It's rough country out there and if he made it to a town, any town, we would have heard by now." He hesitated. "Regarding the police investigation, I believe that Mr. Streeter has raised a number of legitimate concerns."

"You bet your sweet ass he has," Marty concluded, clearing his throat. "As far as being a survivalist, forget it. Hell, Richie gets disoriented when he wanders off the carpeting." He paused. "Mr. Streeter, let's have you stay down there for a while and sniff around. Find out what the real people saw. Your basic Mexican is honest if you treat 'em right." He paused again. "Howell get you a good interpreter?"

Streeter nodded to Rafael sitting across the room. "The best."

"Good," Moats shot back. "Just hang in there and do like you said. I trust your instincts on this, son. Do *you* think the boy's been killed?"

Streeter frowned. "I'm not sure what to think yet, but there don't seem to be too many other options."

"Give me a call if you hear anything. Either way, check in tomorrow night and we'll see where we stand." With that, Marty Moats hung up.

None of the three men in Howell's office said anything for a moment. Finally, Rafael spoke. "You want me back here at nine?"

Streeter looked over at him. "Can you make it earlier? Eight?" When Rafael nodded, the bounty hunter turned to the vice consul. "Any words of wisdom before we take off, Mr. Howell?"

Howell stood and looked at his guests. "Just try not to piss Ruiz off."

By the time Streeter got back to El Cid, it was almost six o'clock. He grabbed a beer from the refrigerator in his room and took it with him into the shower. When he'd finished cleaning up, he smoked a cigar. The air-conditioning felt good after the long day in the dusty Jetta. Sitting in the chair next to his bed, his skin still moist from the shower, he wondered who'd killed Richie. Fat chance of finding the perp on his own. Most likely, the mayor had had one of Ruiz's men do it so he could get the car. His Honor then left town knowing that the attention would blow over in a couple of weeks. Official San Ignacio was hunkered down, covering its ass real good on this one. Still, Streeter was determined to find out all he could. He at least owed Uncle Marty and Aunt Marlene part of an explanation. The body might even turn up, but not at that bogus burial site. Finally, he threw on a pair of khaki slacks and a Banlon shirt and headed to the hotel restaurant.

El Cid's sprawling lobby was broken up into several sitting areas, giving it a catacomb-like feel. Just outside, to the west, was a round pool where you could swim up to a bar and sit in the water and drink. There was another bar inside, in the restaurant, and Streeter walked to it. He ordered a Tecate longnecker. When it arrived, he surveyed the room, leaning back against the bar and sipping casually as he did. It was pushing seven-thirty and the sun was setting off to his left, the last rays of the day streaking in. The place was filling mostly with tourists and Streeter spotted someone who looked familiar.

Evidently finished with her nightly feed to Denver, Lise Abbott entered, kicking back in white shorts and a powder-blue T-shirt with MAZATLÁN embroidered on it. She wore a burgundy NEWS 3 baseball cap and she still managed to look like she was on deadline. That nervousness in her eyes, wide and always scanning. Her movements, quick and almost jerky.

Streeter wondered if she always acted like that. Lise walked through the rounded archways from the lobby and moved quickly toward the bar. Suddenly she stopped and sat down in an overstuffed club chair next to one of the low cocktail tables. When the waitress took her order, Lise pulled a small notebook from her purse and began writing.

Streeter watched as her drink arrived. Chilled blush wine in a tall, perspiring glass. Figures, he thought. He took a last pull on his beer and ordered a second Tecate. When it came, he grabbed it and walked over to her.

"Are you finding anything interesting down here?" he asked, standing across the table from her. His smile was more inquisitive than friendly.

Lise looked up, openmouthed. "Huh?" She frowned. "I mean, pardon me?" Her expression then turned to her version of a practiced on-camera smile.

Streeter took a small sip from his beer. Despite her formality, he sensed that she was friendly. "I asked if you're having any luck with your story. I'm from Denver too, and I recognized you from Channel Three. 'Course, the cap helped me a little with that one."

"Really." Lise sat back slightly and studied him for a long moment. "You were at the American consulate this morning, weren't you?"

He didn't say anything at first, wondering if he should tell her why he was in town. He quickly decided against it. "I've been all over the place today and I'm beat. Mind if I sit down?" He glanced at the chair next to her.

Lise nodded quickly several times and closed her notebook. She put the pad and pencil back in her purse as he sat. Streeter noticed how pale her legs were as she stuffed her purse next to her thigh on the chair. He studied her nose as she took a sip from her wine. She looked younger in person than on television.

"I'm Lise Abbott," she said when she put her glass down. "But then I suppose you might already have known that."

"Not really," Streeter lied. "I recognized your face from TV, but I'm not much with names." He paused and held out his hand. "I'm Streeter."

"Streeter what?" She sort of smiled. "Is that a nickname?"

He ignored the question. "Seeing as how you were with a camera crew this morning, I gather you're not down here on vacation."

"That's true. I don't know if you heard before you left Denver, but Marty Moats's nephew is missing and his truck turned up not far from here. You've heard of Marty? The big waterbed salesman? Everyone in Colorado seems to know him. Anyhow, the missing guy's name is Richie Moats and his blood was splattered all over the truck."

"You don't say? When did all this happen?"

"Well, Richie's been missing for over a week and they just found the truck a day or so ago. I flew right in last night. We've got an exclusive on the story so far. Anyhow, I had a long talk this afternoon with the chief of police in the town where they found the truck. A Chevy Blazer, actually." Lise paused to take another sip from the wine. "He told me that they've arrested a couple of guys who confessed to killing Richie for his truck. Both of the suspects have long criminal histories. They're supposed to be really bad people, but I'm not so sure. Anyhow, they supposedly buried Richie out in the brush somewhere."

"What do you mean, you're not sure about the two men?"

"Well, I went out to where the body is said to be buried and it was pretty weird. I can't believe they're in the right place. And the two guys they arrested are more like playful teenagers. They even tried to get on camera and they were playing golf or something like that. It seemed silly to me."

"I take it they didn't find a body," he asked, smiling.

She looked closely at him and paused, then shook her head

and returned his smile. "Not as of deadline tonight." She perked up. "We got the murder confession for tonight's feed and I got in the golf stuff, too. My cameraman and I are heading back to San Ignacio first thing in the morning. San Ignacio's where the Blazer was found. About all I can do is keep after it."

"I suppose that's true."

Lise glanced around the room like she was expecting someone. Turning back, she said, "The police chief's a piece of work. He's scary. But the guy in charge of the burial site is a regular hoot. He's all dressed up like my father would have been back in the seventies. A white leisure suit or whatever they call it." Her smile was warm and genuine by now.

"You hear all those stories about Mexican police being strange," he said. "I guess it's true."

Lise pulled her head back. "Anyhow, it gives me the lead story for a day or so. At least until the other stations get down here." Suddenly she motioned to a man behind him, near the archways. Looking back at Streeter, she rose from her chair. "You'll have to excuse me. Hal, my cameraman, is here and we have to meet some people for dinner."

"More sources for your story?"

She shook her head. "No, just friends. You ask a lot of questions, Streeter. Maybe you should have been a reporter or a private eye or something. But curiosity is a good thing, in my opinion." She smiled again, then set her glass on the table and got up. "It was nice to meet you. Maybe we'll see each other around. Have a good vacation."

Streeter watched her leave. Nice lady, he thought, but she has a lot to learn. She hadn't even asked him what he was doing at the consulate. At least she wasn't completely fooled by Ruiz and all that garbage in the countryside. But he could tell that she was struggling with the story. He finished his beer and got a table for dinner. Tired from so little sleep the night before, he wanted to eat and turn in early.

If his first day in Mexico was fruitless, the next three were laughable. Rivera and his men went to no fewer than four more "burial sites." Same results: a worker or two would whack away at the hard dirt while the sergeant whacked away at his long irons. Then they'd move on. An AP writer and another on-camera reporter, this one from Channel 10 in Denver, made it to Mazatlán on Friday. By the next morning, a regular little caravan of reporters was setting out from the oceanfront hotels to San Ignacio. Once they were there, Ruiz would feed them their daily load of bullshit and then they'd dutifully head to the newest grave site, hoping to capture Richie Moats's body on film.

After seeing Streeter twice more at the consulate, Lise finally asked Howell exactly who he was and what he was doing there. As the bounty hunter had requested, Ben just said he was a friend of Marty's who was keeping an eye on things for the family. That night Abbott mentioned it near the end of her telecast, although she never did try to interview him.

For Streeter's part, he didn't even bother with the police. He just worked the streets of San Ignacio with Rafael, interviewing anyone who'd talk to him. The two went to other little towns in the area. particularly the three between the main highway and San Ignacio. By mid-Sunday, they'd spoken to over one hundred people. No one had seen the Blazer before it turned up with Mayor Hernández on board. No one had seen any Americans, male or female, in the area prior to the media excitement. And no one expressed surprise that both Hernández and Ruiz were knee-deep in the mess.

"Looks like you're beating a dead horse down there, son," Marty Moats told him over the phone late Sunday afternoon. "Hell, even the bimbos on the local news seem to be getting the message by now. Richie's dead and if the right people get nailed, it'll be pure coincidence and blind luck. The story's dying of natural causes up here."

"I don't get it, Marty," Streeter said. "We still don't have a clue about what Richie was doing here. Absolutely no one saw him or Tina. And these people are leveling with me. It's like the two of them blew into town late one night, dropped off the Blazer, and then disappeared."

"Enough is enough," Marty said. "Get yourself a good night's sleep and then first thing in the morning get a flight back up here. Keep the rest of the advance I gave you. That should cover your expenses. If not, send me an invoice. Richie's gone and that's that." His voice got quiet. " 'Course, Marlene ain't feeling too good about all of it, but there's not much I can do about that."

Streeter thought for a moment. "Listen, when I get back to Denver, let me see if I can at least find out why he came to Mexico. I'll backtrack from up there. We can't just leave it like this."

Marty cleared his throat. "We can and we will, son. Once you get back up here you're off the meter and off the job. Just let it lie. You did your best and we appreciate that. Richie had his own way of doing things and his own reasons for getting himself stuck out there in the rat lands. Marlene and me'll grieve for the boy and then get on with our lives."

"But if I could—"

"But nothing." Moats sounded irritated. "No hard feelings, but you're fired." He coughed once and then added, "Say howdy to Frank for me. Okay?" With that he hung up.

5

She had acted curiously toward Streeter ever since she'd seen the faded SAVE THE WHALES: COLLECT THE ENTIRE SET bumper sticker on his Buick. That was a month earlier, when he'd gone to the music store on South Broadway for his weekly piano lesson. He was just getting out of his car and she was approaching hers. She'd stopped, studied his rear bumper, and then looked at him with a confused half smile, half frown.

"I suppose you think it's funny when they club baby seals, too," she'd said.

Her voice was even, but he couldn't tell if it was anger or amusement in her eyes. Those eyes. Huge, soft brown, and each a perfect almond shape. Damp and dreamy. At first, Streeter could only stare at them. Then he glanced down at his bumper and the source of her concern. It had been on there so long he'd forgotten the stupid sticker. He looked back at her.

"It's just a joke," he'd answered with a hint of a smile himself.

"I see." She'd taken a step toward him, the same puzzled look on her face. Her perfume was lilac, but he couldn't place it.

"It probably isn't all that funny."

She'd considered that for a moment, the smile seeming to win out. "Probably." Then she'd walked away without saying anything else.

It turned out the woman worked at the store in sales. Gave guitar lessons, too. Constance—seldom Connie—is what his piano teacher told him. Streeter had seen her twice inside the store since the parking-lot incident and each time she'd just given him only a perfunctory nod. Still, she looked terrific and he thought he'd caught a hint of a smile both times. Great legs, long hair a shade or two darker than her eyes. Those perfect eyes. He'd asked his teacher about her. Single? Available? The usual bachelor stuff. Apparently, just about a year earlier her boyfriend, a violinist with the Denver Symphony Orchestra, had left her for a close friend. Or someone she *thought* was a close friend. Since then she'd become increasingly distant and brittle with people, especially of the male variety.

"Constance used to be a real treat to work with," Streeter's teacher had told him. "She's still a good person, but not so friendly anymore. I'm sure it takes time to get over what she's been dealing with, but she can be pretty aloof. Don't take it personally." He thought for a moment. "If you think she might have given you a smile, that's not bad for her. Hell, you should be encouraged."

After hearing about her boyfriend, Streeter wasn't sure what his move should be. Still, he thought of her again this particular Thursday night as he left the music store. A couple of guitar cases stood near the front door and he wondered where she was. Once he got outside he saw something that jolted his attention away from Constance.

"Hey, scrub. I stopped by your place, but you weren't around." The big man was leaning against the driver's door of a jet-black 1967 GT Ford Mustang fastback. "*Nice* neighborhood you got up there. Don't you like white people?"

Streeter stared straight into his eyes. "Right at this moment, no." It was Grover Royals. He hadn't seen him in eight years, which wasn't nearly long enough. Streeter hated Royals. He had ever since they'd played football together in high school, which was when Grover'd started calling him "scrub."

Born exactly one year and a day before Streeter, Grover Royals came from the same middle-class background. Right up to junior year, Streeter had idolized him in terms of football. Grover was an inch or two taller, thirty pounds stronger, and even a step faster. And that competitive fire: always the last one off the field. Win or lose, he'd keep kicking ass until there was no more ass left to kick. By senior year, he was a full six feet, three inches tall and college recruiters were sniffing around like hogs in heat. But in his second game that fall, he blew out a knee so badly that he was on crutches for over six months. During that time, his mother died of cancer and his father crawled into a bottle of blended. When he could finally move around again, Grover was all wrong and twisted inside. He started muling drugs around the country and then moved on to prostitution, numbers running, and kiddie porno. By the time he was thirty, his name had been mentioned in the deaths of at least two business rivals. He was rumored to be "connected" or "made" or whatever the street term was for being in bed with organized crime. Streeter's hero had turned out to be pure poison.

Now Grover kept up his smirk, cool and confident. It had snowed that day and he was wearing a knee-length, Gestapo-type leather coat. The thing was black, thick, and must have weighed a ton. Probably cost a ton, too. But it couldn't hide the fact that Royals was built like a bear. His breath fogged as he spoke. "Yeah, real nice neighborhood," he repeated. "Like living in Denver's smoking section. And your place looks like a damned fort. All those red bricks and steeples and shit. 'Course, with as many winos and jigaboos as you got living near you, I suppose you want to keep some of the scumbags out."

"Did Frank tell you where I was?"

"Yeah. We had a nice little chat in his office." Grover adjusted himself and casually rolled his neck. Guys who spend four hours a day throwing weights around have ways of showing off their physiques even when they're bundled up.

"If you got inside, then obviously we can't keep all the scumbags out." Streeter paused to let that sink in. "Exactly what do you want? I'm sure you didn't come out here to take piano lessons."

Grover's smile flattened but he kept eye contact. His thinning dark hair was combed straight back, held in place by what appeared to be pig lard. He also had a tightly trimmed goatee. With his blunt, uneven features and small eyes in such a large face, even his mother would probably admit he was butt-ugly. "You're right. Don't want any piano lessons tonight."

Neither man spoke for a moment. Finally, Streeter spoke. "I'd like to say that it's been a pleasure and then just head home. But that would be a lie and you might follow me anyway."

"You want to go have a beer with me and Sid?" Grover stepped to one side so Streeter could see into the Mustang. It had deeply tinted glass, but the side window was open, exposing the chunky profile of Sid Wahl in the passenger's seat. "This is Sid, an associate of mine." He looked back at the bounty hunter. "We can all go get a brew. I'm buying. There's something I need to talk to you about."

Streeter leaned forward slightly and studied Sid. He wore a cheap plaid coat and his glasses had a Band-Aid around the nose bridge. Compared with him, Grover seemed almost classy. Almost. Casually, Sid looked out at the man on the sidewalk and issued a muffled "Aye" that passed for hello.

"No thanks," Streeter said, straightening up. "I'm not going anywhere in this stupid Batmobile of yours. You want to talk, walk me to my car over there. I'm in kind of a hurry."

Grover shrugged like it didn't matter. "Lead the way."

The day had been so cloudy that there was no actual sunset. It was almost dark as they walked away from the huge music store. Every Thursday night for the past ten months, except for the week he was in Mexico, Streeter drove to the funky shopping center on South Broadway near the freeway for piano lessons. Last year he'd gotten a baby grand when a drug dealer, who had put it up as collateral, left the state without so much as a goodbye. Streeter had always wanted to learn to play and this was his chance.

"I see your tan's all gone," Grover said as they walked west across the nearly empty lot and away from Broadway. "Mexico must be lovely this time of year."

Streeter considered that as he walked. "Get to the point, Grover."

Royals stopped suddenly and faced him. "Okay, scrub. I saw on the TV that you were down in Mexico looking for Richie Moats. Old Marty's nephew. I also saw where they haven't found his body yet." Grover's eyes narrowed and he glanced to both sides before continuing. "I want to hire you to go back down to San Douche Bag or wherever the hell they spotted Richie's car and find out what happened. I'm thinking the guy's still alive. They don't have a body and to me that means Moats is probably still aboveground walking around somewhere. What do you say, scrub? For old time's sake. That and I'll give you a thousand a day plus expenses."

Streeter didn't know if he was more surprised that Grover had anything to do with Richie or that Grover thought he'd work for him. His mouth opened a tad and he winced. "What do *you* have to do with Richie Moats?"

Royals shrugged and his eyebrows shot up. "What's the difference? For a grand a day, you don't need reasons." He could see that that wouldn't fly. "All right, I'll tell you. I couldn't give a good fuck about this Richie clown. But I think he's traveling with someone I'm interested in. A lady who used to sort of work for me. My business is with her and that's all you have to know."

"A thousand dollars a day tells me this is pretty important business." Streeter shifted his weight from one foot to the other. "Why not just go down there yourself?"

Grover looked to both sides again before speaking. "Because if someone needs finding, you're the man. Everyone knows that."

Streeter kept staring at him. "I'm not that good, and besides, you're a pretty persuasive guy. You can handle this yourself."

"Look, I don't want to go down there. Me or any of my guys."

Royals sniffed once. "We've known each other forever, Streeter. You could really play the old game of football and I always thought you were half cool even though I busted your balls most of the time. And you know what you're doing. I really need these people found. Dead or alive, I have to know what happened to them. Fucking Mexicans won't find Richie unless he runs for office. Maybe not even then." He took a half step closer. "I'm willing to give you ten days' advance right now. Sid's got it in the car. What do you say?"

"I say I'd rather shovel horse manure at minimum wage than work for you," Streeter responded.

Royals shuddered and his eyes narrowed so hard that Streeter braced for a punch. "You arrogant little bastard," Grover hissed. "You worked for Marty Moats. Jerk-off waterbed salesman. But my money's not good enough. We go way back, yet every time I see you, you act like you're too good for me. What's with that?"

Streeter said nothing.

Grover was standing so close that the bounty hunter smelled onion on his breath. "You never made nothing out of your life, did you, scrub? Live in a dump church with nothing but spics and coons all around. You bring whores and pimps back to court but you won't work for me. I buy and sell people like you every day of my life."

"Not today, you don't." Streeter swallowed and steadied himself. "I'm not working for you at any price. Pure and simple." Grover's little lecture made him feel like he was a sophomore all over again. Standing in the varsity huddle and getting reamed out for the first time.

The bigger man took a couple of steps back and shook his head. Glancing off to the side again, he took a deep breath. "Come on, scrub. I'll give you one more chance. You gonna work for me and find those two?"

Streeter rolled his sheet music with both hands. Chopin, Nocturne No. 5 in F-sharp, no less. He'd been wrestling with the piece for a month and getting nowhere. "You're dumber than I remembered, Grover. Like the song goes, 'What part of "no" don't you understand?' I'm not working for you. End of discussion."

Royals turned hard to his left and headed back to his car. When he'd gotten about ten feet away, Streeter yelled, "Hey!" Royals stopped and twisted his head back toward the voice, his eyes on the pavement. "Tell Sid it was nice talking to him. Okay?"

When Streeter returned to the church, he went to Frank's apartment at the rear of the first floor. The door was open and he walked in to find his partner watching a World War II documentary on television. Frank was sitting on a recliner, wearing sweatpants and a gray sweater, utterly engrossed in the black-and-white footage.

"Streeter." He slowly looked up and hit the mute button on his remote control. "Your buddy ever find you?"

"He found me. Not that I wanted him to." Streeter set his sheet music on the counter between the kitchen and the living room. He walked to a cabinet next to the refrigerator and pulled out a fifth of Johnnie Walker Red. "You want one?" He held it up as he spoke.

Frank nodded. "Did I do the wrong thing sending him to your lesson? I admit the guy was not what you'd call pretty. Looked like his face was designed by a committee, but other than that he seemed okay."

"He's not okay at all, but you had no way of knowing. Royals is pure trouble."

"Big as that guy was, I figured he was an old lifting buddy. He said you used to play ball together at Central."

"That's true." Streeter poured the Scotch over ice, brought the drinks out, and handed one to Frank. Then he sat on the couch next to the recliner. "If he wouldn't have ruined his knee, he'd have been a hell of a tackle for CU or Southern Cal. One of those places. Maybe even the pros someday. He was the best prospect in the state back in 'sixty-seven. Ate broken glass for breakfast and he wouldn't take an ounce of shit from Godzilla." He studied his partner. "I tell you, Grover Royals was the only guy in a jockstrap I was ever afraid of. He was my hero for a while until I realized what a psychopath he is. One time when I was a sophomore I was out with him and some of the other guys. We were coming out of a restaurant downtown and this kid from another school started giving Grover grief. He was damned near as big as Royals and I thought it'd be a fair fight. But Grover floored him with two quick punches." Streeter paused and frowned. "Evidently, that still wasn't enough punishment. He dragged the kid over to the curb. Then he opened his jaws so that his teeth were mouthing the curb corner. Royals took a step and kicked him in the back of the head. It drove his face into the curb and knocked out half his lower teeth. I never saw so much blood. It happened so fast we couldn't stop him."

"Christ. A high-school kid did that?"

Streeter nodded. "You know, Frank, it's amazing how those old high-school memories stick with you. That was what? Twenty-five years ago. But Royals can still get to me. He always could. See, he was big man on campus in more ways than one. He used to ride me pretty hard at practice and he knew just how to pull my chain. Like I said, I was afraid of him. Royals could hit like a jackhammer in scrimmage. But somehow I admired him at the same time. I played extra hard just to impress him. Funny thing is, talking to him tonight, I felt some of that old crap coming back. He still knows how to pull my chain. Still calls me 'scrub' and I react almost the same way I did back then." He shook his head slowly. "You'd think I would have outgrown that by now.

"Anyhow, Grover became much worse later. After his injury senior year he got turned around somehow and went off the charts. He's been over the line ever since." He studied his drink before taking a swallow. "You name the sin and old Grover's smack in the middle of it. I know for a fact that he's been involved in white slaving. He'd run underage girls from the Midwest to both coasts and set them up as hookers. The guy's dead-solid wrong and I don't ever want to see him again. I just hope that's possible."

Frank frowned. "Why wouldn't it be?"

"He tried to hire me to find Richie Moats. Gave me a line about wanting to get the woman traveling with him. That Tina." He took a sip. "She must be something."

"So? Like Nancy Reagan always advised us: 'Just say no.' "

"I did, but it's been bugging me ever since." He stood up and went back to the kitchen for more ice. "Marty never mentioned anything about Grover. Maybe he doesn't know there's a connection, but I have to find out how he fits in."

"No you don't." Frank's face twisted in impatience. The clank of ice hitting glass in the other room drowned his voice. He waited until Streeter got back to the couch. "I said, no you don't."

"I heard you and yes I do. It's at least worth a call to Marty. I haven't talked to him since I got back from Mazatlán on Monday. Aren't you curious about what's going on here?"

"Not enough to do anything about it," Frank answered. "If Royals is the kind of maniac you say, let the whole thing just lie there. Richie and his little gal are long dead by now. Forget all of it."

"One call to Marty. What's the harm?"

Frank shook his head. "If there is any, you'll find it." He glanced at the television and hit the sound on the remote. "I'm going to get back to the Battle of Stalingrad here. It's less upsetting than talking to you."

6

Grover's arms twitched like they were on fire. Too steamed to talk, he yanked back on the gearshift, shoving his precious ponycar into second while turning left off Broadway and onto Louisiana. The 390 big-block V-8 whined and you could almost hear the beefed-up four-barrel sucking gas and air. Reading the situation, Sid Wahl said nothing and let out a short hiccup. Besides gears shifting and the engine wailing, the only other sounds were the rich groans from Grover's leather coat as he worked the four-speed. The Mustang was moving fast for being on such a quiet residential street. Sid didn't know the exact speed limit, but he was pretty sure fifty-seven wasn't it.

"Getting a ticket won't help find those two," he offered quietly, his eyes fixed on the windshield.

Grover didn't respond at first, although he let up on the accelerator. Suddenly he yelled, "You believe the attitude on that guy?" He shot Sid a glance and didn't wait for a response. "I can live with him saying no, but it's his attitude that corks my ass. Like he doesn't need my money. Guy lives in a barracks, for chrissakes. And that car of his." He shook his head. "Looks like a turd on wheels."

"Did he ask many questions?"

"A few," Grover responded. "I fed him some junk about wanting to find Tina. Didn't mention the robbery." He looked back at Sid. "No way I'm letting him know it was my money in the suitcase that Richie took off my too-cool delivery boys." He flashed a quick grin. "Puked all over them, to boot. I'm embarrassed enough just knowing that myself, much less having it get around town."

This time, Sid returned the look. He adjusted himself in his seat, his face reddening. "We don't need to go over all that again. Nothing me and Dexter could a done to stop it. They knew the drill inside out and Moats was carrying a cannon 'bout the size a your leg. You'd a done the same as us. Even the puking part."

"Maybe." Royals downshifted for an upcoming stoplight. "But we'll never know, will we?" He shook his head again. "*Calley.* Now there's another attitude I don't need. The man loses all that cash and then gives me two tons of grief about it. I was getting tired of all his superspade jive anyhow. I'm glad he's gone."

Sid recalled the horrendous argument Grover and Dexter had gotten into on the night of the robbery. Looking back, he could see that it was only a matter of time before the two muscle heads clashed. He was surprised they didn't fight on the spot, what with Royals calling Dexter a pussy like that. Probably the only thing that stopped it was Dexter being covered with undigested pasta or whatever the hell it was that Richie doused them with. That would have been some fight if those two got into it, Sid thought. Grover's bulk and fury versus Calley's speed and cell-block savvy. Sid wasn't sure if Dexter quit or if Grover fired him, but the net result was that the big Indian was gone and Royals had a hard-on for Richie and Tina that wouldn't go away. Not ever.

"So what do we do now?" Sid asked as they turned north on Logan and headed downtown. "You wanna let me go to Mexico and see what I can turn up?"

"Forget that noise." Grover was silent for a while. "We're meeting Fontana at his office. Speaking of losers. The hell was I thinking when I picked him for a front man? No wonder Tina thought she could pull this stunt. A ten-year-old idiot could steal from Rudy Fontana and get away with it. I tell you, I put a real top-notch crew around me."

Sid ignored that last part and turned to Grover again. "Why you so convinced that Tina didn't know you're the guy behind Fontana? Hell, she had her hands on all the records and stuff. She saw you around from time to time and she's sure smart enough to figure out that a bug like Rudy couldn't run a lemonade stand on his own. My hunch is she knew she was stealing from you when she set up the robbery."

The lighted skyscrapers of Denver were off to their right as Grover worked the Mustang onto the four-lane Speer Boulevard. "Doesn't matter one way or the other," he responded. "My money's gone and I know who's got it. That bullshit down in Mexico was supposed to make everyone think Moats and her are dead so we'll forget what they did and write it off. But we're going to get the money back and take care of those two. How long do you think I could stay in business if I don't do something serious about this? I'd be lucky to last a week. Hell, Calley's probably running around right now telling everyone what a schmuck I am. If I don't take care of this, I'll have guys picking my pockets while I'm asleep."

Sid glanced at the massive brick-and-glass performing-arts complex on the right. Huge banners for *Ain't Misbehavin'* and *Always . . . Patsy Cline* were all over the west walls. No one spoke for a few minutes as they drove past Currigan Exhibition Hall. Then Grover moved the Mustang into a lot off nearby Champa Street. Finally, Sid asked, "What do we gotta see this guy for? You think Fontana was in on it?"

"Not likely. He just about shit in his pants when he found out about it. Rudy doesn't have the brains or the stomach to cross me. But I thought we'd have us a little strategy session." Grover shut the engine off and turned to his passenger. "It's time to shake up a few people and see what happens. Shake them up so hard the truth's bound to fall out." He glanced past Sid to the car parked close on the right. His voice became soft, the closest to gentle that Sid had ever heard it. "Be careful how you open the door. No way I want any dings on this baby."

Rudy Fontana often referred to himself as a "sex addict." He said that's why he'd gotten into the skin business. "If you can't lick 'em, join 'em," he had told Grover once. "I try to do both. Makes perfect sense for me to work around all these girls like this."

Grover'd listen to him spout his nonsense, Rudy trying to sound street-tough. From the first time they'd met, eight years earlier, he'd thought Rudy was fairly pathetic. The more he knew him, the more evidence of that he found. In those days, Rudy was a shiftless thirty-year-old trust-funder who practically lived at a strip joint in North Denver. Finally, he approached the manager about buying a piece of the place.

"I might as well, seeing as how I pay most of the upkeep around here anyhow," he had told Sid Wahl, who ran the Mile Hi Show Lounge back then for Grover.

In Rudy, Grover found just what he was looking for: someone to put his name on the official documents for his expanding empire. Rudy was rich, obtuse, spineless, and easy to manipulate. So Grover let him buy small chunks of his clubs and put the Fontana name on virtually every deed, lease, or corporate paper. That distanced Grover from all sorts of legal liabilities and made it almost impossible for the law to touch him. As compensation, Rudy received a tacky downtown office above a strip club, income, and enough ready access to hookers and strippers to feel like a player. Fontana ate it up. But it didn't take long for Grover and him to sour on each other. Rudy's lack of direction and other weaknesses meant that Grover had to be more involved in the day-to-day operations than he'd planned. For his part, Rudy quickly grew to fear his huge associate. He'd seen Grover's volatile and sadistic personality flare up regularly and often.

Walking into Rudy's office above the Cheetah that Thursday night, Grover was not surprised to find him sprawled nearly nude on his leather couch with one of the dancers, who was completely naked. Ginger, a black stripper who was getting her figure back following the recent birth of her second child, barely acknowledged Grover and Sid as they entered. But Rudy practically went into convulsions.

"Jesus, Grover," he said as he lifted himself up and off Ginger. He put one hand in front of his crotch. With the other, he grabbed his crumpled pants, which had fallen to his ankles, and jerked them toward his waist. "It's not what you think."

That one even caught Grover's attention. "Then what is it? This your idea of cleaning the couch?"

Ginger sat up and slowly grabbed her deep-purple thong panties from the floor, rolling her eyes as she did. Rudy had by now gotten his pants on and was standing between her and his visitors, buttoning his shirt. "Well, I mean, obviously it is what you're thinking, but what the hell? The kind of hours I've been putting in around here, I deserve a little R and R. Right, guys?"

"I don't give a shit what you were doing here," Grover said. "But we have business to discuss." To Ginger, he added without emotion, "Take a hike, okay, honey?" She nodded as she hooked up a matching purple bra. Except for a few tiny stretch marks on her tummy, her coffee-colored body had the look of a twenty-year-old gymnast's. Not that Grover paid much attention. When it came to sex, he was oddly ambivalent. To him, it was just another bodily function. He did it fast and not to make emotional contact or even to actually feel good. More just to shuck tension.

Ginger left silently, almost regally, not bothering to make eye contact with any of them. When Rudy was dressed, the three men sat around, drank house bourbon from smudged beer glasses, and discussed the Richie-and-Tina situation. It was only after a couple of stiff ones that Rudy calmed down from his agitation at being interrupted with Ginger.

"So what do you think, Grover?" he asked as he carefully adjusted his butt on the couch. "If your skip-tracer buddy won't help, you want me to head on down there for a little look-see?"

Royals wasn't sure if he should even bother to reply. The thought of Rudy flopping around Mexico was ridiculous. Finally, he shook his head. "I'd be better off sending Ginger."

Rudy's face showed no response. It hardly ever did when Grover insulted him. The big man wondered if Rudy really didn't know when he was being humped or if he was just smart enough not to make anything of it. Looking now at his vacant stare, Grover decided on the first explanation. Rudy was just under six feet tall, and had a simple, peasant-like face. Flat blue eyes as revealing as raisins and thick hair the color of very dirty snow. Rudy's hair. Funniest damned thing Grover'd ever seen. He combed it from a skinny part on the far left, across the top, and over. It looked like a shiny off-white plate as the front came to a well-lacquered, rounded shelf an inch or so above his eyes.

"We have to get serious about Mr. Richie Moats," Grover continued. "Let's get cracking on our own again here. I know we've had feelers out since it happened, what, about two weeks ago? But it's time to take off the gloves. Bust some skulls if we have to. Talk to anyone who ever knew those two. I'm going to start with that uncle of Richie's. Mr. Waterbed. Tomorrow. I have some special plans for him." He stared at Rudy. "I don't suppose you came up with anything? Any names we should be checking out? I was you, I wouldn't be sleeping all that well at night. Those two thought they were stealing from you, plus the fact that you were so tight with Gillis. You're the one coming off like a real goof here. She was your hire, which makes her your problem."

Rudy took a long pull from his bourbon but pretended he didn't hear that last part. He tended to take long pulls from whatever was handy, having no preferences when it came to alcohol or women. "I'm chasing down these leads, Grover." He nodded his head in almost pained resolution. "Something should shake loose real soon."

"I can't tell you how secure that makes me feel," Grover said, rolling his eyes almost imperceptibly. "Here's what we do. Like I said, I'm talking to Uncle Marty tomorrow. Let him know I mean business. Then this weekend we're going back out there and talk to everyone, even the ones we already did last week. But this time, we go together and we lean on them like our lives depend on it." He shot Rudy another quick look. "In your case, that's about true. Either of you two got a better idea, let's hear it."

Rudy sat there listening, his face passive. Very subtle, you moron, he kept thinking as Grover laid it all out. But when he finished talking, Rudy merely grinned. "That sounds like the plan, big fella. We'll turn something for sure. This time next week, we'll have it all nailed down—absolutely."

7

It was late Saturday afternoon and Streeter sat nursing a hangover and staring idly at the keyboard of his deep-red mahogany baby grand. The memory of last night's activities kept him from practicing the Chopin nocturne. Plus, wine and vodka-tonics had left his mouth dry, his head pounding, and his attention span jangled. He leaned back and yawned, thinking about his dating disaster of the night before and how he'd reacted. Of course, in the first place, going on a blind date is asking for trouble. This one was arranged by a private eye who over the years had thrown some serious business his way. Streeter felt a sense of obligation when she called telling of a friend, mid-thirtyish, who was working her way through a divorce and looking to meet "interesting, evolved men. Like you, Street." He should have been more suspicious when she blew smoke that heavy. Then she described the friend with terms like "wonderful personality" and "deeply sensitive," but didn't provide details.

He had also made the mistake of agreeing to a full dinner date. That meant several hours of his time and attention, not to mention a potentially stiff tab. All with a woman he didn't even know if he wanted to spend twenty minutes with. Or vice versa. If you do jump for a blind date, make it a quick drink and both of you drive. But over the phone, Sally let him know that her favorite restaurant was Adde Brewster in Cherry Creek and that she thought it would be terrific if they went there. Adde's was posh deco and frequented by people who made the local society pages. Streeter couldn't think of a handy counterargument, so he agreed to make a reservation for seven o'clock.

Unfortunately, Sally believed that a "magnificent personality" demands several coats of makeup to be fully appreciated. Not that she was unattractive, although her actual looks were hard to find. So Streeter escorted her into Adde's just before seven. The woman liked to talk and to drink, and moderation wasn't in her repertoire. Sally nailed two quick martinis before the appetizers arrived and she attacked the dinner wine like it was an Olympic event. That was when the "deeply sensitive" portion of her "wonderful personality" kicked in. Halfway through the entrée she was heavily into a tortured postmortem of her marriage. Streeter listened with decreasing interest. She recalled in no small detail the indignities she'd suffered at the hands of her ex. It seems he'd left her for a twenty-two-year-old whose main drawing card was her disdain for wearing a bra. Then, when she tired of that topic, she went into a long riff of her read on why Streeter had been married and divorced four times. Sounded like a self-help marriage manual in the process.

By the time he drove her home, Streeter was a painful combination of bored and agitated. He walked Sally to her door, where they quickly shook hands. Neither of them even bothered to mention another date. She said she was too tired to ask him in and a relieved Streeter simply said goodnight. When he got back into the Buick at the curb, he just sat there for a long time. That same feeling of loneliness that had swept over him in Mazatlán came back with a vengeance. He wondered if he'd ever meet anyone whom he would feel jazzed up about. Then he thought of Constance from the music store. He wondered what she was doing that night. What she'd be like on a date. He also wondered what was behind those shy and cryptic smiles. Thinking about her made him feel painfully alone and more agitated so he started his car and drove to a bar within walking distance of the church. That was when the vodka-tonics portion of the evening began. No wonder married men live longer.

Sitting at the piano now, he made two more never-again promises to himself. These specifically regarded blind dates and solo drinking. Suddenly the cordless phone on the bench next to him rang. He grabbed it on the first ring and promptly dropped it onto the floor. When he picked it up, he heard that the voice on the other end belonged to a woman. Older and delicate, but strong and articulate. He liked it although he had no idea who it belonged to. "Mr. Streeter?"

"Yeah?"

"I'm not interrupting you, am I? I know it's the weekend."

The more he heard the woman talk, the more he liked her. "No, that's okay. Who is this?"

"Oh dear, I'm sorry." A hint of sincere remorse, then she recovered. "My name is Marlene Moats, Mr. Streeter. I believe you know my husband. Martin."

She made his name sound formal, almost majestic. Streeter had a hard time putting the woman behind the voice and Marty together in the same marriage. "Sure, sure." He paused. "You know, I've been trying to get ahold of your husband for the past couple of days. He's never around. What can I do for you, Mrs. Moats?"

"Martin's been quite busy. We'd like to hire you again. Martin and I. He'll be on the line in a minute to tell you all about it." Streeter could hear her softly call out her husband's name. Then she spoke to him again. "There was an incident at one of his stores last night. It was quite ugly, actually. Martin has the details, but it seems that several of his delivery trucks were destroyed." She paused. "Martin has been threatened as well, Mr. Streeter."

"Threatened? How?" He shifted his position on the piano bench and ran his hand through his hair.

"With extreme physical harm. You had better ask him." Her voice became less steady as she spoke.

"Have you called the police?"

There was another long pause, and before she could answer,

he heard the click of an extension being picked up. "Streeter." Marty's voice sounded rough after Marlene's. "How are you, son? Marlene tell you about our little trouble?"

"Sort of. She said your trucks were destroyed and someone threatened your person."

Marty let out a harsh grunt indicating amusement. "You might say that, son. When a fella says he's planning on nailing you to a wall and beating you to death with a baseball bat, I guess that your person's been threatened."

"Any idea who it was, Marty?"

"An old pal of yours. Name of Grover Royals. I understand you two played some ball together back at Central. Royals came out to my downtown store yesterday morning and said that if I don't produce Richie and his girlfriend, he'll be doing that nailing I spoke of a minute ago. Then—I gather to drive the point home good and clear—he had a couple of my trucks torched last night. At least it seems to me that he was the one to have done it and that that was his intention." Marty's voice rose in anger. "That son of a bitch came right to my place of business and did all that like I'm just another one of his pimps to push around."

"Martin, don't be vulgar," Marlene interrupted sternly.

Her voice calmed him. "That's asking a lot of me, darlin'," he responded.

"What did the police say?" Streeter stood up and began pacing his living room. The notion that Grover would do this after Streeter refused to work for him made him queasy and furious at the same time.

"Martin has not spoken to the police, Mr. Streeter," Marlene interjected. "He's being quite unreasonable about it."

"Now darlin' "—Marty spoke gently—"no need to go running to the police with every little problem. Besides, he just made that crack about nailing me up to get my attention. I can't believe he'd really do it."

Streeter knew better. “You’ve got to go to the police. What about your trucks?”

“No problem there. They were insured to the hilt against vandalism and you can bet I’ll make out just fine on that little exchange. Tell you what, son. This ain’t New York or one of them other faggy places where people have to get all hooked up with the law and the government whenever they got a beef. I take care of myself and my family in my own way.”

“He always has, Mr. Streeter,” Marlene Moats said evenly. “Don’t bother trying to change his mind. Martin’s stubborn as an old mule about most things.”

“Thank you, darlin’. ” Marty was clearly pleased with her words.

Streeter ran his left palm over his forehead. “Did he mention that he tried to hire me to find Richie?”

“That he did.”

“Did he tell you why he wants to find Richie?”

“Not exactly. He hinted around about it and I gather Richie and Tina owe him money. Lots of it.”

“How is it that Richie knows Grover Royals?” Streeter looked up at the high ceiling. “You have any idea what kind of sick things Royals does for a living?”

Marty considered that for a moment, so Marlene jumped in. “We gather that Mr. Royals is connected with Tina Gillis and her employer somehow. Miss Gillis works in the adult-entertainment field. Perhaps Richie borrowed money from this Royals. His last business venture did rather poorly and Martin was reluctant to keep financing his endeavors.”

“Got that right, darlin’, ” Marty shot in. “The boy knew he’d touched me for the last time when his telemarketing scheme bellied up.”

“Mrs. Moats mentioned that you want to hire me again,” Streeter said. “I take it you want me to look for Richie and Tina?”

"Among other things," Marty said. "I'd also like you to keep an eye on Marlene and me. Seeing as how you've got a history with this Royals guy, I was thinking you could maybe go have a talk with him. Let him know we're doing all we can to find Richie and that we'll see to it that the boy does right by him if he owes him money."

Marlene stepped in, her voice sounding anxious for the first time. "Tell him you'll find Richie and he'll come back here and straighten everything out. That is, if he's still alive."

"Could be this all is for the best," Marty said. "This Grover seems to believe that Richie and Tina staged that whole Mexican fiasco so everyone would think they were dead and gone for good. If that's true, at least the kids are still breathing."

"We'd practically given up on ever finding Richie." Marlene sounded more upbeat. "We're not proud of what he's done, but at least he may not be dead."

"That's right, darlin'," Marty said and then turned his attention back to Streeter. "I tell you what, son. You come work for me. There's this old business partner of Richie's that I told you about by the name of Eddy Spangler. Even Richie stands out as brilliant next to this mutt. I'd go see Eddy right quick. If Richie hatched up this Mexican deal to get lost, Spangler might know a little about it. Then go have that chat with Royals. Get us some time to bring Richie home."

"Listen, Marty," Streeter said. "You should be having this conversation with the police. We're already dealing with more felonies here than you can imagine. Grover Royals should have been slammed behind bars years ago. This could be a good chance to make that happen."

No one spoke at the other end for a long time. "Marty?" Streeter finally offered.

"We're still here, son." Then, to his wife, he added, "Marlene, darlin'? Would you mind hanging up and letting me have a word in private with the man? I'd surely appreciate it."

"Goodbye, Mr. Streeter." Her voice was calm and composed again. "Thank you for helping us, dear." With that, she hung up.

Marty's voice was hushed when he spoke again. "I didn't want Marlene to hear this, but that crazy fucker Royals didn't actually say it'd be my ass he'd nail to the wall if I go to the police." He sounded genuinely shaken. "He said if I involve the cops, it'd be Marlene he'd come after first. I believe him, too. He said if we get Richie to call him, everyone will come out fine. I have to do it his way, son. Work outside the law. I can't risk getting Marlene hurt. I'll make it more than worth your while—financially speaking, that is."

Streeter was pacing faster now. He wasn't nuts about working for Moats after the way the old man had cut him off at the knees in Mexico. And messing with a severely pissed-off Grover Royals didn't exactly appeal to him, either. But how could he turn down the kind of money Marty paid? He couldn't and he damned well knew it. "Okay, I'll do it," he heard himself saying. "For you and Mrs. Moats."

"I was counting on you feeling that way, son."

8

Eddy Spangler's office was located at the end of an aging strip mall, behind a cluttered pet-grooming store named Doggy Styles. The place was just north of 6th Avenue on Wadsworth Boulevard in Lakewood, a suburb west of Denver. Doggy Styles matched the condition and motif of the entire mall: poorly tended schlock. There was a wig store that never seemed busy, a karate school that never seemed open, a take-out pizza place that never seemed closed, and a liquor store that never seemed to have heard about the legal drinking age. Spangler's decrepit résumé office fit in nicely.

Streeter did a good bit of looking before he found the cramped, windowless room where Eddy toiled as many as three days a week. Luckily, that Monday was one of those days. Streeter knocked on the wood-veneer door bearing a sign in green Magic Marker on typing paper proclaiming EXECUTIVE SEARCH PREPARATION. Spangler wrote résumés primarily for high-school graduates and GEDs looking to crack the corporate bowels of places like Target or Pep Boys Automotive or KFC. A weary "Yeah" came from within ESP's headquarters.

Streeter opened the door and winced to focus his eyes. The room was lit by two dim fluorescent ceiling bulbs, one of which flickered randomly. Spangler sat behind a gray metal desk scouring the sports pages of the *Denver Post* and nursing a Big Gulp the color of turquoise sludge. He barely looked up when the bounty hunter entered. Eddy appeared to be in his late twenties and was good-looking in a retro-disco sort of way. His thick black hair was combed down, highlighted by sideburns almost large enough to suit Elvis in his final Vegas days. But he also had penetrating dark eyes and a handsomely delicate bone structure that gave his face a certain low-rent cool. He glanced up from the paper and studied his visitor.

"You looking for a résumé, hoss?" The words slid out like speaking took great effort, and the rest of his face showed no interest in what his mouth was saying. A trace of a southern accent made him seem even more bored. Streeter stared hard at him without answering. Finally, Eddy shifted in his chair and put down the paper. "I say, hoss, you interested in getting yourself a résumé?" he repeated, almost like this time he cared.

Streeter closed the door and walked the ten or so feet across the room. There was only one other chair, a folding number with duct tape on the seat. A two-drawer file cabinet displaying a bumper sticker that read HUNG LIKE EINSTEIN, SMART AS A HORSE stood in one corner. An IBM clone and an aging printer sat on a card table across from Spangler. The bounty hunter stood in front of the desk staring down at the résumé maker.

"Eddy Spangler?" he finally asked.

The man sat up and his face hardened. "Who wants to know?"

That lazy smugness was still in the voice and Streeter liked him less with every syllable. He decided to see how plugged in the guy was. "Grover Royals, that's who," he said.

The name drew blood as Spangler quickly cleared his throat twice and blushed. Glancing at Streeter's huge forearms, he asked in an almost reverential tone, "You're Grover?"

"No. But I'm sure one phone call would get him down here. My bet is he'd like to talk to you." Streeter looked slowly around the room. "Nice office."

Eddie frowned deeply and a trace of the cockiness crawled back into his voice. "I know it's not all that classy, but you should see the kind of mouth-breathers I deal with out here. It pays the bills." He studied his guest's face. "We know who you're not. Mind telling me who you are?"

"I'm a friend of a friend and I need to find that friend. I was told maybe you could help me."

"That's a lot of friends to keep track of there, hoss. A name or two might help." Eddy's voice was now back up to full-schmooze, salesman strength.

Streeter wanted to get to the point and leave, so he put heavy steam into his voice. "First of all, little fella, my name's not hoss. Save that for those mouth-breathers you mentioned. Second, you knowing who Grover is and being that scared of him is very interesting."

"Just who the hell are you?" Eddy's eyes narrowed and his voice deepened.

"I'm someone who's going to save you and our mutual friends a lot of trouble. And I'm the guy standing between you and Grover Royals. It's very important for you that someone does that because if Grover knew how tight you are with our friends, he'd drop by here. I'm sure you don't want that." He straightened up, keeping hard eye contact with Eddy. "My name's Streeter and I'm looking for Richie Moats and Tina Gillis. Apparently they have something that belongs to Mr. Royals. He wants it back so badly that he's threatening certain people about it. As you know, Richie and Tina have been missing for a while. There was talk that they might have been killed in Mexico. But Mr. Royals is of a different opinion. So am I. We believe they're making themselves scarce on purpose." He nodded. "You're tight with Richie and if anyone in Denver knows where he is, it'd be you. I want you to tell me where he and Tina are, along with anything you might know about why Mr. Royals is so interested in finding them."

Spangler opened his mouth to speak, but Streeter held up both hands, palms toward him, and shook his head. "Before you answer, Eddy, I want to say a couple of other things. I know that you're a bullshit artist. I've heard that and it's written all over your face." His voice stayed low and firm, but not angry. "Also, I know that if Richie and Tina are on the run, they're in deep trouble, because Royals'll catch them sooner or later. That's how he is. And he'll stomp them real good along with anyone who helped them. So think real hard before you tell me what you know. If all you're going to give me is some I-have-no-idea-where-they-are crap, then save it. I don't even want to hear it. I'll just call Grover and you can discuss it with him."

"But it's the truth," Eddy blurted out, his voice hoarse with concern. All of the cockiness was drained from it by now. "I haven't seen or heard from them in a month or more. I don't have a clue where they are."

Streeter winced and shook his head. "I told you not to tell me that, Eddy. You're not a very good listener." He reached into his shirt pocket, pulled out Frank's card, and tossed it on the desk. "How's this? You obviously need some time to think over what I said. You might even want to confer with our friends. I'll give you a day or so, and if you haven't called me with a better recollection of what's going on, then I'll personally arrange it so that Grover Royals comes by and asks you the same questions. That sound like a plan, Eddy? I don't see how I can be more fair."

"Jesus Christ, you're putting me in a barrel here." His features looked more delicate than before, almost frail.

"The name's not hoss and it's not Jesus Christ, either. It's Streeter." He leaned forward, his palms now on the desk. "You think you might be remembering more about Richie yet?"

Eddy slumped down. Streeter's arms looked thick as logs from where he sat and he could see that the guy wasn't joking around. Still, Eddy needed time to think. "Let me check around. Two days. I'll call you Wednesday." He shook his head. "Just don't go talking to Grover. Okay? Give me until Wednesday."

"Tomorrow night, Eddy." Streeter straightened up again and took a step backward. "Give me a holler by about eight tomorrow night. I don't want to waste too much of anyone's time on this. And while you're checking around, keep in mind that Grover's already talked to Richie's uncle. He made some very ugly suggestions about what might happen to him and Aunt

Marlene if Richie doesn't turn up soon. I don't think your friend wants his aunt to deal with that maniac. Have Richie phone home. And fast."

"I'll do what I can." Eddy's voice was sad and resigned by now. "Just don't go running to Royals. I'll do my best to help all our friends."

"That's all we can ask, right? That you do your best."

Eddy sat up a bit. "It was Uncle Marty that hired you. Right?"

"I'll talk to you by tomorrow, Eddy," was all Streeter said before he turned and walked out of the room.

Eddy sat in silence for a long time afterward, nursing his Big Gulp. The room seemed more quiet than usual. Finally, he made a long-distance call to Naples, Florida. Tina Gillis answered on the third ring.

"Hello." She sounded tentative. Not her usual style, but then hiding out in south Florida wasn't, either.

"That was one hell of a plan you guys came up with," Eddy yelled, standing up from his desk. "First, you don't fool anyone with your stupid Mexican ploy. Dropping off the Blazer down there, smearing a little blood on it, and then taking a bus out. About the only people you conned were the reporters. Which leaves the rest of Denver looking for you. Guess who just visited my office?"

There was a pause. Tina cleared her throat and spoke softly into the phone. "A guy named Grover Royals?"

Eddy held the receiver away from his face and frowned at it for a moment. Then he pulled it back to his ear. "Sort of. I mean, how'd you know about him?"

"Last week, Richie and I finally went over every page of those files I took from Rudy's office. It turns out that I was very mistaken about what was going on there. Rudy Fontana was just a token figurehead." Her voice picked up clarity and force as she spoke. "Grover Royals is really in charge. He owns everything and runs the whole operation. It looks like there might be a silent partner somewhere in the background, but Grover's the immediate man in charge. That means it was his money Richie took from those two clowns in the alley." She paused and glanced around the living room of their rented mobile home. "If we had thought Grover was connected in any way, we never would have made the move. He won't let this slide no matter where we run."

"No shit, Sherlock! I'd say you were *very mistaken* about all that stuff!" Eddy walked from behind his desk and started moving aimlessly around his office. "I've heard about Grover Royals, myself. Who hasn't? He's got a big rep in this town and he's nothing like that Fontana guy you told me about. Nothing at all. This is one major screwup, Tina. Royals *kills* people, from what I've heard. That's his rep." His voice was getting high-pitched, so he paused for a moment to calm down.

Tina jumped into the void. "What did Grover say when he came by?"

Eddy frowned in confusion. "He didn't say . . . I mean it wasn't actually him. It was some PI or whatever by the name of Streeter. He wouldn't tell me for sure, but my hunch is that Uncle Marty hired him to find you two. The guy was probably as big as Royals and about as convincing, too. He just left my office. Told me that if I don't come up with you two bozos real fast, he'll sic Grover on me. See, Grover's talked to Streeter and Uncle Marty already. Like I said, nobody bought that Mexican trick. And he's putting heat on Marty and the aunt. Threatened them, according to Streeter. This whole thing's unraveling fast, and seeing as how shit generally rolls downhill, everyone's coming after me."

"You say none of them think we're dead?"

"No one. Except those idiots with the local news. According to both papers and all the TV stations, you two died down there. That should tell you about the quality of information the average citizen gets nowadays." He was picking up momentum again and his voice was rising. "All that crap in Mexico was just a waste of time and money. Not to mention a little of Richie's blood. Grover knows you're alive, which means you're not even close to safe in that little hometown of yours."

"No kidding. Exactly what do you think he wants from us?"

"Who knows? I would guess that he'd like his money back. He might want a couple of pounds of your skin while he's at it. Streeter just wants to know where you are and to have Richie call his uncle and aunt." Eddy paused. "You're no match for either of them. What the hell are you going to do now?"

"Well, for starters I'm not going to panic. You might chill out a little yourself." Her voice was totally calm by now. "When Richie gets back from the store later, he and I'll figure out our options. We've still got some insurance. Those files I took from Rudy. They'll work as well against Grover as against Rudy. Based on these financial records and his ledgers, Grover's implicated in half the vice in Colorado. Not to mention the pictures from his sex parties. A lot of high rollers there. The kind of men who won't tolerate bad publicity. My hunch is Grover Royals wants this stuff back as much as he wants his money. More, maybe."

"Great!" Eddy felt himself getting hyper again. "Another one of your hunches. What am I supposed to do back here? Between Grover and Streeter, I'm right in the line of fire. I'm giving some serious thought to just getting out of town for a couple of decades."

Tina paused before answering. "You can start by taking a few deep breaths. Richie and I'll sort it all out this afternoon and we'll get back to you tonight. No one's going to hurt you. When Richie hears that his aunt's been threatened, he'll want to take care of her. Where will you be later?"

"My place."

"Okay. We'll take care of Grover and make things right. You're going to be just fine, Eddy."

"Knowing how on the mark you've been up to now, that's not all that comforting."

9

Grover and Sid were not amused, but Doggy Styles cracked Rudy up no end. When they saw it that Monday afternoon, it was the first time any one of them had smiled in days. All week-end they'd been hounding people who knew Richie and Tina. Despite Grover's hard-assed threats, no one had any idea where they were. Finally, late Sunday afternoon, one of Richie's old girlfriends mentioned a bogus slacker named Eddy Spangler who Moats had hooked up with a few years earlier. They started a fly-by-night telemarketing company together. It went under, and now Spangler was just scrambling to make a living. She had only his name and description, so it took Grover almost a full day to track Eddy to his office in the run-down Lakewood shopette.

"What a hoot," Rudy said, shaking his head in amazement as they stood outside the pet store. "Doggy Styles! Like the position. You know, for shtupping. Don't you guys get it?"

It was unseasonably warm. The sun had pushed the temperature into the upper eighties, turning the parking lot into a skillet. Typical moody Colorado springtime: from snow to near ninety in four days.

Sid Wahl, being the kind of guy who broke into a grin maybe once every couple of years, didn't respond. Grover studied Rudy, who was wearing silver sunglasses and a white sport coat with the sleeves at least an inch too short. "No, it's way the hell over my head," Grover deadpanned. "Why don't you explain it to us, Moe?"

"That doesn't crack you up?" Fontana pressed on. "Straight from behind like a dog. Hysterical." He grinned like an idiot.

"Yeah, well, if we don't find Tina and Richie you'll get to know all about what that feels like." There wasn't a hint of amusement in Grover's voice.

Fontana changed the subject. "His office is supposed to be right behind the pet store," he said and glanced toward a metal outer door next to the Styles window. "What a dump." He took a few steps toward the door and winced in concentration. "Here it is, all right. Executive Search Preparation."

Grover moved past Rudy and stared at the small metal sign. Then he turned back to Sid and grabbed the door handle. "This better be worth it," the big man said.

Sid nodded. The three walked down the hall, which smelled like animal piss and cleaning fluid, with a strong hint of bird-seed. When they got to Eddy's door, Sid grabbed the handle and found that it was locked. He turned to Grover and shrugged. Royals pushed him to the side and grunted. Then he squared up on the door and shifted his shoulders once. He grabbed the handle, leaned back, and burst forward, with his right shoulder hitting the door a couple of feet above the handle. The thin oak veneer of the door popped through the narrow wooden strip on the other side like it was made out of potato chips and swung inward and open. Grover nodded and walked in with the other two right behind him. The fluorescent overhead light was on but no one was there. Grover looked around and muttered "Shit" under his breath. Then he turned to Sid off to his left. "There has to be a home address or a phone number around here somewhere. Some way to get ahold of this jerk. Let's find it."

With that, the three descended on the desk and file cabinet. It only took about ten minutes before Rudy found a spiral note-book on the bottom of the lowest file drawer. A power-blue book with the words PHONE NO's scrawled in what appeared to be the same Magic Marker that had made the door sign.

"This should do 'er, Grover," Rudy said, holding up the worn notebook and smiling like he just discovered a cure for cancer.

Grover didn't say a word but just grabbed it from Rudy's hand. Then he dropped into the chair behind the desk and started leafing silently through the book. "I don't think his address is in here but there's a pager number inside the back cover," he finally said without looking up. "A few other numbers and addresses in here that might help us out, too." Then he glanced at the phone in front of him and, picking up the receiver, pressed in the pager number.

Eddy was going through his back closet trying to decide what to take with him. Following his conversation with Tina, he'd decided that his best move was to leave Colorado for a month or so. Maybe for good. He had a cousin in southern California who'd let him crash at his place and he still had more than half of the money Richie had given him. Hell with Richie, Tina, Streeter, Grover, and the whole mess. He was reaching into a dresser drawer for a sweater when his pager went off. Eddy frowned and grabbed his belt on the side and pulled out the tiny beeper. His frown deepened when he saw that the call was from his own office. He was the only one who had a key to the door, other than the building maintenance people. Eddy walked to the bathroom just outside his bedroom, where a black portable phone sat on the sink counter. He pulled the toilet seat down and sat on it, thoroughly confused. Should he answer? Why? Hell, why not? Slowly, he picked up the receiver and punched in his office number. The phone was picked up before the first ring was finished, causing Eddy's head to snap back slightly.

"Yeah?" Grover put as much friendliness into it as he could muster, which wasn't much.

Eddy winced in curiosity. "Who is this?"

"Eddy, baby," he answered with more mock charm. "So good of you to call back." He paused for a beat. "My name is Grover

Royals and I'm in kind of a hurry here. Patience never was what you'd call one of my stronger points. Same thing can be said about compassion, too." He paused to let that sink in. "You have any idea who I am?"

"Everyone knows who Grover Royals is." Eddy suddenly sounded very sad.

"And you know about my connection to Richie Moats?"

Silence for a long time. Then, "I got some idea."

"Then you probably know why I'm calling. And you should be able to help me out. Let's cut right to it, Eddy. I hear anything that sounds like bullshit and I might make a few visits." He glanced down at the notebook in his hands. "We've got your address book and I bet I could get ahold of your mother, your sister, and a whole bunch of your friends if I had to. I'm sure you don't want me buggin' all those people. Makin' their lives miserable just because you won't cooperate. Now, I assume it was Richie Moats or Tina Gillis that told you I might be contacting you."

Spangler tried to figure his play. Since Streeter had left six hours earlier, he had spoken to Tina and then spent a couple of hours pacing his office and taking quick hits from the bottle of blended whiskey he kept in his bottom drawer. Even had a bump or two of the flake he kept in the file cabinet. And he'd seriously reevaluated his position. Richie and Tina had given him three thousand in cash the night they had split for Mexico. The money was for Eddy to keep an eye on the fallout from the robbery. But that wasn't nearly enough to compensate him for his having to deal with Grover Royals or now maybe having him come down on his mother and the rest of those folks. All he wanted to do was get out of town with his body intact and make sure Grover left him and his family alone. No point trying to con this guy.

"Among other people," he finally said. "There was some kind of PI or bounty hunter came to see me late this morning. I think he's working for Marty Moats. Richie's uncle. He told me if I didn't cooperate with him and rat out Richie, he'd give you a call. That was a few hours ago." He frowned. "Was he the one who told you how to find my place?"

Grover ignored the question. "His name wasn't Streeter, by any chance?"

"That's the man."

Grover spun hard to his left and punched at the air. Then he glanced at Sid. "At least we know that our little fire Friday night got to the old man." Then he turned his attention back to the phone. "Listen, Eddy. I assume I got your attention now."

"That's damned straight, hoss," Eddy responded. He just wanted to end the conversation and get going. "You got my undivided attention. Ask me what it is you need and I'll see that you get it."

"I assume that Richie and Tina are still alive."

"Right."

"And they would be hanging out where, right about now?" Grover asked slowly, deliberately pronouncing each syllable of every word.

"They would be hanging out in Naples, Florida." Eddy sat up. "They're staying in some rattrap trailer park down there. See, Tina was born in Naples and she knows a few people in town."

Grover turned to Fontana and cocked his head. "Did you know she was from south Florida, Rudy?"

Rudy shifted his weight from one foot to another and glanced off to the side. "She might have mentioned it to me at some point."

"Yeah?" Grover's voice grew lower and the edge got harder. "Terrific. And when were you thinking of mentioning it to me? That's something we should have been working on."

"I forgot, okay?" Rudy looked back.

Grover said nothing and instead refocused on the phone. "Eddy? You got a phone number where we can call them?"

Eddy nodded and said, "I talked to Tina at about one. She

said Richie was out but he'd be back later. Their number should be written down on my notepad there on top of the desk. It's a couple of pages in and the area code is 813. You see it?"

Grover looked down at the pad in front of him and worked his way through five pages before he came to the phone number. "Yeah," he answered. "I might want to just give those two crazy kids a call. I gather that whole Mexican trip was just a dodge."

"From the word go." Eddy stood up from the toilet. "That was Tina's brainstorm. She thought it would throw everyone off the track. 'Course, she didn't know she'd be dealing with you." He paused for a moment wondering if he should go on. Why not? "From what she tells me now, they had no idea you were involved until they went through some files she took from the office." He knew he was answering questions Grover hadn't even asked yet, but he felt like getting everything out. Like it made him safer. "Who knows what they were thinking, huh? They were nuts."

"Yeah, they were," Grover said. "So, they still have those files?"

"That they do, hoss," Eddy said. "Tina called it their life insurance."

Grover stood up, a scowl on his face. "Did she tell you what's in them?"

Eddy shook his head. "No sir. And I didn't ask, either. Look, they fucked up. Everyone's willing to acknowledge that. And now, especially with Richie's uncle and aunt in trouble, I'm sure they'll do whatever it takes to make things right. That's all any of us want."

Grover glanced at Rudy and Sid before talking to Eddy again. "Well, *hoss.* I'll be going now. I want to call down there to Naples." There was a long pause. "I tell you what. Don't get any ideas about leaving town. And give me your home number, too. Might be I'll need to talk to you in the near future." His voice lowered. "I'm not joking around here, either. If you should talk to those two, let them know how serious I am about getting my money back and that I know how to get in touch with their families. Yours, too, for that matter."

By the time Grover finished, Eddy's head was bobbing up and down like one of those little football-player statues with a spring in the neck. "You're absolutely right, Grover. No one wants this thing to go any further. We'll just make things right and get you happy again. Like I said, that's all any of us want."

"You better make that your number-one priority from now on," Grover said. "As far as you and Tina and Richie are concerned, my happiness is a matter of life and death." He looked around. "By the way, nice office." With that, he hung up. Then he quickly grabbed the receiver and dialed the Naples number. When no one answered after about a dozen rings, he put the receiver down and looked at Sid and Rudy. "No one's home. Let's get back to the Cheetah."

Eddy sat quietly on the toilet for a long time. Leaving town was now out of the question. Better try to persuade Richie to get his sorry ass back to Denver. All this for a crummy three grand. Finally, he rose and went back to the bedroom to have a hit from the tiny bindle of cocaine that was supposed to get him to California.

10

To Tina, Eddy Spangler was nothing but a lying, two-faced pretty boy. Any fool could see that. Any fool, apparently, except for Richie, and that always bothered her. The little résumé writer was trouble and always out for himself. Listening to his message now on the answering machine drove that point squarely home. Once again. She and Richie had just gotten back from dinner and they were standing in the long, narrow living room of her father's mobile home. The place was done up in conflicting yard-sale furniture, but kept as tidy and uncluttered as a hospital.

"I did all I could to protect you guys," Eddy was saying. "Grover Royals himself stopped by the office. Brought a couple of guys with him, too." Eddy decided not to tell them he wasn't there personally for the visit. Let them draw their own conclusions. "A guy he called Rudy, I'm guessing Fontana, and some other guy. They called you before but you must not have had your machine on. Anyhow, there was no point trying to con them. He threatened my family, for chrissakes. I leave town, Royals'll go deal with my family. Richie, he said he'll hurt your uncle and your aunt, too. I know Marlene's like a mother to you. They already fucked with your uncle somehow." There was a pause. "It's all over, you guys. Royals is on to you. He'll probably be calling you later or else you're supposed to call him. While you're at it, I'd suggest you drop a dime on Marty and tell him what's going on. Him and Marlene must be scared shitless."

There was a long pause on the tape. Richie's forehead was pleated in concern as he stared at the machine. Then he glanced at Tina, who was watching him. His eyebrows shot up for a second and he opened his mouth to speak. But before he could, Eddy came back on the recorder.

"Look, I'm sorry it has to go down like this. But you gotta understand the position you put me in. Come back and settle up with these guys. There's no other way."

When the message ended, Richie leaned over and turned off the machine. Tina fumbled through her purse and pulled out a Camel Light and matches. "I just bet that worm put up a fight," she said, striking a match. "They probably asked him once and he folded like a cheap card table." She looked off and took a puff. It was almost dark but they hadn't turned any lights on yet. "Where'd you dig that guy up, Richard?" That was the only name she ever called him.

Richie looked at her and slowly ran the fingertips of one hand over his thick mustache. Standing there in his plaid shorts, he suddenly felt vulnerable and stupid. "I know you always said he's pretty much of a dink, but he's right about this one, Teen. No way I'm going to let Aunt Marlene get hurt. Or Marty, for that matter. He's no day at the beach, but I can't get him killed."

Tina considered that but didn't respond. Instead, she let out another long blast of smoke and then stubbed her cigarette in the ashtray on a cocktail table. Where *does* that blind spot for Eddy come from? She walked over and turned on the kitchen wall light. Glancing around the front of her father's mobile home put her in a worse mood. The place reminded her of him and how she wouldn't be able to help him now. Stan Gillis owned a small convenience store and bait-and-tackle shop on the bay in north Naples. He'd had the place for almost twenty years and it was on the verge of going under. Strapped with debt and needing almost a hundred thousand dollars for Health Department upgrades and other overdue improvements, Stan had asked his daughter a few months ago if she had any ideas on how to dig out. Tina adored him. Fifty-one and a decorated Vietnam veteran, he had treated his only child like gold since his wife's death years earlier.

Stealing from Rudy seemed like a reasonable plan. But when she talked to Stan about it, she made it sound as though she and Richie were more or less borrowing the money. Nothing was said about armed robbery and Stan didn't ask too many questions. Take the money from Rudy, she figured, bail Stan out with about half of it, and then go to work for him at his store while they invested the rest. Richie went for it in a heartbeat. Hell, he'd take a whack at swimming up Niagara Falls if it made Tina happy. Plus, being a rabid fisherman since he was ten, he liked the idea of working near the water. But now, Tina realized as she looked around the trailer, it wouldn't happen. She knew they had to go back to Denver and make things right with Grover.

"I don't want to give them the money back any more than you do, honey," Richie continued in a gentle tone. He took a step toward Tina. To him, she was irresistible. That light drift of freckles across her nose. What a face. He loved everything about Tina. The way she walked, the way she slept, the way she ate, the way she made love. But especially the freckles. Gave her a little-girl innocence to go with her high cheekbones and cat-like green eyes. Sometimes Richie didn't like being in love so deeply. If anything happened to break them up, he'd be so lost. It made him act like a hungry puppy around her. Still, when they were together he wouldn't trade it for the world. And the sex. Forget it. Both in quantity and quality, Tina Gillis had simply spoiled him for any other woman. Just look at her there in that yellow halter top and those tight white shorts. "But I can't leave Aunt Marlene hanging like this."

Staring at the middle of his chest, Tina shook her head. Finally, she looked at his face. Richard had incredibly intense eyes. He might be a bit slow on the uptake, but he had a way of looking at her with so much feeling it let her know how much he cared. It's nice being adored. And that open, friendly face of his. Amazing that a scammy mind like Richard's sat behind such a trusting face.

"You're right, of course," she said. "I've been thinking about that ever since Shit-for-brains called the first time. You and I covered it over dinner tonight. It's just that I hate to throw in the towel with an idiot like Rudy, not to mention what it's going to mean to Dad."

Richie's voice was really soft now and he put the back of his hand on her cheek and stroked it lightly. "I know how you feel about that, but at least we'll be alive and we'll be together. Maybe we can think of some other way to get Stan back on his feet." He paused. "We gave it a shot, and now the party's over. Might as well call Fontana."

She nodded. "But if Grover answers, I'm hanging up. I don't want to talk to him yet. Rudy'll tell me how bad it is." She shook her head. "Damned Grover. I pride myself on knowing the score but I didn't have a clue that he ran things. He'd come around from time to time, but I thought he just had a slice of the strip joints. How could I have been so wrong?"

"A lot of people keep two sets of books, and you weren't Rudy's accountant, Teen. Just let him know we're coming back with the money. I'll talk to Marty when you're done."

Tina went to the phone on the salmon-colored Formica counter between the kitchen and the living room. The whining of the window air conditioner was so loud she turned it off. "Richard, get me a Rolling Rock, please?" She looked at him, pulling an ashtray toward her. Then she lit another cigarette. The clock next to the phone showed it was almost eight, which meant it would be six in Denver. He moved toward the refrigerator as she worked the phone. Rudy picked up on the second ring.

"Yeah," he answered. "Yeah!" he repeated louder.

That's our Rudy, Tina thought. Class up the gazoo. Richie sat the Rolling Rock bottle in front of her. She blinked once as she spoke. "Rudy?"

A pause was followed by an explosion of sound that made her pull the receiver from her ear. "Gillis, you . . . Jesus!" He paused. "You got your nerve, you know that?"

Tina rolled her eyes at Richie. "Rudy, calm down."

"Calm down my ass. You're not the one with Grover Royals in your face all day long." He lowered his voice a shade. "At least not yet."

"Believe me, Rudy, we had no idea the money belonged to him."

"That supposed to make me feel better?" His voice rose again. "Thinking you were stealing from me is hardly a consolation here, Tina. After all I did for you. The good pay, the trust, for God's sake. Then you turn around and screw me over like this!"

"Spare me, Rudy. I worked long and hard for you. Then I made one mistake. What's done is done. The question now is: How can I put things right?"

"Yeah, that does seem to be the sixty-four-thousand-dollar question. Grover'd like to run you and Richie through a drill press right about now." His breathing sounded wheezy. A binge smoker, he'd been lighting up like a foundry since the robbery. "And that crazy fuckin' dwarf Sid Wahl wouldn't mind a shot at you, either." He chuckled. "That was really something, Richie puking on him like that. You should of seen him and Dexter when they got out of that trunk. The smell, for God's sake." He paused. "You still got the money?"

"Yes."

"And all that stuff from my file cabinet? You still got that?"

She nodded and answered, "Damned right I do."

"You know, that's the real pisser here, Tina. My own files." He didn't say anything for a moment. "Listen, just stay near the phone. I'm seeing Grover later and he'll probably want to talk to you tonight. Tomorrow for sure. He'll lay down the terms and don't kid yourself. It won't be much of a negotiation. You're going to pay big-time."

Tina blew smoke from her nostrils. "I understand, Rudy. But you and Grover better understand that there has to be a safe way out of this for Richard and myself. No more leaning on his family. This is between us and Grover, and it can be taken care of without people getting hurt. If not, those files go to the police and the media. We've got enough copies of them to paper a courtroom. Are we clear on that?"

Rudy didn't answer for a while, so Tina sipped her beer. Finally he came back in a soft voice. "I don't know what this maniac'll do next, Tina. Just plan on getting back here fast. And don't try to shovel any manure at the guy. You have no idea what Royals is capable of. No idea." With that, he hung up.

Richie, who had been sitting across the table from her during the conversation, stood up. "You did good, Teen. Just the right tone."

She glanced at him. "We'll be hearing from Grover soon and it won't be fun. Speaking of no fun, you better call your uncle."

He nodded and reached for the phone while still standing. Normally jumpy as an overbred terrier, Richie sure as hell couldn't sit still for this conversation. He pressed in Marty's home number, biting on his lower lip and playing with the end of his mustache all the while.

"Hello," Marty's familiar voice boomed through after several rings.

Without hesitation, Richie said. "Uncle Marty?"

There was a long pause on the other end. "Is that you, Richie? How are you, boy?" His voice was more sad than angry.

"I'm good. Really, I'm fine." Richie glanced at Tina and his eyebrows shot up.

"Where are you?" The voice picked up slightly.

"We're down in Florida." He nodded across the table. "Me and Tina. Do you remember her?"

"Yes, I believe I do." Another pause and then in a more

agitated tone, "You really stepped in it all the way this time. What the hell were you thinking, son?"

He shrugged. "What else? I was thinking about money. And don't worry. I'm going to make everything good."

"For chrissakes!" Marty yelled suddenly. "Make everything good? You worried your aunt sick and got me threatened by some gangster or whatever the hell he is. The police in two countries are looking for you, and a couple of my delivery trucks got torched. Now what? You're going to snap your fingers and make everything okay?" He was silent. "To be honest, son, I didn't think you had enough ambition or smarts to try something this far over the top. But I damn well knew that whatever it was you were trying, you'd muck it up somehow. That's generally how you operate."

Richie's face tightened. Just like Marty to treat him like a dim-witted child. Ever since he went to live with his aunt and uncle after his parents died, old Marty'd been riding him like a mule. Pointing out his shortcomings. If it hadn't been for Aunt Marlene, Richie figured, he would have cut bait with that guy years ago. "Look, I understand that you're mad and I'm sorry for all the trouble I caused. But we're coming back to Denver to make good. You and Aunt Marlene are safe and I don't need a lecture."

When Marty spoke again, his voice was softer. "Well, at least your aunt'll sleep better knowing you're alive. She's not here right now or I'd let you talk to her."

Richie toyed with his mustache again. "I would have called her eventually. Exactly how much do you know about what's going on?"

"I know you stole from Royals and Tina's boss, and they want everything back. I know you staged that bullshit in Mexico to cover your tracks. And I know it's all rolling back this way, toward your aunt and me. I also know we want to keep everything under wraps and away from the public eye. Sound like I got a handle on it, son?"

"Yes. Just let me work with these guys and get it straightened out. We'll think of something to tell the cops and reporters later to explain why I'm back in town."

"You do that, Richie. And don't get cute with these folks. Give them what they want and hope they forget the whole thing. First thing tomorrow, give your aunt a call. She's worried half to death. I'll explain it to her later, but you talk to her in the morning."

Richie frowned. "Yeah." Then his voice softened. "And tell her I'm sorry. Okay?"

When he hung up, Richie stared silently at the table. Tina reached over to him and put her hand on his. "Two brutal calls and we came out all right, Richard." He nodded and she continued. "Dad's staying with his girlfriend tonight and I think you and I should relax and enjoy ourselves." She smiled and nodded toward the back of the mobile home, where the bedrooms were. Richie flushed and she twitched her shoulders for dramatic effect. "It feels like a latex-and-body-oil kind of night."

She stood and he followed her through the den, watching her flowing red hair sway in front of him. By the time they got to the hallway, Richie was spellbound. Once they were inside the bedroom, Tina turned to him, frowning. "What is it, Teen?" he asked.

"I want to talk to you about something, later. I think we can keep a lot of that money, after all."

Her words bothered him, but as she slipped out of her yellow halter top, he was way too juiced to speak.

Streeter was tapping on Frank's desktop with a pencil and listening to Marty on the phone. From time to time, he'd nod. Finally, he spoke. "Must have been Spangler who gave Grover Richie's number. He must have tracked him down today after I left. Eddy just about gagged when I mentioned Royals's name this morning."

"Don't see where it matters much, son." Marty sounded like

he was in a hurry. "The main thing is the boy's alive and he's coming home with what he stole. Don't matter to me who got ahold of who first."

"I guess this means you won't be needing me anymore," Streeter said.

"Not necessarily. This thing won't be over until the money and those papers are returned and Royals and his friends are happy. Might be I'd like to get you involved in all that. We can't go to the police and I want someone I can trust working on our side."

"Whatever you need, Marty. I'll take care of it."

"Good, son. With Richie involved at that end, it ain't going to be over until it's over. *All* over. You follow my drift?"

11

About the last thing Streeter expected to find at Grover's house that Tuesday morning was a wife. Grover's wife, at any rate. His being married made as much sense as putting a Democrat on a budget: it had to be in name only, so why bother? But more baffling was that the Royalses had tied the knot sixteen years before and had produced two sullen offspring. One, nominally, from each gender column. The girl was fifteen, the boy two years younger. They'd inherited their father's crooked features and both were androgynous in a Russian swim team sort of way.

Streeter pulled his old Buick to the curb in front of the West Denver bungalow. He rechecked the address he'd gotten from the Department of Motor Vehicles. The house was not what he would have expected. Located in a working-class neighborhood between Federal and Sheridan in the low Forties, Grover's place looked more like a plumber's home than that of Denver's sex-for-sale baron.

Marty had asked him the night before to talk to Grover as soon as possible. Find out what he expected of Richie and Tina before they came back to town. Streeter was not authorized to negotiate, but rather to get the terms and, primarily, to assure Royals that old Marty would make good.

"Don't rile up this piece of shit if you can avoid it, Streeter," Marty had instructed. "Let him know he's going to get everything back. We sure as hell want him calm and reasonable. It'd be a good idea to go right to where he lives. That always tends to make a fella more cautious."

"I still think you should tell the cops what he did to your trucks," Streeter had responded. "Grover's the kind of man who understands the law leaning on him and not much else. Don't expect him to do the right thing just because you're nice to him."

"You might be right about that, son, but we'll do this my way. You know what Royals said he'd do if we called the cops. Plus, bring the police in and we have to explain what the hell Richie's been up to lately. My nephew sharing a cell with Grover down in Cañon City isn't anyone's version of a good idea."

Hence, Streeter arrived at Grover's first thing that morning. Patty Royals looked like an aging prom queen who took ownership of a liquor store somewhere along the line. She was a blonde, although Streeter was nearly dead certain that wasn't nature's original intent. Her once-pretty face had hardened and smiling seemed nearly out of the question now. Soft little bags under her eyes testified to a life of rage, fear, and day drinking. It was a face that had come to grips with utter disappointment and turned it into a living scowl. Too bad, Streeter thought as he stared at her. She had been stunning long ago. Living with Grover Royals had changed that forever.

"What?" Patty asked sternly through the front screen door. More of a command than a question. A freshly lit cigarette hung off her left hand like a sixth finger.

"Is Grover in?" Streeter shifted his weight.

"Who wants to know?" Her scowl deepened.

"I do. My name's Streeter." He paused. "I went to high school with him."

"How touching." Her voice kept its bored monotone and her eyes remained lifeless. Suddenly she let out a deep cough. "Why don't you come in and wait? I'm sure he'll be home from his paper route any minute now and we can all have some Ovaltine together."

Streeter shifted his weight back to his other leg and cleared his throat. Despite her attitude, he found himself liking the woman. He smiled at her. "That sounds nice, but if you could just tell me where he is, I have to talk to him about a few things. It's important."

Patty took a long drag from her cigarette and coughed deeply again. Then she shrugged. "He's probably down at one of his clubs. The Cheetah. You know it?"

"Sure. Thanks." He thought for a moment. "If I don't catch him there, could you tell him to give me a call? Streeter. He's got my number. Like I said, it's important." He wondered if maybe there was a hint of a smile creeping across her face. Probably not.

She nodded slightly. "I'm sure it is. With him, it's always important." Then she closed the door without another word.

Streeter drove to the Cheetah and parked in one of the semi-honor downtown lots where you're supposed to shove singles through tiny slots in metal boards. He never used to pay, figuring that even if he got caught every third or fourth time he'd still come out ahead. To Streeter, it seemed unfair to pay to park on public property. But since they'd raised the fine to fifteen dollars, he now shoved the singles in every time.

The Cheetah was located in an ancient, freestanding two-story building deep in downtown. To the south was a camera shop. A new state-of-the-art Burger King was located immediately to the north. The Cheetah's front door was locked when he got there shortly before ten, so he walked around back to the alley. As he got within a few feet of the rear door, it swung open and Grover Royals stormed out of it. They glared at each other, filling the alley with so much hostility that the green Dumpsters almost rattled. Finally, Grover took a step forward and spoke.

"Still working the case? What with Richie being found, I thought you'd be out of a job." He shifted his shoulders and squinted slightly.

"Marty wants me around to make sure everyone's cool." Streeter waited a beat. "And that no more trucks get torched."

Grover frowned. "Whatever that means."

Streeter kept an even gaze. "Right."

No one spoke for a moment and then Grover again broke the silence. "So what do you want with me? This sure ain't coincidence, running into each other back here."

"Marty asked me to find out how we're going to handle this thing. Make sure you get back what was stolen and that Richie and Tina get off the hook. What is it you need in order to forget this whole thing ever happened?"

Royals looked up and squinted into the sunshine bouncing off the top of the building behind the Cheetah. It was going to be another warm day, although not as hot as the last few. Then he glanced back at Streeter.

"How does one really ever forget something like this?" His voice was forced, snotty, and he was smiling now. "I mean, I feel so very *violated* by what happened. You have no idea how traumatic it is being victimized like that."

Streeter took a deep breath. "What is it you want?"

Grover's face returned to its normal smirk and any hint of humor left his voice. "I want that little cocksucker and his girlfriend to fry for this, is what I really want. But what I'll settle for is getting my money back. And I want the originals of all the stuff they took from Rudy's office. They don't get to keep any copies, either. And I'll want something else which I haven't even thought up yet. Something to show me that they really regret what they did. A token of remorse. I'll have to get back to you on exactly what it'll be. Later today I plan on calling those two down in Florida and laying it all out for them. I haven't called yet because I wanted them to squirm for a while."

Streeter considered that in silence. He wanted to come back with something, but Marty had told him not to rile the big man. The two were now about a foot apart. Royals's body shuddered once and he inhaled deeply. "You got all that, scrub? Run along now and tell old Marty that I'll be laying down the terms to Richie and there won't be no room for discussion. Think you can handle it?"

Streeter felt anger building inside. At least he was pretty sure it was anger. Might be a little fear thrown in, too. He flashed on a time during his sophomore year when he and Royals had squared off in a "nutcracker" drill. That was where the two faced off in their line stances with Streeter trying to block Royals for the running back behind him. Grover had come off his four-point defensive position and knocked the hell out of him. One serious concussion. Almost broke his jaw, too. It was the hardest Streeter had ever been hit in his life, including his two years playing varsity ball at Western Michigan.

Speaking again, he was relieved that his voice stayed calm. "I'll tell Marty what you said and we'll be back in touch after everyone talks to Richie." He thought for a moment and then added, "Say hello to Patty for me, okay? We had a nice little chat earlier this morning over at your place."

Grover flushed and seemed about to open his mouth to speak. Instead, he just turned and headed down the alley.

Driving back to the church, Streeter squirmed in his seat. He would dearly love to screw with Royals. But what good would it do? His job was to help Richie and Tina get things straightened out. Pissing off Grover any further wouldn't help. But it sure would feel good. He even thought of some desperate move against the man. Years ago, he'd heard that Royals had a collection of Ford muscle cars from the mid-sixties. A former client of his who also was a Mustang fanatic had told the bounty hunter about them. Grover kept almost two dozen of them locked away, taking them out sparingly to show them off. They were about thirty years old but looked as fine as the day they'd rolled off the Detroit assembly line. Streeter thought it might be fun to find out where he kept the cars and then pay a visit. Torch a couple of them for Marty. Sugar in the gas tank: that was supposed to ruin the engine for good. Hell, take a leak in the gas tank, for all Streeter cared. What was it the kids in high school used to do? Cheese. A couple of cases of Velveeta cheese spread all over the leather interiors of his precious cars.

Especially damaging in a warm garage. Royals would be scraping it off for weeks and they never would come back to the way they'd been. I can get to your house, Grover, *and* to your cars. Anytime, Grover. But that was childish and crazy and he knew it. By the time he pulled up next to the church, he'd cooled down enough to think clearly. He didn't need Grover snarling after him, too.

12

Richie and Tina sat on the side stoop of Stan's mobile home shortly after noon on Tuesday, taking in fumes from the latest mosquito spray dusting and nailing their first Rolling Rocks of the day. The pesticides were compliments of the City of Naples, the beer they bought for themselves. With summer coming, the city sent out low-flying airplanes almost daily to dust the town with a light chemical that looked and smelled like talcum powder with an attitude.

They had a portable phone with them, as they'd had all morning while they waited for the inevitable call from Grover Royals. Tina felt ready, while Richie was nervous. But, despite all that had happened in the past couple of weeks, his faith in his girlfriend was still unshakable. Late the night before, after several hours of sexual mayhem, she'd described her plan to salvage a slice of money for her father's business. It might not have been the most brilliant proposal Richie had ever heard, but in bed listening to her go over it, he had to admit it had a chance. Of course, with Tina in her green French-cut teddy, almost anything she said sounded reasonable to him. Spreading all their cash out on the bed, they had re-counted it. Three hundred and sixty-eight thousand dollars and change. They'd already spent about ten thousand getting to Florida via Mexico and paying off Eddy. Luckily for them, Sid Wahl had put his ledger book inside the suitcase and he hadn't begun to total the amount of the pickups.

"That means," Tina had explained to Richie, "no one has an

accurate figure on how much money was in there. The places Sid stopped pretty much run on cash and I know for a fact the managers don't keep very good records. Rudy used to complain about it all the time. Plus, I'm sure that he and Grover realize there's a certain amount of skimming going on everywhere. Now, Sid Wahl has all the brainpower of a gopher, so I doubt that he was counting it up in his head as he and Dexter went along. They made eight stops and I'm sure he lost track before they were even halfway through.

"Those pickups usually net anywhere between two hundred thousand and maybe twice that. Rudy never knows what to expect and we always have a hell of a time accounting for everything. It never bothered him much because he usually skimmed a chunk for himself. This is going to help us a lot. See, he's been stashing it away for years and it's always been an unspoken secret between us. He knows that I know. I thought he did it so the IRS wouldn't find out, but he was really skimming from Grover all the time.

"Keeping all that in mind, I figure we have two sources of money here. First, we dummy up Sid's ledger to show that they only pulled in, say, three hundred and thirty thousand. It's not too low and I think Grover and Rudy'll be satisfied. That gives us a nifty profit of nearly forty grand right there. Secondly, we're going to put Rudy's feet to the fire over his skimming from Grover. His stealing. When we get back to Denver, I'll get him aside somehow. Then I'll demand another thirty-five thousand to keep me from telling Grover about the skimming. Rudy'll scream and holler a little, but he must have ripped off ten times that by now. In the end, he'll pay us just to keep Grover from tearing his head off."

She'd sat back when she'd finished and waited for Richie's reaction. At first, he had just nodded, considering what she said. Then he shook his head and stood up from the bed. "This puts us out on a whole different limb. Them finding out about us and the robbery was bad enough, but this could get us killed for sure. Don't you *ever* get scared, Teen?"

Blowing out a long stream of smoke, she said matter-of-factly, "I try to avoid it. The last thing we need now is to let our emotions do our thinking for us. This is business." Then she leaned forward, giving Richie a chance to appreciate the full view of her in the small teddy. "We're already out on a limb, Richard. After what we've gone through so far, I can't see coming away empty-handed. And I'm not going to let my father down. Stan said if he had fifty thousand up front, he could borrow the rest from the bank to get himself out of trouble. I intend to see that he gets it." She took a deep breath. "I figure we're owed at least that much for all the work we put in. Don't forget who we're taking the money from here, Richard. These guys can afford it and it's not like they actually worked for it. They exploit women and human weakness. Why not exploit them?"

When he didn't respond, she pulled him back onto the bed. "Remember the files, Richard. As long as we have them, those guys'll keep their distance. We've got enough to put all of them away for a long, long time and they know it."

That logic combined with the teddy was enough to bring him around. Then she made one other suggestion. To make it appear that they were being honest, they'd tell Grover that they were about five thousand short. That would seem legitimate, given the cost of Mexico and all. "We'll make a big deal out of asking your uncle for a loan to cover it. My read is that Marty'll go along with that. It's chump change to him and you said he sounded pretty relieved that you're alive. For Marlene's sake, anyhow. If Grover thinks we're borrowing to pay him back, it'll sound more sincere and he'll be less suspicious of the amount we come up with. We can always pay Marty back from what we have left over."

Richie didn't much care for asking his uncle for a loan, but he knew she was right about the appearance of it. Before the night was out, he'd agreed to do it.

Now, as they waited for Grover she walked him through the plan one more time. She was wearing her hair up, Gibson Girl–style, to keep the back of her neck cool. Richie liked the look. Even the back of her neck was sexy to him. She was wearing a short red silk robe, with her legs flowing out from it, all smooth and tan. "Just let me do the negotiating, Richard," Tina concluded. "I know how these people operate."

Grover Royals and Sid Wahl both bellied up to the desk in the basement office of Grover's house shortly before noon, Colorado time. The big man stared at the phone for a second and then picked it up. "No point dragging this out." He glanced at Sid. "It's time those two found out what's in store for them."

Tina answered on the third ring. Grover heard her voice saying a cautious hello, but he didn't respond at first. When he finally spoke, his voice was low and hoarse, but under control. "That you, Tina?"

"Grover?" Her voice stayed even. "Yes, it's me."

Royals jumped right into it. "You got some set a stones on you, Tina. You know that? Pulling a stunt like this." His voice rose. "You definitely went after the wrong people and now your butt's hanging out there in the wind with that jerk boyfriend of yours. More, maybe, seeing as how you probably wired the whole thing."

She didn't respond at first. Then, "We'll make good, Grover. I don't suppose it would help if I said we had no idea it was your money. We never would have tried this move against you. We thought we were dealing with *Fontana*, for chrissakes."

"Whatever you were thinking, you did steal from me. I personally don't give a good rat's ass what you knew going in. But now it's over and you're coming back here. And I mean soon." Grover nodded to the man with him.

Sid leaned back in his chair and let out a quick hiccup. Then he moved closer again. "St. Louis," he grunted, his voice sounding cocky. "St. Louis," he repeated for emphasis.

Grover nodded. "Yeah, right." Then he said into the phone, "Look, you're going to give me my money back along with all your copies of those files you stole. How much was in the case when you took it off Sid?"

"I'll have a complete accounting when we get back there," she answered evenly. "Let's just say it's in the midrange of the usual pickup."

Grover considered that for a moment before speaking. "Damned right you'll account for everything. There's something else, too. You and Richie are going to eat a little shit to show me how sorry you are about this whole situation. To show me how much you regret what you did."

No one said anything for a while. Finally, Tina broke the silence. "Exactly what do you have in mind, Grover?"

"I'll tell you *exactly.*" He switched the phone to his other hand and other ear. "On the way here, you're going to stop in St. Louis. I'll give you the name and number for an associate of mine who has something for you to pick up and bring back to me. There's six thousand Swiss Quaaludes out there that I've already paid for. The whole batch should fit in your trunk. When you get back here, you give me the ludes and the money and those files. All of them. That *exact* enough for you?"

"Yes, it is." She paused. "Richard and I have incurred some expenses along the way. We've spent some of your money but don't worry. It's only a few thousand and we plan on borrowing it from Richard's uncle Marty. With that, you'll be completely covered."

"I better be" was all he said.

Tina spoke again, her voice low and soothing. "We get the message, Grover, and you'll get your money and your Quaaludes, too. We'll talk to Uncle Marty and call you tomorrow at the Cheetah with our travel plans." She paused. "But there is one thing we definitely cannot agree to."

“What’s that?” Grover frowned into the receiver.

“We keep the originals of those files tucked safely away so that you don’t get a wild hair and come after us later. It has to be that way or else I’d never get another good night’s sleep.” Her voice was firm enough to leave little room for discussion.

Grover considered that for a moment, glancing at Sid. “We can talk about that last part when you get back here. Just call Rudy later and let him know when you’re leaving. Either me or him’ll give you the details about St. Louis then.” With that, he hung up. “Yeah, sure,” he said out loud to the basement in general. Then he turned to Sid. “We’ll talk about the files when they get back to Denver, all right. Where’d Rudy find that woman? She’s telling me what’s what like it’s her call. I tell you, Sid. They come home, they’re dead within a day or two. Tops. I know someone that’s going to help us with that. They’ll never know what hit them.”

For her part, Tina hung up and flashed Richie a smile warmer than the Florida afternoon sun. “It’s going to work, baby,” she said. “I know it is. Let’s go back to our room and celebrate. Dad won’t be home for hours.”

Richie couldn’t argue with that.

13

Constance studied the label on the bottle of dry herbs like she was splitting an atom. Frowning a deep V in her forehead, she nibbled the corner of her lower lip. For his part, Streeter scrutinized her shapely legs below the short black skirt with the same intensity. They stood there a few feet apart near the front of Alfalfa's, a health-food supermarket in Denver's Capitol Hill section. He didn't like the place. The Generation Xers who worked there treated customers like annoying interruptions to their endless conversations with each other. If you were lucky enough to get their attention, they acted like you'd just pulled them away from sex. "May I *help* you?" they'd ask with a pain-in-the-ass deadpan that must have been part of their employee training. But Alfalfa's was on the way to Marty Moats's office, so Streeter stopped off late that Tuesday afternoon to pick up vitamins. His glance worked its way from Constance's legs quickly up past the white blouse and to her face. Those killer almond-shaped eyes so deep in concentration. Her hair was lighter than he recalled, probably sun-bleached from the nice weather they'd been having.

Suddenly she looked up and broke into a quick smile of recognition, even though she couldn't place him at first. Within a couple of seconds, once she remembered him as the piano student with the bumper sticker, that familiar quizzical look shadowed her smile. He didn't know what to make of it, but her round face stayed open and warm, and the laugh lines around her eyes betrayed a kindness she normally tried to hide. She looked pleased to see him. Streeter flashed on what he was told about her boyfriend's leaving her and it made him feel a twinge of tenderness toward her.

"If it isn't the whale lover," she said. "I didn't peg you for an Alfalfa's kind of guy." She walked toward him to where they were only a couple of feet apart. "You look more like the type to get his groceries down at the Sizzler. Meat and potatoes all the way."

Streeter glanced around the store for a moment. "I get a healthy impulse now and then. But you're right. This isn't my kind of place. The employees are mostly condescending vegetarians with nose rings and purple lips. Order the chicken salad or anything with meat at the deli and they act like you're asking them to slaughter a puppy. How about you? Come here often?" He immediately realized that it sounded like a bar pickup line.

She nodded. "From time to time, Streeter. I don't live far from here."

Now he smiled and leaned closer. As he did, he recognized her perfume as Donna Karan. A good fit for her. "You know my name. Have you been asking about me, Constance?"

She shot one eyebrow up for a second. "You know my name, too."

"That must mean something."

"It means we both were checking each other out," she responded.

They stood there for a long moment in silence. Finally, he spoke. "You've given me the strangest look the last few times I've seen you. Ever since you commented on my bumper sticker. It's almost like we're sharing a joke together, only I don't know it. Either that or maybe you're laughing at me. What's that about?"

"I'm not sure, Streeter. For one thing, you sort of remind me of someone. Sort of. Plus, I don't know what to make of you." She glanced down at his hands. "A big guy like you. Shoulders a mile wide and hands like a foundry worker, and here you are struggling with classical music. And you dress nice enough, but then there's that car of yours. I gather you're not too image-conscious." She flashed her big grin again. "I think that's kind of . . . I don't know. Sweet."

"*Sweet?* My Buick's been called a lot of things, but never that."

"I don't mean your car's sweet. And forget the bumper art. I just mean it's kind of endearing the way you come down to the studio every week in that old clunker, all serious, and work so hard at learning to play the piano."

He had to think about that for a moment. As he did, she frowned slightly. "You're some kind of bounty hunter, aren't you?"

He nodded. "Some kind."

"Do you find people?"

"I do a fair amount of skip tracing."

Her smile reappeared. "Are you any good at it?"

He nodded. "Why?"

"Would you find someone for me?"

"Who?"

"A deadbeat former student of mine. The bum owes me over three hundred dollars and I want to drag him into small-claims court. Trouble is, I have no idea where he is. All I ever had for him was a phone number and that's been disconnected."

"What's his name?"

"Ernie Lomeli. L-O-M-E-L-I. I think he lived way north, but I'm not sure."

"How old is he?"

"About twenty-five, I guess." She studied him, the quizzical grin working its way back on her face. "Think you can track him down, Streeter? I'll take you out for a nice dinner if you do."

That set him back. "Dinner? Us? I usually charge by the hour."

Constance took a step back, about to leave. "What fun is

that? As long as we're checking up on each other, we may as well just go out sometime and ask our questions face-to-face." With that, she nodded and turned to walk away. Then she paused. "Keep me posted on Mr. Lomeli. I don't know anything else about him except that he plays a rotten guitar and that he's going to pay for our dinner if you find him." She smiled once more and then walked away.

By the time Streeter left the store and got to Marty's, it was almost six-thirty. Marty actually kept two offices. The first one was a small working facility in the rear of his largest store just off the 16th Street Mall. The second was located in an older row house near Washington Park, in the middle of town. It was barely an office and he didn't keep a receptionist there. More like an elaborate den where he could get away from Marlene and the demands of business, and hoist a few in peace while working on his stamp collection. Judging by the rumpled condition of the side bedroom he spotted when he walked in, Streeter also assumed that stamp collecting wasn't the only recreation that old Marty pursued there.

Marty was in a good mood, holding a glass of what appeared to be bourbon and offering the bounty hunter a drink the minute he arrived. He did not, however, give a tour of the office suite and he casually shut the bedroom door before serving the Scotch.

"Things are taking shape real nicely, son," Marty said as he settled into a recliner and pulled a cigar from his shirt pocket. "I just got off the phone with Richie and his lady friend and they're coming home. Probably leaving tomorrow. 'Course, it'll cost me a few thousand bucks, but that's to be expected. Not much that boy's done in the past twenty years that doesn't end up screwing with my P-and-L statement. But I told him this time it's a loan." He stared at Streeter for a moment. "You speak to Royals?"

The bounty hunter nodded. "First off, this morning. He

seems to want to get this thing over too, but I know he's going to be trouble. Somehow that guy's always trouble. I went to his house and I don't think he likes me knowing where he lives. But I figure that's all right."

"Good," Marty said. "I'm glad that miserable son of a bitch understands that we know how to get to him. Gives him a little something to chew on before his head hits the pillow at night. I don't like it that we're the only ones on the defensive all the time. Just don't get him all mad about it."

"I have to be careful around Grover. There's some bad blood between us and he knows how to get me worked up."

Marty smiled. "It won't hurt if you're a little on edge. Keep you on your toes."

Streeter considered all that as he drained his Scotch. "So what now?"

"In a nutshell? Tina and Richie come back to Denver and we give the money and everything else back to Royals."

"When I talked to Grover," Streeter said, "he mentioned making Richie do penance or something like that."

"The boy didn't say anything to me about it. I'll leave that up to them to work out." He stared at his guest for a long moment. "We'd like you to serve as the bagman here, Streeter. Richie and Tina shouldn't even get in the same room with Royals and I'm too old for this kind of stuff. Think you'll be able to do that?"

Streeter nodded.

Marty ran one hand thoughtfully along the side of his face. "Might be a wrinkle or two we have to iron out first."

"Such as?"

"Apparently, Grover wants the originals *and all* copies of those stolen files. Tina and Richie don't much care for that notion. Especially her. Me and her got into a big flap about it on the phone just now. She sees keeping the originals as protection against Grover coming after them down the road."

Streeter stared hard at him. "She's right. Grover Royals'll never be happy with what they're giving him. Sooner or later, he'll kill Tina and Richie unless they have something on him. They shouldn't give up those files under any circumstances."

This seemed to bother Marty, as he frowned like his stomach hurt. "I told them just to do what Royals says and not piss him off any further. But Tina won't hear of it and Lord knows Richie'll do whatever that woman tells him to do. In my entire life I don't believe I've never seen a man so pussy-whipped. Anyhow, they'll be back soon and I have a place they can stay here in town where Royals won't be able to find them. I also said that if they insist on keeping the original files, they can store them in my office safe." He paused. "For now, just sit tight, Streeter. I'll call you when we make all the arrangements."

"You seem awfully concerned about those files, Marty."

The old man shrugged and studied his drink. "Just trying to help, son. That's all."

14

Richie looked at the three fifty-pound iced wooden crates of fresh Florida stone crabs in the back of their rented minivan and shook his head. Stealing from Rudy was supposed to be the move that would rescue Stan and set him and Tina up financially. Instead, they're hauling crabs and drugs around the country. Might as well strap live chickens to the van roof and hang a sign off the side saying IDIOT BANDITS ON BOARD.

Tina's father had given them the fresh crabs half an hour ago as a token of his gratitude for what they were trying to do for him. He said to take them to a fish market in Woodville, some backwater town off the freeway south of Tallahassee. It was only twenty minutes out of their way and the owner would give them seven hundred dollars for the three crates. Cash. Stan had gotten them free from a longtime customer who owed him a big favor. Take all the profits, he had told his daughter. Tina finally convinced him to let her wire half the money back to him. He needed it more than she did, but he wouldn't hear of taking it all. Secretly, she planned to send it all anyway.

It was almost noon that Wednesday as Stanley Gillis stood silently in front of his trailer watching Richie and Tina put their luggage into the green van. He was a balding, thick man of five foot nine, wearing his usual work clothes: bib blue-jean overalls with a gray T-shirt underneath. His skin looked like weather-beaten saddle leather and he appeared to be ten years older than he really was. The only physical trait he shared with his daughter was his long, though receding, red hair. Tina, wearing blue shorts and a T-shirt, approached from the driveway and Stan opened his arms to her.

"I'm going to miss having you two here, baby," he said as he circled his chunky arms around her. "Mostly you, but Richie was starting to grow on me, too."

Tina hugged him and then pulled back. He smelled of grouper, cigars, and Budweiser. She looked up and smiled. "We might be back sooner than you think. Richie loves it here and I've had about enough of Colorado myself."

"Sure," he said with little conviction. He studied her for a moment. "You guys be careful up in Denver. If it gets rough, either call me or head back home. This isn't right, you taking all the heat for trying to help your old man out."

"We'll be fine." She looked away. Tina had told Stan little about their situation other than that they had to return some of the money. He hadn't heard about Grover and his threats or about their side trip to St. Louis. She certainly hadn't mentioned her plan to skim part of the money and get more from Rudy. All Stan knew was that they had run into trouble with her ex-boss, who wanted his money back, and that Tina had arranged to keep fifty thousand dollars. "Take care of yourself and keep the drinking down." She studied his sad, dark eyes. "This is going to work out. The bank gave you time and I'll send the money in about a week or so."

Stan smiled and shrugged. "I don't know how you did it, baby, but then you always had a way with people." Just then Richie walked up behind her. Stan spotted him over her shoulder. "You drive careful, mister." Then he stepped back and looked at them. "Art's expecting you tonight. It's about seven hours up there and you should miss rush-hour traffic in St. Pete. Art'll try and talk you down on the price for the crabs. He's like that. He'll bitch and moan some, but he'll end up paying it."

Then he nodded, turned, and walked toward the house. As Tina watched him leave, she wondered if he'd ever open up more. That was about as much conversation as she could get from the man. She turned to Richie, her eyebrows shooting up for a second. "Let's go. He never was much for long goodbyes."

They walked to the van and she glanced through the side window before getting in. Their two suitcases, all they left Denver with, were stacked on the back bench seat. "Where did you put the money briefcase?" She asked once she got inside.

Richie motioned behind himself toward the backseat. "It's way in the rear. Under the crabs." He started the engine and they headed north.

The afternoon drive along the Gulf Coast went fast. Tina particularly liked going through Sarasota, her favorite city in Florida. The highway runs right along the beach and with the tall, expensive condos on their right and the luxury boats bobbing in the bay to their left, the place looked like a postcard. They only stopped once, for gas and burgers, as they hit the Panhandle and headed west. By the time they approached Tallahassee, it was after seven. They turned off the freeway and moved south. Two miles down they stopped at a four-way intersection. An elderly man in a red windbreaker was leaning against the stop sign. He waved to them and moved toward the van.

"You mind giving me a lift to Woodville?" he asked as he got to them. "It's just down the road a few miles. My truck broke down back there."

Tina frowned, trying to remember if she'd seen a stalled truck as they got off the freeway. "We're in kind of a hurry," she said.

"This won't be out of your way." His voice sounded as tired as the man looked. He squinted into the van and added, "You got plenty of room."

Tina glanced at Richie, who shrugged and rolled his eyes. Her call. She looked back out her window. The man appeared to be in his sixties and small. "Okay."

The old man nodded wildly. "Thanks, ma'am."

Richie pulled away from the intersection and no one spoke for a few minutes. Finally, the new passenger said, "You folks just passing through?"

Richie nodded once but neither of them answered.

"Folks call me Sonny," the old man said. "Yourselves?"

Tina looked back briefly, a stench from the old man reaching her now. Body odor so strong it was practically visible. "I'm Tina and this is Richard," she said quickly.

Sonny considered that as he looked around the back of the minivan. He saw the wooden crates. "Whatcha hauling?"

Tina answered without looking back. "Stone crabs."

Sonny's eyes darted around. That's when he spotted it. Under Tina's seat directly in front of him, the nut-brown handle of the huge Smith & Wesson .357. He looked up and saw that they weren't paying attention to him. Slowly he bent over and eased the gun from under the seat. He waited another minute before speaking. "Nice leather luggage. My bet is you folks aren't wanting for things, Materially, that is." The strange comment caused Tina to look back again. She let out a short gulp at what she saw. Sonny was holding the .357, pointed midway between the two in the front seat. His left hand was draped over the top of it and he slowly pulled back the hammer. "Wouldn't mind having some of your possessions to take with me," he added.

The heavy click of the hammer caught Richie's attention. He quickly twisted around in his seat and when he saw what was happening he let out a quick "Jesus!" He now spun between the passenger and the windshield, trying to keep an eye on everything.

"You've got to be nuts," Tina said without emotion. "We know your name and, plus, that thing's not even loaded."

Sonny frowned and glanced at the gun. He examined the cylinder. Then a quick grin worked its way back across his face. "That's not entirely true, ma'am. I believe I see one bullet in there. That's damned near fully loaded for my purposes." Now he paused for effect. "Which one of you wants the pleasure of taking it?"

Tina looked over at Richie, who stared at the windshield. "I thought we agreed that you'd keep the bullet in the glove box. That way, no one could possibly get hurt."

"Come on, Teen. What good is it going to do us in there?" He hated the subject. Hell, Tina had only let him put the one bullet in the .357 when he robbed Sid.

"Not nearly as much good as it's doing us where it is," she now answered. Suddenly she reached into her purse, pulled out a small blue canister of Mace, and aimed it at the hitchhiker. "Why don't you just put the gun down and we'll drop you off and forget this ever happened. I spray this, it'll make you sick for a month."

The old man studied the tiny can. "Whatcha got there, ma'am? Nerve gas?"

"Just about. Shoot me and he'll break you in two. Shoot him and I'll gas you."

The hitchhiker frowned and shifted in his seat. "Looks like we have us a standoff here, ma'am. But there's no way I'm getting out of here as broke as when I got in."

Tina considered that as Richie drove in silence. "Take my wallet," she finally said. "There's fifty bucks in there. Probably more than you've earned in a month."

"You don't have to insult me, ma'am." The old man paused, mulling over her offer. Then he glanced to his left. "I'll take your wallet and the suitcases."

"Come on, old-timer." Tina's eyes widened as she spoke. "Don't push your luck."

"Don't push *yours,* ma'am. This cannon here's getting awfully heavy. I'd hate to have an accident to where it went off and you got hurt." He was smiling.

At that, Richie jumped into the negotiations. "Teen! Give him the damned suitcases *and* the fifty. Whatever he wants. It's not worth getting shot over."

"The young man's right. Silly to die for a few pieces of luggage."

But Tina was heavily into the process now. "The fifty, and one suitcase." She paused. "And you leave the gun. That's my final offer."

Sonny nodded. "Fair enough. But I get to pick the bag and I take the bullet with me. Wouldn't do to get shot the minute I step out."

"Done," Tina said.

Richie stopped at the side of the road and they made the exchange. The old man carefully closed the sliding door behind him. "Have a nice trip, you two," he said, speaking as pleasantly as when he'd first approached them. "Enjoy Florida, now. Ya hear?"

Tina glared back at him. "Take a shower. Ya hear?"

Richie pulled away from the shoulder with her staring straight ahead. Finally, she spoke. "This is not a good sign and now we don't even have our bullet anymore." She paused. "You and me definitely were not cut out for this outlaw life."

"You can say that again." Richie wiped at a band of sweat on his forehead. It was nearly dark by now. "When that old fart was aiming the gun at you, Teen, I nearly lost it. I'd just die if anything happened to you."

She reached over in the darkness and wiped gently at his forehead. "The same for me, Richard." Then she smiled and leaned toward him, her voice suddenly husky. "But I have to tell you, all this gunplay sort of got me excited. Worked up romantically."

His head spun in her direction. "I know what you mean." Richie was smiling back now, and without another word, he pulled the van back off the road and onto the shoulder. They stayed there for over an hour, making love like it was their first time. In fact, for the rest of the trip to St. Louis, they made a fair number of roadside stops. Just outside of Birmingham, due north of Memphis, in a rest stop on 55 across the river from

Cairo, Illinois. Turned out that the outlaw life wasn't totally without its benefits.

It took Streeter about two hours to find Ernie Lomeli late Wednesday afternoon. It was a fairly typical skip trace and he followed his normal routine. He pegged Ernie as someone who doesn't particularly want to be found, but who isn't in deep hiding, either. Undoubtedly, he moved around a lot, never leaving a clear trail like forwarding addresses with the post office or updated information at voter registration. If he stiffed Constance, he'd most certainly stiffed other people. But probably not enough that he'd change his identity.

First, Streeter checked the latest Denver residential phone book. He'd learned long ago never to overlook the obvious. No Ernie. Then he called directory assistance. Same result. So he drove to the Department of Motor Vehicles and pulled a copy of Lomeli's driver's history. It showed his most recent address, nearly three years old, as being in the southeast part of town. There was a unit number, so Streeter assumed it was an apartment or a condo. Maybe a town house. It turned out that the address was in a huge development of triplexes off Monaco Parkway. He went there, and from the current renter he learned that Lomeli had moved out about ten months earlier. The tenant had no idea where he'd gone, but he gave Streeter the name and phone number of the unit's owner.

When he got back to the church he went to Frank's empty office, called the owner, and explained what he was after. He assumed the guy, being a landlord, would be sympathetic to people looking for deadbeats. He was, but about all he knew was that Lomeli used to work as a bartender at a Cheery Creek singles bar called Butterfield Eight. Streeter then called the club and asked for Ernie. He was told he had quit in February. Streeter said he was a distant cousin of Lomeli's who'd just moved to town and needed to contact him quick. The manager put him on hold and asked a couple of the bartenders where

Ernie was. When he got back on the line, he said that the best they knew, the guy was tending bar at the Proof of the Pudding, another huge singles bar, in South Denver.

Streeter called the Proof. "Is Ernie Lomeli on duty?" he asked.

There was a pause and then "You got him. Who's this?" The voice was tight and cautious.

The bounty hunter now knew where Ernie worked, so he tried to finesse the guy's home address out of him. "I'm looking for the one who lives in the Breakers, near Aurora. We were in the army together twenty years ago. He'd be about forty or so. Would that be you?"

"No, no. Not even close." The fake description worked as Ernie, thinking he had the wrong man, loosened up immediately. "Sorry, pal. I don't live near the Breakers."

"No? What part of town are you in?"

"Over in Capitol Hill. On Lafayette."

"An apartment?"

"Yeah. In the Cheesman Arms. Why?" Then the voice tightened again. "Like I said, I'm not the one you're looking for."

"Just curious." Streeter had enough. Better back off. "Sorry to bother you."

When he hung up he jotted down the information and then got out the phone number for his music school. But he decided not to call Constance yet. It had been only a day since they'd talked and he didn't want to appear too eager. He'd wait until the next night, when he went for his piano lesson, and tell her in person. As he sat there, Frank walked in.

"Hey, Street." He dropped into one of the chairs facing his desk. "Haven't seen you in a couple of days. What's up with old Marty and all that?"

"Looks like it's going to get taken care of soon," Streeter answered. He then filled his partner in on what had happened since Monday. "I still don't trust Grover not to go after those two when he gets his money back. But as long as they keep the file originals, he'll probably behave himself. At any rate, once the exchange is made, I'm out of it." He thought for a moment. "Uncle Marty seems pretty interested in getting all the files back to Grover. I can't quite figure that out."

Frank shrugged. "With an old farmer like Marty Moats, it could mean anything. So, what you been doing today?"

"I just did a skip trace for someone. This gorgeous guitar teacher down at my music school. I told you about her. Constance. The one who got dumped last year for her best friend. The one who looks at me in that strange way all the time."

"Yeah, yeah." Frank straightened up. "You mentioned her. She gave you a job?"

"I ran into her last night and we got to talking. She said if I find this deadbeat for her she'll take me out to dinner."

The bondsman grinned at that. "All right, Street-aire. This is good news. You've been kind of smitten by her for a while."

"Smitten. Jesus, Frank. You *are* old. Nowadays people don't get smitten anymore."

Frank frowned. "Well, whatever they get, you've been leaning that way. Now you'll get a chance to do something about it."

"I suppose." Streeter shrugged.

"You don't seem too happy about it."

"You know me, Frank. I always get panicky when a woman seems interested in me. To paraphrase Groucho, I wouldn't want to go out with any woman who'd go out with me. Something like that."

"You're nuts. You know that?" Frank shook his head. "You've been moping around here for all these months complaining that you're alone and can't find anyone interesting. How you're sick of being by yourself and how nice it would be to have someone cool in your life. Blah, blah, blah. Then you find her and you're not sure it's what you want. One of these days you better figure out exactly what you're after. Like they say, if you don't know where you're going, that's where you'll end up."

15

As Dexter Calley drove, he toked on the tiny joint pressed between his thumb and index finger and wondered what that little ass-kisser wanted. Rudy had called the day before and suggested meeting at the Esquire Lounge on East Colfax at ten on Wednesday night. Dexter had asked why, but Fontana had played it cagey. All he'd say was that he would make it worth Dexter's while. That'll be the day, Dexter thought as he wheeled his pickup truck into the Esquire's parking lot at twenty to eleven. He sat in his truck, smoking and thinking about the man he was meeting. Rudy with the slicked-down slab of hair and those stupid leisure suits or whatever the hell they were. And the way he let Grover Royals dump on him whenever he felt like it. Guy like Rudy'd last maybe half an hour locked up in Stillwater before they'd have him wearing a bra and mascara. Dexter finished his joint and headed toward the Esquire's front door.

Sitting in a booth in the restaurant, Rudy was deep into his third gin and tonic when the big Indian blew through the front door. Look at that guy, he thought as Dexter squinted into the darkened room. Flat nose and square jaw, wearing that jailhouse scowl. Chest muscles packed so tight into his black T-shirt that you could bounce new forks off them. That *would* have been one hell of a fight if he and Grover had squared off the night of the robbery: both dumb and viscous beyond description. Probably would have killed each other and not even noticed. As Rudy motioned to Dexter, he imagined both Grover and Calley dead. Like winning the lottery twice, as Rudy didn't know which of the two he hated more. But he knew that Dexter was the one he needed right now.

"There's the man," Rudy said a little louder than he'd intended. He lifted his butt a couple of inches off the red vinyl bench seat and leaned forward by way of a greeting. "How they hangin', Dex?"

Dexter slid into the booth and merely nodded. Both men sat there for an edgy moment. Rudy wore a green silk shirt and a tight grin and Dexter sported a frown.

Finally, the newcomer spoke. "So, what's this all about?"

Rudy's smile widened and he glanced toward the waitress. "Over here, nurse." Then he looked back. "A little something to loosen you up?"

By this time the waitress had arrived and was standing beside the booth. Dexter shot his eyes toward her without moving his head. "Coke, no ice." She nodded and moved away. Dexter glanced around. The Esquire was a hard-drinking, blue-collar joint where the bar seemed to stay almost packed no matter what the time of day whereas the restaurant part never saw more than one or two full booths. The clientele consisted mainly of aging Charles Bronson impersonators and cranky women who were willing to overlook details like poor personal hygiene and wedding rings if the guy was buying the rounds.

"Not a drinking man, huh?" Rudy asked as he lit one cigarette off another. Then, without waiting for an answer, he added, " 'Course not. You being a football player."

Dexter rolled his eyes. "Yeah, right. You never know when the Forty Niners are gonna call." His voice was as bored as his expression. He idly pulled his ponytail from the side to the back of his head. "Let's get to it. What was all that 'make it worth my while' crap you were telling me yesterday?"

Before Rudy could answer, the waitress returned with the Coke. Rudy held up his glass and nodded for another drink. When she left he turned his attention back to the question at hand. "First of all, Dex, I know you left our little organization under less than ideal circumstances. Grover giving you all that friction about the robbery." He shook his head and frowned in pained concern. "I wasn't happy, the way he handled that. Believe you me, I told him as much later that night."

Now *there's* a crock, Dexter thought.

"Yessir, I told Royals that I wouldn't stand for any more of that. Like it was your fault that Richie and Tina pulled that crazy stunt. What the hell, maybe he thought you were supposed to get blown away for our money. Give me a break."

"Give *me* a break, Rudy." Dexter shifted his seat, more irritated as he remembered those odor-filled hours in the trunk. He practically didn't eat for a week after that one. "Where the hell you headed with all this?"

Just as Rudy leaned in, about to speak, the waitress reappeared with his drink. He looked up at her and smiled. "Thanks, honey." Then he watched her butt as she walked away.

Fontana straightened his shoulders and cleared his throat. "Fair enough. Dex, I can imagine how you feel about Grover. Truth is, I probably feel about the same way. He's a shitheel from way back and he always will be. And now he's all worked up about this Richie Moats thing. We found him and Tina down in Florida and Grover convinced them to bring the money back. They should be in Denver by the weekend." He winced like he was confiding something major. "I think that's our chance."

"Ours?" Dexter frowned. "As in you and me? The hell you talking about?"

Rudy leaned into the table again. "I'm talking about us taking Grover down. Hard and fast. I'm saying that with him so pissed off and with all those files Tina stole floating around like that, Grover's vulnerable." He sat back when he'd finished and took a long sip from his drink.

"Are you really saying we should make a move against Grover?"

"Yea-uh." Rudy's eyes widened in mock surprise. "You got a *problem* with that? It's not like you're about to get your old job back. Let's face it, Dex, you sure didn't have any future working for that prick. Grover would never let a half-nigger get too deep into his operation." Then, seeing Calley grimace and tense up, he quickly added, "No offense intended with that racial crack. It's not like I invented the word, you know."

"I hear you say it one more time you'll wish you never even heard it before."

The booth fell silent again and Rudy lit another cigarette. Dexter drummed his fingers softly on the table, deep in thought. Then he looked at Rudy. "Why am I the lucky one you called about this?"

"Because if I'm going to need any muscle, you're the perfect choice. You hate Grover, you think good on your feet, and you know what's what with how he runs things." He nodded sagely. "Plus, I trust you, Dex. And I like you. Always have."

Right. Still, the idea of getting something out of Grover intrigued Dexter. Not that numb nuts here, on his best day, could take over a Sunday-school picnic. But the little goofwad definitely had something in mind. "Just how you planning to pull this one off?"

"I haven't figured out all the details yet, but when Richie returns, we lay in the weeds and let Grover set up his plan for getting everything back. There's even a bunch of ludes they're bringing in from St. Louis. We wait and when the time is right we step in." Rudy had to force his voice down as he worked into the subject. "My hunch is Grover will make the pickup himself. Personally. When he walks away he'll be carrying several hunnard thousand in cash and all the ludes. Maybe more. I'll let you know where and when." He paused. "That's when you make him dead and take what he's carrying." Rudy never looked more serious. "No one would think of you doing that. You're out of the picture as far as him and Sid are concerned."

Dexter grinned incredulously. "Just where will you be while all of this dead-making is going on?"

Rudy nodded like he knew what was behind every door. "I'll be dealing with Tina and Richie. I have to get those files back or I'm in as much trouble as Grover."

"Oh? You going to make them dead, are you, Rudy?" Dexter shook his head slightly. "Where the hell did you learn to talk like that?"

The man across the table ignored the question. "Grover's working up his plans now but he told us that no matter what, Tina and Richie are history. He doesn't know how yet, but my hunch is that he's going to let Sid deal with them while he's making the pickup. If I keep nosing around and we catch a couple of breaks, you and me'll come out of this just fine. Maybe half a mil and Grover dead. Tina and Richie, too. And his whole business coming our way." He glanced around the room, calm again. "Why not give it a shot, Dex? You got something better lined up for the next week or so?"

Dexter considered that as he finished his Coke. "We need to know a lot more before I start running around making people dead." He got out of the booth and looked down at Rudy. "This is so far out of your league, you may as well be planning a trip to Mars. But I've got plenty of unfinished business with Royals and it might be we can handle it together. Somehow."

"Does that mean you're in?" Rudy drained his drink.

"It means I'll think about it. It also means that you better come up with some very clear information about what Grover's got in mind with this. Call me when those two morons get back to Denver and you know something solid."

"That's fair enough, Dex." By the time he'd said those four words, Dexter was walking toward the door. Rudy sat there studying his empty glass. Then he picked it up and spotted the waitress. "Nurse!" He shook it in the air. "One more time."

As he waited, he lit another cigarette and thought about the Indian. Watch it with Dexter. Getting all testy about the racial slur. Be cool with him. You need the man. For now, anyway. Rudy wasn't sure how, but come the big day everyone connected with Royals would go down and he'd take over. Sure, Grover terrified him, but it was that fear combined with his burning hatred that fueled his plans. The blond waitress came back to his booth and he laid two twenties on the table, grinning boldly. "Just exactly when do you get off work, honey?"

She placed the gin and tonic next to his ashtray and scooped up the money. Stuffing it into the pockets of her skirt, she barely looked at him. "About two o'clock." She waited a beat. "May forty-eighth." Before Rudy could come back with anything, she was gone.

Dexter turned over the pickup but didn't move for a moment. Rudy's big score. Be worth the price of admission just to see what he comes up with. All that make-Grover-dead crap. Rudy definitely watched too many bad movies. But Grover Royals deserved it and Dexter would love to be the one to do it. Might end up like that anyhow. Only he wouldn't be doing it with Rudy Fontana. Call the man when you get home, Dexter told himself as he put his truck into gear. That's what he's paying me for: to watch everyone and find out what they're doing. And he had to admit the man was giving him good money for not much work. Still, listening to Rudy talking about taking the ludes and money made Dexter think about freelancing. Hell, it can't be that hard a job if even a bimbo like Rudy thinks it's possible.

16

St. Louis turned out to be more like a Mary Kay party than a drug deal. Not at all what Tina and Richie had anticipated as they drove up from Live Oak. And their contact was certainly nothing like they expected, either. Grover gave her name only as Liz, but "Hart" appeared on the apartment's lobby directory. In a light-pink pants suit, her hair in a neat graying beehive, and chattering away like a schoolmarm on speed, Liz had a hell of a front for her line of work. So unlikely and innocuous, she could probably deal dime bags from the trunk of her car at a police station and not raise an eyebrow.

"Mr. Royals told me you'd be punctual," Liz said as she showed them into her spotless apartment. Her voice was professionally friendly, the way a realtor sounds at a showing, and she had that rasping shortness of breath common to elderly heavy smokers. "He said to expect you at about dinnertime on Thursday and here it is almost five-thirty. I didn't cook anything, but I've got coffee, herbal tea, and some refreshments ready for you."

What the hell is this? Tina thought as she studied the silver serving tray on the cocktail table in front of the sofa. Liz had laid out two pots, saucers, cups, and spoons, along with a plate of small sugar cookies and linen napkins. Tina cleared her throat and glanced at Richie, who was frowning in confusion. Then she surveyed the huge sunken living room. Located in a high-rise with a knockout view of the Mississippi River to the east through floor-to-ceiling windows, the place had to go for an easy two thousand a month. It was furnished like a Hyatt lobby and the thick scent from at least four vases of cut flowers was everywhere. On their way to town, they had pictured either a fortified subbasement or a run-down public housing project. Before leaving Naples, Richie had even pestered Tina about taking a gun to the meeting. Of course, with them losing their bullet near Woodville, the gun would be pointless.

Seated on the overstuffed white sofa, Tina finally noticed some of the trappings of a drug dealer's home. Standing quietly in the corner behind the wet bar near the fireplace was a huge man with a shaved head and a trimmed goatee. He'd been watching them silently the whole time, his face as impassive as cardboard. Another, slightly smaller man wearing tiny gold wire-rimmed glasses was coming down the hall from the entryway. His eyes moved cautiously between the two guests.

Richie finally spotted the two men and he glared at Liz. "What's this all about? We're just here to pick that stuff up and get going. Didn't Grover tell you about us?"

Liz backed off her matronly smile a tad and there was now a decided edge in her voice. "Yes, he did, Mr. Moats. He told me that you took a great deal of money from his people at gunpoint. Now, if you'd both please stand, these two gentlemen will do a quick search." She glanced at the man from the hallway. "Sheldon?"

That task completed, Liz's voice became kinder. "Very good. That's much better now, isn't it?" She pointed to the sofa, indicating that her guests could be seated again.

Tina sat back down, keeping tight eye contact with Liz. "We just want to get our goods and leave." Her voice was soft but there was a clear no-bullshit undertone. "Our car is parked a few blocks from here and it contains Grover's money along with other very important items. The sooner you stop this silly intimidation and give us the product, the sooner we can get everything to Mr. Royals."

Liz sat back and nodded. “Would you like cream or sugar in your coffee? Or would you prefer tea?”

Tina rose from the sofa again, with Richie following suit. “We’d prefer Quaaludes and then we’d prefer to leave.”

Liz shrugged, while looking at Tina. “Sheldon,” she said suddenly. “Bring the containers, please.”

The smaller man moved noiselessly to the kitchen door and through it. About a minute later he came back into the living room carrying two large red Igloo coolers. They were the flat-top kind and he had them stacked one on top of the other. He set them down near the hallway leading to the outer door and glanced back at Liz, his arms crossed in front of him.

“Six thousand Quaaludes. You can count them if you’d like, but that might take a while,” the hostess said.

“I’m sure they’re all there,” Tina responded.

She and Richie both turned to look at the coolers. Then Richie walked over and lifted one. “It weighs a ton.”

Liz drew her head back with obvious pride. “I’ve packed them in batches of two hundred inside Tupperware containers. Then I put ice packs in each cooler so the capsules won’t melt while you drive.”

“Not to belabor a point, Liz,” Tina interjected, “but if you try to follow us when we leave, we’ll just keep walking and dump those pills out individually into the river over there. I’m serious. We have to do it this way as a precaution.”

“I understand. My job is finished once you walk out the front door.”

“What did you make of all that, Teen?” Richie asked once they got back onto Interstate 70 heading west. “Tupperware! A tea service. Unreal. And Liz. She was something. Perfect little hostess dealing drugs like that.”

When Tina didn’t answer for a while, Richie glanced over. They were holding hands. They usually did that when they drove together. She liked the attention and he liked the connection. Looking at her face, the freckles wrinkling across her nose as she squinted slightly into the setting sun, he felt like pulling the car over and holding her close. Never letting her go. They'd been together for eleven months and it still amazed him that every day found him more in love with her. She always surprised him and he always seemed to find something new to like about the way she looked. Lately he'd been concentrating on her mouth. Perfect shape. A little puffy and a hint of a pout. He squeezed her hand gently. "What're you thinking about?"

Her eyes widened as if she was coming out of deep thought and she looked over at him, squeezing his hand back as she did. "That *was* strange, all right. Liz has to be the world's most anal-retentive drug dealer. We could have eaten off the floor, it was so clean."

They drove in silence for a long time before Tina spoke again. "You know, Richard, *most* of the people we deal with are crazy. Rudy, Grover Royals. Look at Sid and Dexter. Then there's your friend Spangler. Not much maturity in that whole crew and they're all half psychotic. Now we meet Liz and Sheldon and his partner." She turned toward him. "We shouldn't be around people like that." She studied his profile as he drove. "We're in over our heads, Richard. If we get out of this alive we have got to get away from these kind of people. I can't go back to work for Rudy and you don't have anything going right now, either. You'll probably just let butthead Eddy talk you into another one of his get-poor-quick schemes. I want us to have a normal life. A house, children, and everything."

He looked over at her. "That's what I want, too."

"But first you have to get yourself going with a career. I love you, Richard, but I'm not going wait around until you and Spangler figure it all out. And I'm certainly not taking my babies to see their daddy in prison."

Richie nodded silently.

"Then go talk to your uncle when we get back. Tell him you want to go to work for him. Let him know you're serious. When he sees that you're really trying, he'll get you going. Aunt Marlene'll see to it."

Richie considered that for a long stretch of highway. Finally, he squeezed her hand extra hard. "That's what I'll do."

"And *promise* me you'll lose Eddy. For good."

"You got it."

After a moment, she scrunched her shoulders up and smiled. "For now, tiger, let's get a room. I've had enough of the car for today and all this heavy drug running's got me excited again. Like back at Woodville."

Richie just about fainted behind the wheel. They pulled into the next motel, a Days Inn about forty miles west of St. Louis, and stayed there until almost noon the next day. The trip back to Denver was dotted with more roadside stops. When they hit the Colorado border, Tina pointed out that they had made love in every state they passed through on the way from Florida. Their best guess was fourteen stops in six states, which they figured must be some kind of record.

Streeter had just walked into the music store that Thursday night as Constance was heading toward the large glass front door to leave. She seemed preoccupied and in a hurry, but glad to see him.

"Alfresco's sounds good to me," he said as she walked up to him.

Her smile wrinkled slightly. "Alfresco's?"

"For that dinner you promised."

"You found him already? Good work, Streeter. I'm impressed." She sounded like she really meant it.

"That's why I did it. To impress you. *And* for that free meal."

"You get both." She stood back for a moment studying him. "Where is that jerk hiding these days?"

"He works at The Proof of the Pudding as a bartender. He

lives over in Capitol Hill, at the Cheesman Arms. I don't know the unit number, but that'll be easy enough to find."

"A bartender. That figures." She thought about that, briefly looking away. "If I gave you the papers for my small-claims suit, would you be willing to serve Mr. Lomeli?"

Streeter looked at the sheet music in his hand and then back at Constance. He shot her a grin. "I don't much like serving papers. Besides, you don't believe in paying money, so what's in it for me?"

Her eyebrows shot up. "Finding him gets you a dinner." Then she stepped toward him and moved her face up to his, giving him a light kiss on his right cheek. "Serving him gets you dessert," she said as she pulled away.

Streeter touched the spot she'd just kissed and shook his head slightly. "The more I know you, the less I understand you. When we met you were pretty distant. And then, out of nowhere, you promise me dinner. Now dessert. You can't be all that impressed with my skip tracing."

She shrugged. "I wasn't really *very* distant. And don't read too much into that dessert offer. I meant it literally. Besides, like I told you before, you remind me of someone. That's got me confused because I have very mixed feelings about that person. We can talk about it over dinner. A little mystery never hurt anything. I'm sort of tied up for the next couple of nights. How about Alfresco's on Sunday night at seven-thirty. I'll bring the papers. Does that sound all right to you?"

He nodded. "I'll be there. One other thing."

"What's that?"

"Can I call you Connie? Constance sounds so formal. To be honest, it's a little old-fashioned for you. Connie just suits you better."

"Okay. Connie's fine." She stepped toward the door. "And Streeter. Don't look so worried. You might actually enjoy yourself Sunday night."

Then she turned and walked outside, heading toward the

parking lot. He watched closely, rolling his sheet music tightly in his hands. As she moved smoothly across the lot and then disappeared into her car, Streeter wondered if he really looked worried. And why.

17

As Streeter pulled into the parking lot just before seven that Saturday night, Marty Moats was leaning against his car looking worn and crumpled. When he got closer, Streeter also noticed a hardness to Marty's eyes that he'd never seen before. The sun was setting fast over the mountains off to their left. Still, its last rays were strong enough to make the old man squint. He took a shot at straightening up, but his shoulders didn't have their usual squared certainty and his belly pushed hard against his green zipped-up windbreaker. It also was the first time the bounty hunter had seen Moats wearing glasses. Square-framed, silver wire rims. The whole package looked weary and wound up at the same time.

"Streeter," Marty said as he held out his right hand. "Glad you could come on such short notice."

He seemed about to say something else, but instead he glanced at the door to the warehouse. They were in the west lot of a long, low building that Marty owned off Santa Fe Drive, a mile south of Denver. They were in a remote area consisting of all kinds of commercial buildings. That part of town felt shut down at night. Completely still. It had nearly hit eighty that day, but the temperature was dropping fast. A slight breeze was kicking up from the mountains and Streeter wished he'd worn a jacket too.

"No problem," Streeter said. They shook hands, but he could feel that Marty's heart wasn't in that, either. "Have you talked to them yet?"

Marty considered the question. "Just on the phone this afternoon. Seems they got into town this morning. They finally got around to calling me shortly after one." He shook his head and his eyes hardened. "They've got their nerve, I'll hand 'em that. I set 'em up with a place to stay and they're making demands on me like I'm an errand boy."

"What kind of demands?"

"Oh hell." Marty shifted his stance and frowned. "They're telling me what goes where and how the delivery'll be made. Then I ask them where's the stuff they brought back and Richie tells me 'it's someplace else, where it's secure.' That's it. Just bring the money I'm loaning him and shut up. Same old story with that boy. I tell you what. It wasn't for Marlene thinking so much of Richie, I'd let the little peckerwood hang out there to dry. Yes I would. 'Course, it's that damned Tina who's calling the shots. Left to his own, Richie'd more than likely do what I say. The woman's got him by the balls so tight the boy's probably grown a twat by now."

"You might want to calm down some before we go in there, Marty."

"Calm down, my ass." Marty got into Streeter's face, his eyes wide. "That ungrateful little shit had the nerve to—" Suddenly he stopped talking and backed off. His shoulders heaved as he took two deep breaths. Then, his features softened. "You're right, son. I'm too worked up to be much good right now." He glanced back at the side door. "What the deal is, they called me this afternoon and said they're back and they want to take care of this business fast. Made sense to me. So I put them in here to be safe. This was my first warehouse. It holds mostly junk and not that many people even know about it. Plus, there's a little living space right up front. Kitchen, place to sleep, a phone. The whole nine yards. Richie said he wants me to bring the money over here tonight. I say fine. Then I ask him if he'll have the other cash and those files of Grover's so I can see everything laid out. That's when he says no, he won't have it here. Won't tell me where it might be, either."

"Actually, that makes sense," Streeter interrupted. "If Grover somehow finds out they're here he can't just come over, shoot them, and grab everything. Takes you out of danger, too. Royals can't get information from you that you don't have."

Marty didn't seem impressed. "That's about what the boy said. Anyhow, he says they'll lay out the plan for us tonight." He paused. "Let's do it." He turned and walked toward the door.

The warehouse was an ancient, glorified Quonset hut with boarded windows. Marty pounded on the door and they waited. Muted sounds came from inside, and after a minute or so, a man's voice came out to them. "Uncle Marty?"

"Yes it is, Richie," Moats answered, his voice completely under control by now.

Suddenly, the large steel door swung out, with Richie's curly head following. His eyes looked huge to Streeter. "Uncle Marty!" he yelled and walked outside. He threw his arms around his uncle and gave him a hug. The old man gingerly reciprocated but said nothing. Richie's eyes were closed as he hugged, but when he finally stepped back, they opened and he stared at the other man. "Mr. Streeter?"

The bounty hunter nodded and extended his hand to be shaken. Richie's grip was as eager as his eyes. He was wearing a brown-and-tan fifties-style Banlon shirt with wide vertical stripes down the front, and tan jeans. That and the deep wrinkles around his eyes made him look older than Streeter expected. But he was as tall as his uncle and as earnestly handsome.

"Good to meet you," he said as his right hand then unconsciously reached for his mustache and began to pull one end. Then he glanced back at Marty. "Come on in."

Inside, the living quarters consisted of one large room with a bathroom off to the side on the far end. There was a door next to it that led to the warehouse. The place was dimly lit and

Streeter had a difficult time making out the figure sitting at a table near the kitchen area. Squinting, he could tell it was a woman: long hair the color of red-brown silk. She stood up and hit the overhead light switch. Studying the curve of her hips and the way her breasts struggled against the deep-green sweater, he now could plainly see that this was a lot of woman. With her eyes and that mouth, Streeter knew why Richie went so far out on a limb. For Tina Gillis, he'd consider it himself. Her eyes alone would get him to Mexico. Emerald-green and outclassing her sweater by a mile, they were offset nicely by the full features around them.

"Martin, it's good to see you," Tina said in a husky, authoritative voice that added to her considerable sex appeal. She moved gracefully toward him, her arms stretched out for a hug.

"Miss Gillis." Marty nodded. His voice was not unfriendly but he only extended a hand to be shaken.

Tina took that in stride and her smile stayed even. Then she turned to Streeter. "And you must be the bounty hunter everyone's talking about."

He nodded. "My name's Streeter. It's good to finally meet you." He shot a side glance at Richie. "You two caused a lot of excitement around here."

Tina's smile dropped as if she didn't know how to interpret what he said. "I suppose we have." Turning back to Marty she added, "Let's sit down and talk. Would you gentlemen care for a beer? All we have is domestic. Rolling Rock."

Streeter saw that she was drinking one. "That'll work. Thanks."

Marty sat down at the round wooden table, unzipped his jacket but kept it on. "We didn't come here for any party, Miss Gillis. I'll just have a glass of water."

Streeter could see Richie tensing at that one as he and Tina glanced at each other. Then he went for the beer and water. Streeter and Tina sat down, with her sitting directly across from Marty. No one said anything until Richie returned and handed out the drinks. Streeter liked the way his hostess kept eye contact with Marty. Here she was, mastermind of one of the biggest screwups he'd ever seen and she still comes on like we're all just a bunch of pals playing a little gin rummy.

"First off, Uncle Marty, I just want to say how grateful I am—that me and Teen both are—that you're coming through for us like this," Richie said after he'd sat down. "Secondly, we intend to have this whole thing taken care of tomorrow." Then he turned to Tina, pulling on his mustache as he did, "Honey."

As he watched Richie, Streeter tried to imagine driving all the way to Mexico, Florida, and back here with that nervous bug in the car. He seemed decent and he was clearly nuts about Tina. Practically melted into his shoes whenever she looked at him. But what's with all that twitching and fiddling of his mustache? Streeter turned to Tina, not surprised that she was going to talk for them. She wouldn't get unglued if Marty didn't like what he was hearing and started honking off about it.

Tina lit a cigarette and took a quick sip of her beer, casually shaking her long hair to the side. Then she leaned into the table. "Richard and I definitely don't want to be in the same place with the money and the files. If we are and Grover happens to get to that place, we're finished. He'd kill us on the spot. So about noon today we stored everything in a safe place. All the cash we had left, the originals of Rudy's files, and the Quaaludes. Everything's downtown. We figured—"

"Just what in hell are you talking about?" Marty practically came off his seat when he heard about the drugs. "Quaaludes? Barbiturates. They're illegal."

Tina and Richie glanced at each other. "Why yes, they are," she responded. "Remember Grover saying that he wanted something extra, above and beyond what we took, to show how much we regret it? 'A token of remorse' is how he put it. Well, those ludes are it. We had to stop off on the way back here and pick them up for him."

"How many Quaaludes did you bring?" Streeter asked evenly.

"Six thousand," Tina said. "Give or take."

"Damn!" Marty yelled and glared at his nephew. "When you fuck up, boy, you do it big-time. Now you're a drug runner. Keep it up and you'll end up in a prison cell at Cañon City. I'm just glad your aunt isn't around right now to hear all this."

"Martin, there'll be plenty of time for your criticisms and ranting after this problem is taken care of," Tina continued. "For now, let's try to stay calm. As I was saying, we stored everything at the bus station downtown in several lockers. When Grover gets it, we don't plan on being anywhere near the place. We figure that's what Mr. Streeter is here for. To make sure the transfer goes smoothly."

"Whoa," Streeter interrupted, "I didn't know I'd be dealing drugs when I signed on for this job. I've never moved drugs and I'm sure not going to start now. Hooking Grover up with some files and cash is one thing. Drug dealing is another."

"In the first place," Tina responded, "even if you had to deliver them, it wouldn't make you a drug dealer. But more to the point, we have it set up so that you won't have to touch them. In fact, you'll never even see them."

He frowned. "How'd you work that?"

"Simple. Everything Grover wants is in three big lockers and we've got the keys. With Martin's contribution of five thousand, that makes us free and clear. When you leave here, Mr. Streeter, you take the cash and the keys with you. Go to the station first thing in the morning and put the money into the locker with the other cash. Then deliver the keys to Grover. You never touch the drugs. End of story."

Both Marty and Streeter thought about that. Finally, the Waterbed King nodded. "Sounds like it might work, at that. When do we tell Royals about all this?"

Tina glanced at her wristwatch. "We'll be talking to him any minute now. I called Rudy Fontana a couple of hours ago and said we'd call his office tonight at seven-thirty. I told him to have Grover there."

"One other thing, Miss Gillis," Marty said. "If copies of the files are in one of the lockers, then I take it you still have the originals."

"Why are you so interested in those files?" Richie broke in.

The old man turned to his nephew. "I'm not *so interested* in anything, son. It's just that Royals told you he didn't want any copies made."

"Martin, we don't particularly care what Grover Royals told us. We're keeping them for our own protection."

Marty backed off and said nothing.

Tina looked at Streeter. "The phone's over on the counter by the sink. I'd prefer if you made the call. Is that all right?"

Streeter's eyebrows shot up for a second and he shrugged. "Talking to him isn't my favorite thing, either, but that's why I'm making the big bucks." He got up and walked to the kitchen area. Then he picked up the receiver and turned back toward the table. "What's the number?"

Tina gave it to him as he punched it into the phone. Grover answered fast. He seemed to be in a good mood, something Streeter could barely imagine. When the bounty hunter told him what they had in mind, Royals simply said, "I'll do it."

Streeter's eyes widened for a second and he smiled quickly at Tina. "Good. Meet me in front of the station at eleven tomorrow morning, on the south side. We'll get this thing over with."

"I'll be there," Royals said and then hung up.

After the four of them agreed to talk again in the morning, Streeter left. Walking to his Buick, he had the five thousand dollars in his pocket. He thought about Grover's quick yes to Tina's plan. That didn't sit well with him. Anytime Grover Royals agrees with you, the best thing you can do is seriously rethink whatever it is you just said. Pulling out of the lot, he was too deep in thought to notice the white Subaru station wagon parked in a side alley across the street. And he certainly didn't notice Sid Wahl slumped behind the wheel, watching the building he'd just left.

18

Before leaving for the night, Marty actually hugged Tina goodbye. She and Richie had no idea why, but whatever the reason they were happy with his change of attitude. Particularly given that Richie would be asking him for a job soon. Of course, neither of them saw how sour the old man's face became the instant he turned away from the building. Sid Wahl didn't see it either, because he was parked too far away. As if he cared. He downed the last of the three beers he'd brought and watched Moats drive away. Starting his engine, Sid thought about just heading across the street right then and shooting that spoiled little shit and his girlfriend. Serve him right after he threw up on Sid and left him locked in the trunk with Calley. Jesus, he still got nauseated thinking about it. But Grover had told him to only follow Marty, locate his nephew, and stay until the old man left. So he threw the last can of beer out his side window and headed downtown to meet Grover.

Rudy Fontana stood at the front window of his office above the Cheetah looking out over Champa Street. He was barely paying attention to what was happening outside, which was just about nothing. The relentless throb of the bass and drums from the sound system below softly pounded the room. White noise that he seldom noticed. Particularly now with so much on his mind. Grover was down the hall in the can and Sid was expected back any time. Rudy had just called his own apartment for maybe the two hundredth time. About a minute after Tina had called asking him to get Royals ready to talk that night, he was on the horn trying to get hold of Dexter Calley. The first few times he tried, no one was there. But shortly after four, Dexter's girlfriend had answered. Rudy made her swear that she'd have Dexter call him at home and leave word as to where they could meet later. He couldn't risk having Dexter phone his office.

Now, looking out the window, casually swirling the Jack Daniel's in his glass and smoking, Rudy started to put together another plan. He thought about what to do if Dexter never called back. Was there another way to nail Grover? Maybe he wouldn't need Dexter after all, which would be more than okay. On the phone just now Streeter had told Grover that he would deliver the locker keys to him the next morning. Calley certainly couldn't take Grover out right there in front of the bus station. Old Tina had come up with a way to get the job done without putting anyone's ass too far out on a limb. Just like her to wire the deal like that. Damn, he missed having her around. He felt bad that she was going to be killed. Not real bad, but something like sympathy, which is what Rudy generally *never* felt for anyone but himself. Screw Dexter, Rudy thought as he looked around the room. He could hear Grover in the hallway walking toward the office. Be cool and see what the big idiot has planned for tomorrow. Take it from there. Just then, the big idiot himself walked into the room. Rudy tensed, as he always did when he saw Grover.

"How can you stand that noise?" Grover frowned as he spoke. "Makes it hard to even sit on the toilet and stay focused on what you're trying to accomplish." He waved a giant paw in the air. "Can't you give it a rest? You must run through about a carton of those a day. You working on your own lawsuit against the tobacco companies?"

Guy's a regular charmer, Rudy thought. "I didn't know that sitting on the crapper required that much concentration." The words came out automatically, and immediately he wished he had them back.

Grover studied him for a second and then snorted out something close to a laugh. "Just open a window and let a little oxygen in here, okay, Seinfeld?"

Rudy turned to the window overlooking Champa and put his drink on the ledge. Then he pulled up the frame a few inches and a rush of cool air swept toward him. From there he went to his desk and the Jack Daniel's bottle and freshened his drink.

"Lay a little low on the stuff," Grover ordered. "You been drinking way too much lately and I want you at least reasonably sharp for tomorrow."

"Why's that?"

"Don't wet your pants yet, no one's going to put you to work."

The two of them sat there in the office for about ten minutes before Sid arrived. "He went right to them, like you said," he told Grover. "They're off Santa Fe about a mile or two south of Evans. Looks like one of those army barracks they used on *Gomer Pyle.* I think they're living there for now. I didn't see the broad"—he shot a look toward Rudy—"but the puker, Richie, he came out to let them in. Marty was with your buddy Streeter but they came in separate cars. Left that way, too. About fifteen minutes apart."

Grover stood up and stretched. "Is there someplace out there you can park for a couple of hours in the daylight and not get spotted?"

Sid nodded. "There's a field just to the west. It should work fine."

"Good. Here's what we do." Grover moved around the desk. "I want you and someone you trust to be out there in that field by eight in the morning. Sit on that building. At eleven straight up, you go inside and put your guns to their heads. Richie and Tina both. Tell them you'll blow their fucking brains out if they don't produce the original files. Tina might give you a hard time, but Richie'll probably talk right away. Then, the minute you get the files, you kill them. Don't get cute. Just stash the bodies somewhere in the building, torch the place, and get out. No torturing anybody first."

"What if they leave before eleven?" Sid let out a short hiccup.

"Follow them. Take the Subaru again. No one pays attention to a piece of shit like that. We'll play it by ear. Follow them all day and let me know on the cell phone what's what. Just don't call me at eleven straight up. I'll be with Streeter then."

"What if they don't have the files with them? Even with guns in their ears, they might not have the stuff there."

"If they convince you the files aren't there, just shoot them and look around on your own. My hunch is they haven't had time to put them anywhere safe yet. Turn the place upside down. That and their car. If you don't find them, that means they're hidden so good they're probably gone forever. Torch the place either way. No doubt about it, those two go down tomorrow."

"Who should I use for this?" Sid asked.

Grover glanced at Rudy but spoke to Sid like he wasn't even there. "I'd like to have you take the Terminator here, but we want this done right."

Rudy perked up. "Wait a goddamned minute. I'm no hit man."

"No shit," Grover said. "The way you been drinking and jumping around here lately I can't see you even dressing yourself tomorrow." He turned back to Sid. "Use someone dependable. That crazy Irishman with the Mohawk. He's nuts but he seems to know what he's doing."

Rudy took a step back and studied the two men in his office. He glanced at his phone and wished he could call home for his messages. Also, he wished that he had never mentioned any of this to Dexter. Right now, Rudy had a whole new idea in mind for bringing Grover down.

Dexter Calley wasn't surprised when his girlfriend told him that Rudy had been calling all afternoon. So when he got home that night he telephoned the boss man on his private line at about ten o'clock and was told to get back to Rudy as soon as he could. Find out what the clown had in mind. The boss man said he knew what Grover was up to, seeing as how Grover worked for him as well. But he wanted Dexter to see if Rudy had figured out his plan for destroying Grover.

"I doubt that the little pissant could cause anyone much trouble," the man had told Dexter over the phone. "But it wouldn't hurt to know what he has in mind. He gets a wild hair and he's just crazy enough to make trouble for everyone. Call him back and see what sort of bullshit he's up to. Then let me know first thing tomorrow what you found out."

It wasn't until shortly before midnight that Dexter finally got Rudy on the phone at home. By then, he was too drunk to make any sense. Hell, Dexter thought as he hung up, the idiot probably won't even remember that I called. He decided to drive over to Rudy's early in the morning and see if he could wrestle something out of him. Then he had another beer himself and went to bed. He figured he'd hear what Rudy had in mind, have the man tell him what Grover was up to, and then see if there was any wiggle room in all that for him to make a play. A lot of money and drugs on the table. Might be a way to get some of it moving his way. Dexter wanted to stay loyal to the man, but he always liked to keep his options open.

Frank was waiting in his office when Streeter got back to the church that night. He was sitting at his desk reading a Louis L'Amour novel and nursing a Johnnie Walker Red when his partner walked in. Without a word, he held up his glass and raised his eyebrows, his way of asking if the bounty hunter cared to join him. Streeter nodded and Frank turned around to his credenza and grabbed a glass. He dropped in a few ice cubes from the bucket and then poured a couple of ounces. They sat drinking for a while, with Streeter filling his partner in on the plan for the next day.

"Sounds like you got all the bases covered," Frank said when he'd finished. "But there still might be one problem. Richie drew a lot of attention with that stunt down in Mexico. Doesn't he have some explaining to do to the State Department and the local cops? Not to mention that the media's gonna have a field day bugging him about it."

"We talked a little about that just before I left." Streeter took a sip from his drink. "He and Tina came up with some elaborate story about how Richie was going down there on vacation and he got robbed. Hence the blood on his car. Then it took him forever to get back to civilization because they banged up his head and he wasn't thinking too clearly. Finally he hitched his way back to the States. It sounds ridiculous to me, but that's none of my concern. Plus, as far as anyone knows, he didn't break the law, so no one should be very worried about details."

"You don't seem too thrilled. I'd think you would be," Frank said. "Not much for you to do but hand over some keys and you're out of it."

"That's true. It's just that Marty was acting so strange tonight. So pissed off and disagreeable. You should have seen him. He acted like he wanted to kill someone. Namely, his nephew. It was ugly, plus he'd switch over and be a nice guy without a moment's notice. I wonder what's really going on with that guy."

Frank leaned forward, his voice getting serious. "Look, Marty comes off like your best pal when he's pitching waterbeds on TV, but he can be a son of a bitch. You don't become a multimillionaire like that without being able to turn the screws on people or without taking care of yourself first and foremost. He's moody and he's got a temper. The only thing that saves him from being a total bastard a lot of the time is Marlene. On his own he's capable of damned near anything."

"I thought you two were such good old buddies."

Frank shook his head. "We got a lot of history together, but we were never that close. You don't see me socializing with him, do you?"

"I guess not." Streeter sipped his Scotch. "That Tina Gillis is something. A knockout and she's got nerve, too. My hunch is this whole thing was her doing and only Richie screwing up the night of the robbery kept them from pulling it off. He seems harmless, but I can't see why she'd be with him." He looked up at Frank. "Of course, I can't understand what women think and do around men most of the time. You see it every day: gorgeous women who have it all together and they're with some joker who basically doesn't know his ass from a hole in the ground."

"I hear you, Street," Frank responded. "There doesn't seem to be any end to that blind spot women have for certain men." He smiled. "But maybe that old blind spot has a reason behind it. Like it appeals to a woman when a man's dead certain what he wants and what he's doing with her. Take this Richie character. Could be Tina likes him because he wants her so much. Appears to me that you could use a little of that certainty yourself when dealing with the better gender. Decide what you're really after and then just go get it for a change."

"Yeah?" Streeter pondered that. "Could be. Anyhow, it seems that the guitar teacher I mentioned might have a blind spot for me. I talked to her Thursday and we're having our big date tomorrow night." He flashed a grin. "Maybe there is a God after all."

Frank nodded and tipped his glass toward the bounty hunter. "Could be you'll find out tomorrow."

19

Rudy's hangover was about an eight and a half on scale of one to ten, with ten being dead and almost buried. He squinted at his watch and saw that it was time. Forty-five minutes before Streeter was to meet Grover. Time to set part one of his plan into motion. No way he'd let Grover have what was waiting in those lockers. Rudy would rather see the money burned and the ludes dumped into the Cherry Creek Reservoir than to have Royals get his hands on them. Plus, Rudy wanted the files back to cover his own ass. To hell with Dexter Calley. Stupid Indian never returned his calls.

On to phase one all by himself. Phase two, he'd think up later.

Streeter had gone to the bus station that morning right after he'd finished his daily weight workout in his basement gym. He'd gotten to the station shortly before nine, still in his sweats. Then he put Marty's cash into locker B-38 and opened the other two lockers. Glancing inside each, he wanted to make sure that Richie and Tina were leveling with him. Sure enough, both contained papers held with rubber bands he assumed to be the files, two accordion folders stuffed with Grover's cash, and a couple of huge red Igloo coolers. The inspection completed, Streeter walked around the station for a few minutes checking out the exits and the layout in general. He also watched to see if Grover had sent someone to follow him. Frank Dazzler sat in the Buick on the southeast corner, watching as well.

When they got back to the church, Frank went to his office and Streeter headed upstairs for a shower. A few minutes after ten, he came back downstairs and checked addresses for a bail jumper that he'd look for that afternoon. It was about half an hour before he was to leave for the station when the desk phone rang. Frank grabbed it.

"Bail Bonds," he said, still looking at the papers in front of him. "He's here." He glanced over at Streeter and extended the receiver to him across the desk.

Streeter took it and frowned. "Yeah?" His voice sounded annoyed.

"Jesus," Rudy said. "Some way to talk to a guy who's calling to do you a favor."

Streeter's frown deepened. He didn't recognize the voice but it had a certain street flatness to it. "Who is this?" he asked, even less patient.

"This is a guy that knows exactly what the hell's going on down there on South Santa Fe. I also know about your business with Mr. Royals over at the bus station in a little while. I know about the whole fucking deal, Mr. Streeter, and I know that Grover's gonna screw you over and kill Tina and Richie this morning. Does that sound like someone you might have a couple of minutes to talk to?"

"Yes, it does. Do I know you?" He held up his hand, palm facing Frank to get his attention. The bondsman stared at him.

"No. But I know all the other players in this deal." He paused. "Royals is gonna be at the station at eleven, all right. And while you guys are busy breaking the law, a couple of his playmates will be moving on those two out at Marty's place. They're out there right now keeping an eye on things. See, Royals might talk a good game about just wanting to get his stuff back, but what he really wants is to crush those two. His main thing is that he's really, *really* pissed that Richie and Tina stole from him. All he thinks about is payback."

"How do I know you're telling me the truth?"

"Why would I bullshit you? Look, Streeter, you do what you gotta do here. But if I'm right, Grover gets everything he wants and those two are dead."

Streeter worked the fingertips of his right hand over his forehead, thinking. "Give me some assurance that this is on the level."

"Assurance!" Rudy hollered. The sharp noise stirred his hangover, so he toned down his voice. "To hell with assurance. You know, you're not as bright as everyone says. How would I know about this in the first place? 'Less your head's completely up your ass, I'd get down Santa Fe and check it out. You leave now, you might have time to stop all the fun." He hung up.

Streeter stood up and stared ahead. Frank leaned forward. "The hell was that all about?" he asked.

"That was about Richie and Tina getting killed today." He looked at his partner. "Or it might be just a lot of horseshit."

"Who was it?"

"He wouldn't give his name but he sounded like one of Grover's boys. You know, trying to pass stupid off as tough. He said that when I'm meeting Grover, two of his guys'll be killing Richie and Tina. They're watching the warehouse right now."

"That's nuts. Killing them might expose himself and his business."

Streeter shook his head. "If Royals gets mad enough, he'll let that anger take over his common sense. Which explains why he was so agreeable last night. He was setting us up. He must have had someone follow Marty or me down there." He studied Frank for a second and then picked up the phone. He called the warehouse number and let it ring about a dozen times. No one answered. Then he called Marty's main number and was told that Mr. Moats would be out of the office until about three.

"Marty's not in and no one's at the warehouse." Streeter put down the receiver. "They must be outside. Look, Frank, I can't take a chance that this guy was lying. I'm heading over there. Go to the bus station with a cell phone and these." He pulled three keys from his pants pocket and dropped them on the desk. "Watch for Grover. When he gets there, keep an eye on him. I'll be at the warehouse by eleven. If it's a wild-goose chase, I'll call and let you know and you give the keys to Grover. If it's a setup, either I won't call because I'm busy or I'll call and let you know what happened. No matter what, watch Grover. My hunch is he won't hang around long if I don't show."

Streeter went around to the side of the desk and started fishing through the credenza. He found Frank's Baer .45 automatic and then he headed for the door.

Sid Wahl and Dub McCullough sat in the old Subaru, drinking and belching, and watching the front door of Marty's warehouse. All that while doing an occasional bump from the bindle of cocaine Sid had brought. The coke kept them on a reasonably even keel, although Sid noticed he was having more difficulty focusing on the building and Dub was slurring his words. They'd been there for over three hours. Sid was so tired of Dub's idiotic biker ramblings that he was half ready to shoot the son of bitch, toss the body into the tall prairie-grass field next to them, and go deal with Richie on his own. But he might need the crazy Mick at crunch time, so he just concentrated on the warehouse. The rented minivan hadn't moved since they'd gotten there. At about nine, Richie had come out and put a small suitcase into the back before returning to the building. Sid figured it held Grover's files.

So the two men sat in the Subaru getting wasted. Occasionally, Sid would actually listen to what Dub was saying. Big mistake. The jerk was always off on some dopey riff about how he got this tattoo or that body part pierced. Faggy hipster voodoo doll with a dumb name, Sid thought. Spiky green hair cut at all different angles. Metal sticking into his face and every inch of the exposed arms sticking out of his T-shirt covered with tattoos. Smelled like old gym socks, too.

"I'm plannin' to get me nipples pierced next," Dub was saying. He had a habit of saying "me" instead of "my" to sound more Irish. Like that fooled anyone. In his entire twenty-three years, he had never been east of Kansas City.

Sid glanced at his wristwatch and saw it was five to eleven. Close enough. He looked over at Dub, who was working on his fourth sixteen-ounce can of Guinness and a Camel nonfilter. "Let's saddle up and do it." Sid drained his own stout. "My bet is that what we're looking for is in the van." Then he shifted himself in his seat to face Dub. He reached over and grabbed his left shoulder, squeezing hard. "Remember. The guy is all mine. I really owe that prick and he's going to take a little time to die. You can do whatever you want with the broad."

"You only tole me that about fifty times." Dub looked at the hand on his shoulder and jerked himself free. "You can kill both of them if you want. Grova pays me the same no matter who does what."

Sid started the engine and drove out of the gravel driveway past three huge Dumpsters. He moved the car slowly across the street and parked roughly behind the van. When they got out Sid felt the earth spinning under him. Damn, he was more toasted than he'd thought. Then he looked over to the other side of the car and realized he wasn't nearly as bad off as McCullough. The crazy Irishman had opened his car door and fallen facefirst onto the asphalt. "Sheet!" he screamed and got up brushing hard at one leg of his blue jeans.

Sid walked around to him. "You gonna be able to handle this?" He hiccuped the question out.

"Don't worry about me, Jazzbo." Dub's face was red with rage. "Just make sure you don't fuck up again. I don't want to end up in no trunk with puke all over me shirt."

Sid cursed silently. Then they both walked toward the front door. When they got next to the building, Sid jiggled the handle. It was locked, so he tapped at it softly with the silencer end of his nine-millimeter handgun. He waited a moment and then tapped again. From inside, Richie and Tina didn't know what to make of the intrusion. They had been out in the warehouse looking around and they'd just gotten back inside. Marty was supposed to swing by at noon for lunch, so they assumed he was knocking. When Richie opened the door, he was pulled out by his shirtfront into the harsh sunlight. It took him a few seconds to recognize Sid Wahl.

Sid had grabbed Richie's shirt with his left hand and now he came across hard with the butt of his nine on his nose. It broke instantly and sent a spray of blood straight onto Sid's right shoulder. He was drawing his gun back for another swipe when the brown Buick rolled into the lot, its horn honking. As he wheeled in, Streeter could see Richie going to his knees with Sid beating his face. They were standing in front of the door with an armed punker about ten feet off to the left. Streeter gunned his Buick and headed toward the man with the green hair. At first, Dub couldn't believe that the big car was even coming toward him, much less moving that fast. By the time he got oriented, the Buick's bumper was within two feet of him. He let out a loud curse and then backpedaled three steps until he was up against the building. Still the Buick came. Streeter hit the brakes and stopped within inches of Dub's knees. Then he eased ahead until his bumper pinned the screaming man against the wall.

"Motha focka'!" Dub yelled in pain and shock. He aimed his nine-mil at the driver. Streeter saw what was coming, so he shoved the car into park and threw himself across the front seat. Once down, he grabbed Frank's Baer. Dub squeezed off two rounds, the bullets moving through the windshield and into the front seat. Seeing that there was no one to shoot at, he stopped firing and started cursing again.

Streeter pulled the action back on the Baer to make sure there was one in the chamber. His breath felt like it was sucked out of him at what he saw. The gun was empty. In the excitement he and Frank had both forgotten that the bondsman never kept his guns loaded. They made him nervous. Above

Dub's screaming, Streeter heard Richie yelling. Evidently, Sid didn't interrupt the beating to help his partner. Richie's face was bleeding from several cuts, along with his crushed nose. By now he was on his knees. Suddenly, the door to the warehouse opened and Tina, purse in hand, blew out into the lot. She took three quick steps and glanced around. Dub was off to her right, pinned by the Buick. Immediately in front of her she could see Richie being beaten. Dub saw the redhead come out. Since he couldn't get the guy in the Buick, he leveled his nine at the woman and fired. For his part, Sid knew that the interrogation Grover had asked for was not going to happen. Still, he intended to kill Richie and Tina, so he opened fire on the woman, just a few feet before him, as well.

Tina dropped to one knee and was about to lean forward to help Richie. Her sudden movement saved her life and ended Dub McCullough's. Both men fired. Dub's slug whistled over her head and a few feet past Sid, whose shot flew over Tina and hit Dub in the Adam's apple. His dead body slammed back against the wall and then slid down in front of the Buick.

In the crossfire, Richie and Tina scrambled toward each other, then toward the minivan. Sid stared in disbelief at what he'd done, but regrouped and aimed his gun at Richie.

"Hold it, asshole!" he yelled. Richie stopped but Tina kept running. Half drunk and completely stoned, Sid aimed at Richie's profile and squeezed off a round. But he was so low that the bullet went into Richie's thigh, dropping him to the ground again.

Sid took a step toward him. Beyond the Buick, he could see the van back up and smash into his Subaru. Undaunted, Tina pulled forward, spun the wheel hard to her right, and floored it. This time she barely swiped the station wagon. She spun the van around hard and then crammed it into forward. Sid squeezed off a round in her general direction, hitting nothing. The rented van flew out of the lot and took off toward South Santa Fe Drive, leaving Sid a couple of feet from the passenger's door of the Buick. He stood over Richie, who was squirming facedown on the asphalt. Sid then tried to salvage one thing from what had turned into a very bad morning. The nine-millimeter shook in his hand.

Streeter could only guess at what was happening. He decided to stay low and come out the passenger's door. Maybe with his empty Baer he could finesse the punker. He grabbed the handle and pushed out as hard as he could. The door swung open, with the handle whacking Sid in the small of his back and pushing him forward. He turned around to see where the interruption had come from. Streeter leaped from the car, dropping his Baer as he did. He dove at the little man, running his shoulder into Sid's gut, and dropping him fast. That caused Sid to squeeze off the round that he'd intended for Richie. With his gun arm bent, the nine was at waist level when it went off. The shot ripped into Sid's own stomach. He was unconscious before his body had settled to a stop on the asphalt.

Streeter could tell that the little man would be out for a while. He saw Richie lying off to the right. Reaching out, he gently shook him. "You okay?"

Richie was almost out, too, but he managed to turn his head in the direction of the voice. "Yeah. Go get Tina and make sure she's okay."

Streeter knew he'd better not be there when the police arrived. Richie was right: go find Tina. He grabbed the Baer and got back in the car. Once behind the wheel, he started his engine and jammed into reverse. When he was about a car length away from the building, he saw the punker slumped against the wall. He reached into the glove compartment as he dropped the Buick into forward. Pulling out his cell phone, Streeter punched in 911. He was moving fast toward Santa Fe by the time he started giving the police dispatcher the location of the shooting. That was the only thing he told her that was truthful.

20

"If this don't beat the hell out of anything I've ever seen," the police detective said as he watched the last ambulance leave shortly before noon. Hooper had just made the rank, but surveying the blood-splattered asphalt in the lot, he wished he was back on foot patrol at the Arapahoe County Fair. He looked at one of the uniforms. "Makes no sense at all. The best I can figure out is that the little guy with taped glasses beat the snot out of the guy with the curly hair. Then the skinhead—or whatever the hell he was, with the green hair—got himself shot by the little guy. Once that was over, the little guy again turned back and shot Curly in the leg. Something like that, or maybe he shot him first. Then, just to make sure that everything was all totally fucked up, the little guy shot himself in the gut. How the hell am I supposed to make sense out of all this?"

"Maybe you better wait until the lieutenant gets here before you start panicking," the uniform said, not looking at the detective.

Hooper stared at the uniform for a long time before he turned and headed toward his car. He walked up to Sergeant Steinke, the man in charge of the scene. "You getting anything here, Carl?"

Steinke was watching the uniforms measuring distances with the walking tape machine. He shook his head without looking at his new partner.

"You want to head over to the hospital and get a statement from Curly?" Hooper pressed. "The little fat guy looks like he'll be in surgery or recovery for quite a while. He maybe won't come out of it ever. Curly's our best bet at getting something. What do you say? Go over and ID him and find out what the hell happened."

Steinke, twenty years older than Hooper and about to retire, finally nodded. Once they got to the hospital, they were told that it would be over an hour before they could speak to the injured man with the curly hair. They had an orderly get them the guy's wallet so they could check for identification.

"No wonder I thought Curly looked familiar," Hooper said as he handed Steinke the driver's license. "That there's Richie Moats. Marty Moats's nephew. You remember all that horseshit a few weeks ago when he was missing down in Mexico or Central America or wherever it was. Everyone thought he was killed down there."

Steinke studied the driver's license and finally looked up at his partner. "That's him, all right. Let's you and me talk to him before we call the lieutenant in."

Actually, it was almost four by the time they got to interview Richie. Still groggy from surgery, he didn't have much to say to the two suburban detectives. "It's been a rough two or three weeks," Richie muttered with his eyes closed. "Lemme sleep, okay? Some kind of robbery . . . I guess." With that he nodded out.

Once the local media got hold of the story, they camped out in front of Littleton Hospital and chased Marty down at one of his stores. The old man gave them a couple of sound bites about being in the dark regarding what had happened to his beloved nephew.

"I'm just as surprised that he's alive as all of you folks are," Marty said, staring thoughtfully into the news cameras as he stood on the showroom floor. "My wife, Marlene, and I have gone through pure hell over these past few weeks. Pure hell," he repeated sadly. "And suddenly last night the boy shows up asking for a place to stay. This morning I was headed over to take him to lunch. I can't tell you how shocked I was at what happened. It's a combination of delight and agony that swept through me and Richie's aunt over the last twenty-four hours. She's down at the hospital now and that's where I'm headed." He made a sweeping motion with his arm toward the showroom. "Even if that means my being away from our annual 'April Showers' weekend sale, featuring the biggest savings in Colorado waterbed history." He allowed himself a quick smile. "That's at all thirty-four of our convenient Front Range locations."

"Marty didn't get those thirty-four locations by not knowing how to blow serious smoke," Frank told Streeter as they stared at the five-thirty television news in his living room. "There's times that guy makes even Bill Clinton look sincere."

The bounty hunter was leaning into the Formica that separated the kitchen from the living room. He was nursing his third Johnnie Walker Red since he got home a couple of hours ago. Normally, he never drank alone, but he was rattled. Most of the afternoon he'd spent trying to track down Tina. That and calling his lawyer to see what kind of trouble he was in. The television anchorman was saying that the identity of the man shot to death was still not known. Nor was the identity of the man who killed him. That second man was in Littleton Hospital in critical condition with a gunshot wound to his stomach. Inexplicably, the second wound was self-inflicted.

"Self-inflicted my ass." Streeter spoke to the screen from across the room. He looked like he was about to say more, but instead merely took a sip of his Scotch.

Frank studied him for a moment. "What did Bill say about your situation?"

William McLean had been the bounty hunter's personal attorney and close friend ever since they'd lived next door to each other during Streeter's last marriage. He'd only been able to talk to Bill briefly that afternoon. McLean was in Aspen for the weekend and would not be back in Denver until the next afternoon.

"Not a whole lot," Streeter answered. "We only talked for a few minutes long distance, but I gather I'll be visiting the police sometime soon."

"Might make sense," his partner said, turning his attention back to the television. "These guys play rough." He nodded toward the screen. "Even old Marty's working his own angles here."

Streeter considered that as he watched the anchorman. "What I'd like to know is what Grover's got up his sleeve now. This has got to go down as one of the worst days he's ever had. One man dead, another practically there. And nothing from the lockers. Richie and Tina still alive and it's only a matter of time before the police come sniffing around. Shouldn't be hard to connect Sid to him."

"You got any idea where the girl is? Tina."

Streeter shook his head. "I tried a few places, like her apartment house, but no luck. She might even be heading back to Florida, or wherever the hell's she's from, by now. I have to talk to Marty later. I phoned Marlene before she went to the hospital and she said she'd have him call me when everything settles down. I didn't tell her I was at the warehouse this morning. No one knows about that but you and Sid and Richie."

"And whoever it was that called you in the first place," Frank added.

"Right. Grover doesn't know about that, although I'll probably be hearing from him before long."

Tina settled into the chair next to the bed and opened the Rolling Rock twist-off. The television reporter in front of the hospital listed Richie's condition as serious but stable. Not life-threatening, which was exactly where she'd find herself if she tried to visit him. Grover certainly has someone planted there to watch for me, she thought as she lit a cigarette. Better to lie low and communicate with Richie through his uncle. She had called the Moatses' home a few minutes earlier, after she'd heard that Richie was out of danger. But she got the answering machine, so she left word that she'd call back later. Now, glancing around her motel room, she was anxious. The original files were in the suitcase in the entryway. But they didn't bring her the same comfort they had before the attack. If Grover was willing to come after her and Richie without knowing where the files were, that meant he was nowhere near as concerned about them as she'd thought. Crazy son of a bitch, working off of anger more than reason. About all Tina could count on was that he'd keep coming after them. She picked up the phone.

"Bail Bonds" came through and she was glad the voice that answered was familiar.

"Mr. Streeter, it's me. Tina." She took a sip from her beer. It sounded like he had his hand over the receiver and was talking to someone who was with him.

His voice finally came back. "I was hoping you'd call. Where are you?"

She answered with a question of her own. "You're not alone, are you?"

"No. My partner's here. Don't worry, he knows what happened today."

"Exactly what *did* happen today?"

"Tina, I got a call shortly before eleven," he said. "Some guy telling me that Grover knew where you were staying and he was going to have you killed at about the same time I was handing over the keys. I drove down and I got there just as Sid Wahl was whaling on Richie. Then I pinned some punker against the wall and I'm not sure what all happened right after that. When I finally got out of my car, the punker was dead." He paused. "Sid and I got into a little scrape and he ended up putting one into his own stomach. Richie said he was all right and that I should go find you."

Gillis considered that for a moment, so Streeter continued. "I'm getting together with my lawyer tomorrow night. He'll probably have me go to the police. You might consider coming with me when I turn myself in."

"I've been thinking about that all afternoon," she said. "This is getting too far out of hand. Someone has to put a leash on Grover. Apparently those files don't scare him as much as I thought they might."

"It seems that way. Where are you now?"

"I'd rather not say, Mr. Streeter."

"Can you at least give me a phone number?"

"Let me sleep on it. I'll call you tomorrow. When will you be there?"

"One time's as good as another."

Tina chewed on her lower lip. "This is one strange standoff we've got here. Whatever you do, hang on to those locker keys and don't give them to Grover. You know he'll probably come after you for them."

"That occurred to me."

"I'll call Rudy Fontana," she said. "He might have a line on what Grover's up to."

"Just be careful. Royals won't let up until you're dead or he's in jail. *Or* until he's dead. There's nothing in between for him."

When he hung up, he looked around and saw that Frank had left the room. Streeter stared at the phone for a couple of minutes. Finally, he picked it up and dialed Connie's phone number. They were supposed to meet for dinner in less than two hours, but there was no way he could do it. As he waited for her to pick up, he really wasn't sure what he'd say. The truth seemed too dramatic and he didn't want her to know he was involved with the morning's shooting. But he didn't like the idea of lying to her either.

"Hello." She sounded upbeat.

"Connie?"

A pause. "Streeter?"

"Yeah, right. Listen, Connie. Something's come up. Business. All hell's breaking loose on a case of mine and it looks like I have to work tonight. I wouldn't do this our first time out of the blocks if it wasn't important, but I can't make it." He looked away for a minute. "I'm dying for a rain check, though. Don't be too mad. Like I said, this is really important." When she didn't respond, he continued. "Connie? I'm sorry."

"If it's business, it's business." Her voice betrayed nothing but she didn't sound mad. "We'll make it some other time."

"Good." He nodded. "That's really good. Look, I have to go. I'll call you in a day or so when things settle down. Okay?"

"Okay, Streeter." Her voice had its original bounce back. "This is a school night, so my mom wouldn't let me stay out too late anyhow."

When he hung up, Streeter drained the rest of his Scotch and thought about what a truly depressing day it had been all the way around.

Rudy was sprawled out on the couch in his office with the phone on his right ear, listening to Tina bitching about what Grover had tried at the warehouse. She was being cagey, but he could tell she wanted information.

"I know that we put you in a jam with that robbery, Rudy," she was saying, "but Jesus, we're talking about murder now. Grover wanted to *assassinate* us." She paused and lowered her voice. "Did you know about that setup ahead of time?"

Fontana thought that one over. If he told her he was the one who'd called to warn Streeter, he'd gain her trust. That might help him get the locker keys for himself. But if he told her and somehow it got back to Grover, well sir, Rudy might as well just hang up now and go join Dub McCullough down at the morgue. So he did what he always did in a tight spot: he lied.

"Tina, if I knew ahead of time, it would a been me that called the bounty hunter." His voice sounded hurt, like how could she ask such a thing. "No doubt I was very mad at what you two did to me, but I'm no killer. You know that."

"Right." Her voice sounded like she didn't know that at all. "I better get going, Rudy. You tell Grover for me that—" She didn't finish the sentence.

"Tell him what, Tina?" Rudy sat up.

"Never mind." She hung up without saying another word.

Rudy put the receiver back and stared at the ceiling over the couch. Not a bad day's work. Wahl nearly dead, Richie on his back, and Grover empty-handed. Not to mention that the cops should be breathing down the big man's neck soon. Normally, Sid was as loyal as a beaten German shepherd, but this time the police wouldn't let up on him until he told them what was behind that parking-lot massacre. Rudy stood and poured himself a drink. Grover was extremely vulnerable and, with phase two of his plan now in motion, Rudy felt better than good.

Speaking of Grover, he thought as he glanced at the door, he should be back here anytime now. They'd talked on the phone about an hour earlier. Not much of a conversation. Just his boss ordering him to be in the office at six-thirty. Rudy sat behind his desk drinking for another few minutes until Grover arrived. He was more subdued than usual, but in his leather jacket he looked to be in a war mode.

"You still hitting the sauce?" Grover asked when he first walked in.

"Hello to you, too," Rudy responded. Bad approach. Don't want to seem too confident tonight. "I mean, you want one?"

Grover nodded and stared at him, although his attention seemed elsewhere. "What the fuck happened this morning? Streeter never showed up and the next thing I know, some asshole on the TV's talking about Richie Moats being shot, Sid's in the IC ward, and that harp buddy of his from Mars is dead. No Tina, no money, no ludes." He took the drink Rudy offered him, his eyes wide with disbelief. "I tell you one thing, I'm going to find out what went wrong and take care of everyone. Streeter, Richie, Tina. I got a man down at the hospital now. If Gillis shows there for a second, she's dead."

Rudy sat back in his chair behind the desk and tried to sound concerned. "What about Sid? He comes outta that coma and those cops are gonna be on his ass like wet hair. What if he lays it all out for them?"

"Then I take care of him, too." Royals leaned over the desk. "Don't make any mistake about this one, Rudy. I don't care who you are or how we're connected. After today all bets are off. I'm going to find out what went wrong and then crush anyone who had anything to do with it. If there's a shit storm coming my way, I'm gonna make sure that everyone around me gets to enjoy it as much as I do."

Grover downed his bourbon in one long gulp and glanced away. "Now I gotta go talk to the guy I report to. My *partner.*" He shook his head. "He'll only take about two pounds outta my hide for this."

Rudy sat up and studied Grover. He'd never seen the big man look so worried. Rudy knew Grover had another investor, but he had no idea who it was or that the man could actually command that kind of attitude. Hell, he thought, that's Grover's worry. But it was worth the price of admission just to see him jangled like that.

Marty Moats used a pay phone just outside the hospital to call Streeter. At seventy, he didn't want to be inside a hospital any longer than absolutely necessary. He put the quarter in and dialed Frank's number. Luckily, the bounty hunter answered. Marty was in no mood for small talk with the old bondsman.

"Streeter? That you?" Marty shivered slightly. The ten o'clock temperature was in the upper forties and he didn't have a coat on over his white shirt. "Marlene said you wanted to talk to me. What the hell's going on around here, son?"

"All I know is what I see on the tube. And one other thing. I never made it to the meeting with Grover this morning."

"Why the hell not?" Marty sounded furious.

"Someone called me just before I was going to leave for the bus station and warned me off." Streeter decided not to mention the part about being sent to the warehouse.

"So you still have the keys to the lockers?"

"Yes. And I'll keep them until I decide what to do about all this. I'm talking to my attorney tomorrow and it might be that I'll hand everything over to the Littleton police."

Marty could feel the pressure on his temples increase. He'd had a headache for hours and listening to Streeter didn't help. But he was too drained to argue. "We'll talk about it in the morning, son. For now, I need some sleep. Richie's doing much better but he's still pretty knocked out. He's under police protection." He paused. "You have any idea where Tina is?"

"She called me before but she wouldn't say where she was. I'll be talking to her again. Said she'd call here tomorrow."

"Then I guess all the excitement's over for today. We'll talk in the morning."

21

That storm Grover was waiting for didn't take long to develop. It hit Denver at precisely five-thirty-two the next afternoon. Once again, Streeter and Frank were watching the local news in the downstairs apartment when they saw the whole mess go down. And Lise Abbott, of all people, delivered it. Her eager young face was set in its most serious, professional-journalist expression as she stared into the camera.

"News Three has learned that Richard Moats—nephew of Colorado's legendary 'Waterbed King,' Martin "Marty" Moats—is part owner and a driving force behind a string of sex-for-sale businesses and is also a suspected kingpin in one of the state's largest illegal drug operations. Moats, thirty-three, allegedly has partial control over three strip bars, four adult-book shops, four lingerie-modeling stores, and numerous massage parlors. According to accounting documents obtained by News Three, Moats is in partnership with Grover Royals in all of the businesses.

"News Three also has learned that Royals, forty-seven, has been the subject of several state grand jury probes into illegal drugs and prostitution and at least one federal RICO investigation. Thus far, he has not been charged with any wrongdoing.

"Richard Moats recently made national headlines when his Chevy Blazer was found in the rural Mexican town of San Ignacio. Mexican police originally said that two young men confessed to killing Moats and taking his truck. However, a subsequent investigation failed to turn up a body or any real evidence against the men, who later recanted their confessions and were released.

"Then, yesterday morning, Moats was shot and seriously injured in a bizarre incident in an Englewood parking lot that left one man dead and another in critical condition at Littleton Hospital. Police investigators have linked the injured man, Sidney R. Wahl, forty-three, with Royals, which has led to speculation that the shooting may have been drug-related. It is not known if Moats's disappearance and yesterday's violent shootings have anything to do with his alleged drug-and-prostitution empire. Englewood police refused to comment this afternoon when confronted with the documents obtained by this reporter."

Streeter flew off the couch, staring at the TV screen in utter disbelief. "Where do they get all that crap?" he asked Frank. "Richie couldn't even handle a simple phone scam. And how could he work with Grover? The two never met each other. They've never been in the same room and she's got them running a multimillion-dollar porno ring." He pointed to Lise standing before the camera in front of what appeared to be Littleton Hospital. "I met her when I was down in Mexico. I didn't think she was capable of this. Where's she getting these supposed documents?"

Back on the TV, Lise's voice deepened and her eyes narrowed dramatically as she went off on another tangent. "When contacted by News Three this afternoon, Martin Moats expressed surprise at the allegations. Moats, perhaps one of the state's most recognized figures, said he—quote—doesn't care what's written on some papers. Richie's no drug dealer and that's all there is to it. End of quote."

Suddenly, Marty's face appeared on the screen. He was standing in front of one of his stores looking lost and pale. "This has to be some big mistake. For one thing, my nephew doesn't have the sense to run a business that big. You're talking millions of dollars. Richie'd more than likely get overwhelmed operating a hot dog stand. For another thing, he doesn't even know this supposed partner of his. This is nothing but a lot of horse manure." He turned to the frowning Abbott and added, "Can't you people get your facts straight and leave the boy alone? He's in the damned hospital."

The old man was so shaken that he didn't even plug his stores this time.

Streeter shook his head, his eyes still fixed on the screen. "This is crazy, Frank."

Lise's voice provided a verbal explanation and the camera panned what appeared to be accounting ledgers and official documents from the Secretary of State's office. The name Richard M. Moats was typed in next to a scribble that was supposedly his signature. "According to state registration documents and personal notes on ledgers for the various sex-for-sale businesses, Richard M. Moats has had dealings with Royals going as far back as 1990. Because these documents were obtained only recently, the meaning of the ledgers is not yet completely known to News Three investigators. However, they would seem to point clearly to a partnership between the two men."

Next, the perplexed face of the Denver District Attorney appeared on camera. He was sitting at his desk when Abbott stuck a microphone in front of him and asked for his reaction to the allegations. "I cannot, of course, comment on an ongoing investigation, but our office has had—historically—an interest in Mr. Royals's business affairs. How this is connected with yesterday's shooting incident on South Santa Fe per se, well, I'm not at liberty to discuss that just now."

"I'll bet he's not," Streeter said to the screen. "Look at that fool. His office has been trying to nail Royals for years." He turned back to Frank. "And as far as Richie's concerned, the DA doesn't have a clue. That 'ongoing investigation' junk is his way of saying we don't know nothing about nothing."

"Trouble is, it all sounds legitimate." Frank walked to the kitchen sink and ran some cold water. He filled a glass with it, all the while staring at Streeter. "It sounds real and looks credible. That means people will believe it. Doesn't much matter if it's true. It also means that someone who knows Grover's operation must have talked to this Lise."

Streeter nodded and walked slowly toward the door. "I'm meeting Billy McLean down at the Wynkoop to discuss this whole situation. Right about now, I really wish your old pal Marty had never stopped here that night he found out about Richie in Mexico."

Frank broke out into a small grin. "Say hi to Wild Bill for me, okay?"

William McLean was sitting at one of those high tables scattered around near the front of the Wynkoop Brewing Company. The Wynkoop is probably the senior pub in Lower Downtown. By several years, it predates Coors Baseball Field and the rash of sports bars now surrounding it on three sides. The first floor contains a huge kidney-shaped bar and a large restaurant, as well as the brewing facility itself. The second floor holds an enormous pool hall and tavern catering mostly to the under-thirty crowd. Streeter hardly ever went upstairs, as he wasn't too fond of Yuppie pool sharks *or* Generation Xers. But he liked the downstairs with its wide range of beers and its European-style saloon food.

McLean had gone to the Wynkoop right after a court appearance and he was wearing a dark gray business suit. The tall table suited his six feet five inches fine. Being one of the last professional men Streeter knew who still smoked cigarettes, McLean had a glass of amber ale in one hand and a lit Marlboro in the other when the bounty hunter first spotted him.

"Hey Bill," he said as he walked up. "What's to it?"

McLean put his beer on the table and stood up. With silver hair and a deep, booming voice, he could make reading from the phone book sound important. "Street man," he said. They shook hands and McLean nodded to one of the televisions over the bar. "It looks like you're in even deeper shit than we thought. I just saw something about the Moats clan and your buddy Grover Royals. It wasn't flattering. If you're involved with all that, you have yourself some trouble."

Streeter shook his head and sat down. A waitress was passing by, so he ordered two more amber ales. When they came, he and Bill touched glasses and drank in silence for a couple of minutes. Streeter then broke into a long story of his complete involvement with Richie, Marty, Tina, and Grover. He concluded with what had happened at the warehouse on Sunday morning.

"Jesus," McLean said as he snuffed out a cigarette. "If the DA's in a real good mood and hasn't opened a statute book in a few years, he's only got you for attempted murder, conspiracy to transport a controlled substance with intent to sell—the Quaaludes are yours, technically—leaving the scene of a murder, aiding and abetting a felon, withholding evidence, assault with a deadly weapon, and littering—you left a lot of bodies out there. Now, if he's got a hard-on and there's a statute book nearby, he can probably find eight or ten additional charges. As far as Richie and Tina are concerned, forget it. They can throw the proverbial book at those two and it'll all stick." He gestured toward the TV. "You say that was all bullshit on the tube tonight? About Richie and Grover?"

Streeter nodded. "Royals is probably into most of that stuff, but putting Richie with him like that is complete nonsense."

"Well, then." Bill smiled broadly. "If that's the case and little Richard gets a good lawyer and a sympathetic judge, he should be out in about three or four lifetimes. Tina, maybe as few as two."

"You're cheering the hell out of me, Billy." Streeter took a sip from his beer.

"You want cheer, go rent a video. I'm your attorney and I'm telling you what you're up against. My advice is get your friend Tina and all the evidence you have on Royals—plus those locker keys—and meet me tomorrow morning. We'll have a session with the Arapahoe DA. I think I can get one of the heavyweights from the Denver DA's office to join us, too, seeing as how some of this involves them. We'll lay it all out, say how the three of you are willing to testify against Royals and Sid and Rudy What's-his-name. We dangle those two in front of them and chances are really good that they'll drop what they have on you three. Do Richie and Tina have attorneys?"

"He probably does." Streeter shrugged. "Her, who knows? Look, the problem is that I can't get ahold of Tina Gillis. She said she'd call me today and she never did. I have no idea where she is and chances are good that she's left the state by now."

"To hell with her, then," McLean said. "Talk to Marty tonight, tomorrow at the latest. Convince him that Richie should roll over on Royals. We'll cut the best deal we can with or without Tina."

Streeter nodded. "I'll see what I can do. Marty sure looked terrible on TV just now. This whole thing is taking a toll on him, and his business is going to suffer if people identify the Moats name with drugs and prostitution."

"Nothing we can do about that, Street. From what I saw on Channel Three, there's going to be a lot of pressure to bring Grover down. That report may have been complete BS, but the pressure on the DA to nail the people mentioned is going to be real enough. The quicker we cut our deal, the better. Even if it's just you and me sitting down with the police, we'll still have considerable coin. They'll be drooling to get into those lockers." He paused. "This could get rough on you, pal. But you'll be all right if you stick to the truth and cooperate."

Streeter looked around the room. "I suppose. Let's get something to eat so I can go back to the church and call Marty."

Rudy sat at his desk and wondered what the hell was going on with Grover. Not that he was complaining. The big man had called him minutes after the Channel 3 report aired, screaming about suing the station for libel. Grover suing? That wasn't his style. Rudy was surprised enough that Grover hadn't gone after Streeter the night before. But now, not moving on him all day and then threatening to sue over the news story? Made no sense. He'd pegged Grover to go out and litter the city with bodies by noon at the latest and then sort out who he meant to kill. Streeter should at least be in the hospital. But Grover sounded almost subdued on the phone. Rudy figured it must have something to do with his late meeting with his partner last night. All day, Fontana tried to figure out who the hell was in business with Grover. He'd never seen any names on the corporate documents other than his own, Grover's, and Sid Wahl's. Whoever the man was, he sure knew how to keep Grover in line. Rudy wouldn't even allow himself to think of what that partner could mean to his plans when Grover went down.

For now, Rudy felt so good about what the big man was going through, he didn't even care if the moron figured out that he was the one who fed the story to Lise Abbott. Dummied-up Secretary of State papers, phony ledgers, and everything else. He'd deal with Grover eventually, if he had to. No sir, he'd just enjoy his drink and savor the big payback for Mr. Royals.

22

Bad cop, bad cop. Dumb cop.

That's how Grover pegged them as he walked out the side door of his house that Tuesday morning. He could tell they were the law the minute he spotted them through his front window. The hell do they want? Grover thought he knew the older one. A longtime Denver investigator with an Irish name. The other two were strangers. One was in his late forties. The other—the dorky one—looked to be about thirty. They were leaning against a mud-colored car at the end of his driveway, although the young one straightened up and started to play with his tie as Grover approached.

"You mind moving that thing?" Grover glanced at the unmarked car. "Some of us have to get to work today."

The older cop stepped away from the car and pointed to the rear door. "Your business can wait, Royals."

Grover stopped about ten feet from them and frowned, glancing at the two cops he didn't know. Then he looked at the one who'd just spoken. "You're Denver, right?" The man nodded. "So who are Moe and Larry here? They can't be state or federal."

"I'll tell you who we are, asshole." The young one took a step forward. "We're the guys who're gonna mess up your life so bad you're gonna wish you never heard of Englewood."

Grover broke into a quick smile. "Ouch. That hurt." He walked up to the man, his smile fading. The cop glanced at

Grover's shoulders, the two thick arms coming out of the short-sleeved shirt, and took a half step back. That's when the third cop broke in.

"Let's everyone calm down," he said, pulling his wallet from his back pocket. He opened it to show Grover his badge. "I'm Sergeant Steinke, Englewood Homicide. This is my partner, Detective Hooper." He turned to his right and nodded at the last cop. "That there's Sergeant Haney, Denver PD."

Grover had been in a stare-down with Hooper while his partner spoke. Now he glanced over at Steinke and Haney. "Let's not get too dramatic about this, okay? If you're arresting me, I'll get in the car and we can drive downtown. If not, move away from my drive. I got places to go. This ain't L.A. and you guys ain't all that scary." He shook his head and smiled again. "Englewood."

Haney now took over for their side. "Royals, we've got a file on you as thick as your skull. Some of it's pretty damned interesting. What with all this excitement down in Englewood on Sunday and your boy getting caught in the middle of it, we're about to turn something fairly soon. Oh yeah, there's one name we wanted to run by you, too."

Grover took a step toward Haney, his smile narrowing. The chunky old cop smelled like tobacco. Cheap cigars. Not as cheap as the brown suit he was wearing, but pretty rank. "Is this where you say Sid Wahl and I'm supposed to cave in?"

Now it was Haney's turn to smile. "No, this is where we say Eddy Spangler. What you do with that is your own business."

Grover was obviously surprised. His jaw dropped slightly. Hooper saw the opening and stepped up again. "Didn't expect *that* one, didja? Late last night, Mr. Spangler got stopped for a D.U.I. and driving under revocation. No insurance and a bunch of other stuff. Too bad for him, he had some pot and coke on his backseat. All of a sudden he's in trouble. Seems he'd seen a certain television news story earlier in the evening and that gave him a bright idea. Now he figures it's better to talk to us about you than to face a drug charge and all those driving problems."

Haney stepped between the two men. "Bottom line," he said reaching into his coat pocket and pulling out some folded papers, "is that the DA's requesting the honor of your presence at a little grand jury he's holding this week." Slowly, he handed the subpoena to Grover. "Friday morning. Don't be late. It's more of a command than a request. You might want to bring your lawyer, too."

Then, one by one, they got into their car. Hooper kept staring at Grover, so as they drove off, the big man lifted his hand and flipped out his middle finger.

"Assholes," Grover mumbled. Eddy Spangler was not something he'd planned on. He'd figured he could keep Sid in line and deal with whatever else the police came at him with. But Eddy could be the missing link between Grover and the shootings. Not to mention what was in the lockers at the bus station. As he walked up the drive toward his Mustang, he shoved the subpoena in his back pants pocket. Time to have a talk with his boss again.

Rudy couldn't believe how stupid she sounded on the phone. Don't reporters have to go to journalism school or something? Ain't that like college? He took a long pull from his cigarette and studied his coffee, barely paying attention to Lise Abbott's voice. He debated whether to pour a pinch of whiskey into his cup. Normally, Rudy prided himself on never drinking before noon and seldom before four. 'Course, he'd fudged on those guidelines a bit lately, but these were unusual times. Still, there was no way to justify an eye-opener at just a shade before eight-forty-five in the morning, even if he was awakened by a call like this.

"I suppose I should have studied those so-called papers from the Secretary of State," she was saying, "but we didn't have much time before I went on the air. Let me ask you, did you fill those out yourself?" Then without waiting for an answer, she continued. "And those ledgers. Our accountants went through them late last night and they can't make sense out of them." She took a long pause. "I have to ask you, was this stuff all phony? Did you set me up?"

By now, he didn't particularly give a damn if Lise knew he'd bullshitted her. Rudy was savvy enough to know that once a story like this gets out there, well hell, it's like unringing a bell to try and downplay it. The truth was more or less irrelevant when it came to matters of public opinion. And with both newspapers legitimizing Abbott's story in their pale follow-ups that morning, the impact was all the more profound. Richie and Grover would be forever linked as drug-dealing pimps and pornographers to all of Denver. No denials or clarifications would change that. Mission accomplished, so fuck you very much, Lise Abbott.

"Set you up? That's the thanks I get, is it?" Rudy took a sip of coffee. He hadn't gotten to bed much before three and his temples were pounding. "This is probably the biggest story of your career, honey, and here you are calling me in the middle of the night to split hairs about accuracy. Jesus Christ, you act like we're talking about the Pentagon Papers. Let me ask *you* something. How's your boss treating you today? Since the story broke."

"That's not the point." She paused. "Actually, he's been in a good mood."

" 'Course he is, honey. You had the scoop of the month. You think your boss really gives two shits whether Grover and Richie are in business together?"

"Like I said, you're missing the point." Her voice was softening. "The point is that this story's unraveling like a Kmart sale sweater. I've gotten calls from the state, the FBI, everybody. They're furious and it looks like you fed me a lot of garbage. This could be the end of my career."

"No, no, sweetheart. You're the one missing the point here. First off, if they fired every TV reporter who unloaded a line of horseshit on the air, there'd be no one left working in front of the camera. The real point is that you made a big splash and your boss is happy. Hell, all the denials will just give the story more wheels. Milk it for a few days and then move on. You're a star, honey. Enjoy it and no thanks are necessary."

"I suppose . . ." Her voice trailed off.

"Damned straight, you suppose. One more thing, sweetheart."

"What's that?"

"Don't be calling me ever again." He hung up and thought how he was glad he never gave her his real name. To Lise, Rudy was just a voice at an unlisted phone number and the guy who had some documents delivered to her office.

Tina had called Streeter shortly before ten that morning. She wanted to meet him for lunch. She'd buy if she could pick the spot, so they met at a crowded Arby's Roast Beef in far West Denver, almost out of town. They each ordered just a coffee. Cups in hand, they took a booth near the streaked front window. It was going to be a warm day, maybe into the low eighties. The sun was so intense, they kept their shades on as they talked.

"Have you been to see Richie yet?" Streeter asked.

Tina shook her head. "That could be dangerous. We've been on the phone, though. Have you talked to him?"

"No. Marty keeps me posted. I gather he's getting better. Might be released in a week or so. Of course, now the police are all over him to find out what happened and to shed some light on that story about him and Grover. He'll probably be in front of a grand jury Frank just heard about as soon as he's better. Marty said he's stonewalling them so far. Saying he doesn't know half the story and that he's forgotten the other half." He paused. "They don't know about you, and my hunch is Richie'll go to the gas chamber before he'll tell them anything like that."

She nodded. "I've never doubted his loyalty to me."

Streeter leaned forward and lowered his voice. "Why are you still in town?"

"Mr. Streeter, to you I may be just another slut working for Rudy." Her voice was firm but not bitchy. "But I'm not. I'm still here because this is where Richard is. And I'll stay until he's all better physically and out of Grover's crosshairs. I'll stay even beyond that if this is where he and I decide to live."

"I never saw you as a slut for anyone, Tina," he responded. "Look, I talked to my lawyer. He thinks I should be down spilling my guts to the cops right now. I put him off for a day until I could talk to you, but tomorrow he and I are going to lay it all out for the DA. This is too serious to let slide. My suggestion is that you come with me. If you, me, and Richie all give up the truth, Grover's in a hole for good. The only way to get out of his crosshairs is to get him behind bars. Plus, it'll take all the heat off of Richie's family. His uncle and aunt don't deserve the grief they're getting."

"We've been thinking about that, too," she said, her voice gentler. "When are you going?"

"First thing in the morning."

"Count me in."

Streeter smiled and took a sip of his coffee. "Good. Bring those files, too. I'll bring the locker keys. Denver Vice is going to think it's Christmas in April. Tell you what. Come over to my place with me now. We'll call Richie and let him know what we're doing. You can spend the night there for safety. We'll fix you up with your own room. Do you have the files with you?"

She nodded.

"Good. Maybe Marty can go with us. It would be nice to have him there to speak for Richie."

"Are we going to tell the police about how Richie and I stole from Grover?"

"We'll probably have to. My attorney told me that if we cut a deal with the DA, they might not care about the robbery. It's not like Sid'll file charges."

"Let's go call Richie."

Tina followed Streeter back to the church. He had her park in the garage. There was a chance that Grover had someone watching the place, although there were no strange cars nearby. The bounty hunter also made sure they weren't being followed. Once inside, they went to Frank's empty office and called the hospital.

"How are you, baby?" she asked when she got through to Richie. Then she smiled. "That's good." A slight wrinkle of her brow. "Oh he's there, is he? I wish I could stop by." She looked at Streeter and mouthed "Martin" silently. "Listen, Richard. I'm at Mr. Streeter's right now. I'm going to stay here tonight with him and his partner and then we're going down to talk to the police in the morning. Yes, like we discussed before."

Tina turned to Streeter. "He's telling Martin and Marlene. They're both there." Suddenly she frowned. "They're arguing." She paused. "Hello, Martin. Yes, you heard right. Mr. Streeter and I are going to talk to the Denver DA and police in the morning. Yes, it's the best way to handle this." She listened for a moment, her forehead still creased with concern. Then she looked over at Streeter across the desk and held out the phone for him. "He'd like to speak with you."

Streeter took the receiver. "Marty?"

"Yes, it's me, son." Marty sounded hoarse and tired. "What's all this district attorney nonsense. I never said you could do that."

"Probably because I never asked if I could." The irritation was clear in his voice. "I'm old enough to make up my own mind and, besides, I'm the one out on a limb with the law, not you. We're just letting you know what we're doing and asking you to join us and speak for Richie."

"But that'll just put the boy in even deeper water. We tell the police about that robbery and it's goodbye nephew. He'll go away for sure."

"Not according to my lawyer. The cops want Grover Royals and if that means turning their backs on that other business, they'll do it in a heartbeat."

Marty didn't speak for a long moment. Then he let out a loud exhalation. "If you think it's for the best. Do me one favor first? I'll be over at my downtown store tonight about seven. Stop by with Tina and we'll go over everything before we talk to the police."

"Okay."

"And have her bring Grover's files, too. You and me'll want to look at them before we go running off at the mouth tomorrow."

"Fine. Seven tonight, downtown."

Dexter Calley was sick of waiting for the boss man to call. The last time they'd talked to each other was Sunday afternoon. The old man had gotten ahold of him, all pissed off about the screwed-up exchange at the old warehouse on South Santa Fe. He wanted Dexter to know that he might be needing his services in the next day or so. Promised a load of cash for some heavy work, too. And then nothing. Dexter had kept cool for two solid days. He hadn't gotten in touch with Rudy, although he was tempted. But then, that afternoon, he started phoning the man to find out what was what. A load of cash sounded like a pretty good idea right about now. Who cared what the work was?

It was now almost six on Tuesday evening and Dexter was getting anxious. Maybe he should just go over to Marty's store and confront the man personally. Moats's secretary had told him only half an hour ago that the man would be there tonight. Head down there and ask Marty face-to-face why he's jerking him around. Not returning the calls. See how the old fart likes that. Dexter toked on the tight little joint and looked around his apartment. Yes sir. That's just what he'd do. Finish the pot, eat the last of the pizza, and then head on to Marty Moats's big downtown store and find out why the old man was ignoring him. If he wanted to be treated like that, hell, he could have stayed working for Grover.

23

Most of the time, Marty's downtown store was like the man himself; rambling, big, loud, and busy. But at night it quieted to almost another world. As Streeter and Tina walked down the west end of the 16th Street Mall, the evening wind kicked up. It was clear and the sun was setting in a barrage of orange light off the mountains in front of them. The store, a two-story former sporting-goods shop, had just closed when they arrived a little after seven. Two salespeople were locking up and one, a woman, let them in and told them to go back to the loading docks, where Marty's office was.

"He's expecting you," she told Streeter. "Take the rear-exit door over there." She pointed toward the back corner. "Then head down a long hallway. Marty has an office off to the left at the end. We'll be leaving in a minute and locking the front door. You can go out through the loading dock when you're finished."

They walked to the rear of the huge store and Streeter opened the back door for Tina. The wide hallway leading to the loading docks was well lighted but church-silent. When they got to the time clock and a large rack of time cards on the back wall, they took a quick jog to the left. There were large doors with a sign above them indicating that the loading docks were straight ahead. After passing through them, they could see the darkened docks straight ahead and light from a windowless room off to their right.

"Marty," Streeter yelled out just above his normal speaking

voice. They kept walking toward the lighted room, although no one answered. "Marty," he repeated, louder.

About five feet from the door, they heard an "I'm here," coming from inside. Marty sounded different. But they kept walking toward the light. When they got to the door, they turned into the office. It took their eyes a few seconds to adjust to the glaring brightness. The office itself was about fifteen feet square, a cinder-block cubicle you'd more likely expect to find in a punch-press factory. There were three rows of fluorescent overhead lights, one large desk, and several black metal file cabinets. On the floor, slumped against the desk, lay Marty Moats. Pale and unconscious, with dried blood on a lump on his forehead. Streeter could see that he was breathing. That was the last thing he viewed clearly for a while.

For just a second, he saw Grover Royals's angry face coming at him. Then he caught a flash as Grover's giant right fist smashed into his jaw. Streeter could feel the blood rushing to his face and everything went white for a few seconds. The base of his skull crackled in pain as his head shot back. Behind him, he thought he could hear Tina scream. He almost went down, but managed to steady himself by grabbing the corner of a file cabinet with both hands. He blinked furiously to focus better, but before he could clear his vision, Grover came across with another hard right, a hook that connected with his left temple. Streeter's head twisted off to the left and everything went white again. This time, he dropped to the floor, almost unconscious.

Tina stood behind Grover watching the punches. Her eyes shot furiously around the room. On the desk just to her left lay several lengths of metal pipe, each about two feet long and more than an inch and half around. They looked like part of a furniture assembly, as there was a large rectangular cardboard box leaning against the desk, with a long steel crowbar leaning on it. When Streeter dropped to the floor, Grover, who had his back to her, reached for the desk with his left hand. He picked up a pipe and transferred it to his right hand. She couldn't see the smile on his face as he watched Streeter moan and struggle to his knees in front of him. He raised the pipe to shoulder level and then brought it quickly across from the side and down. Streeter looked up and had just enough time to lift his arms to protect his head. The pipe struck his left forearm, inches from his wrist, and dug deeply into the skin, breaking the bone. A searing pain shot up his arm, through his shoulder, and into his left ear. Then the arm dropped uselessly to his side. When he looked up again, Grover was pulling the pipe back for another swipe.

Adjusting himself slightly on his knees, Streeter turned to his right and drew that arm back as far and fast as he could. Just as the standing man was about to unload with the pipe again, Streeter struck. With all the power he could muster, he shot his right fist into Grover's groin. Royals groaned like all the air was let out of him and leaned forward, almost doubled over. His pain caused him to drop the pipe to the ground. Grover went down on one knee and was almost eye-to-eye with Streeter. But as his breath started to return, Grover reached to the small of his back as though looking for something. In front of him, Streeter had sat back on his butt, too groggy and in too much pain to attack further. Just then Grover smiled as though he'd found what he was looking for. The smile didn't last long.

Moving behind him, Tina had picked up the crowbar in both hands and brought it down squarely on the top of his skull. His eyes flared in pain and he fell forward on his face. That motion caused the back of his shirt to rise up, exposing the .38 pistol in his waistband he had reached for just seconds earlier. Streeter, whose arm throbbed wildly in pain, saw the gun and managed to grab it. Grover suddenly reared up to his knees and leaned back, staring at him. He winced in concentration and pushed himself to his feet. That's when he looked down and saw that the other man now had his gun. Streeter had begun to aim it at Grover when another spasm of pain shot out from his wrist and up his arm. This one was so intense that he blacked out for several seconds. When he came to, he saw Royals moving toward the door leading to the hallway. Before Streeter could move, another jolt of pain in his forearm left him dizzy. By the time that one had passed, Grover was gone.

Streeter managed to get to his feet. Tina was standing off to his left, still holding the crowbar. She was too upset to speak and he was in too much pain. Slowly, he moved out into the hallway. It was empty. He walked toward the loading dock and got there in time to hear the squeal of tires pulling out of the alley next to the building. When he turned around, he could see that Tina had followed him. He held up his left hand, with the pinkie finger twitching and the wrist twisted. "He broke my arm. Better get me to a hospital before I pass out."

Dexter Calley was sitting in his pickup truck on Market Street just around the corner from the waterbed store, watching Marty's car and debating whether or not to talk to the man when he left for the night. His pot high was sliding and he thought of how Marty had warned him repeatedly against any meetings. "You and me get seen together in public, I'm screwed," the old man had said over the phone. "That can never happen, son."

As he sat there thinking, he was surprised to see Grover's red 1967 Mustang convertible move out of the back alley and onto Market. The alley entrance opened up right behind where Marty's car sat. Dexter watched as Grover moved quickly into the street, only to have his engine die. The Mustang lunged forward once and stopped. What the hell? From about thirty feet away, Dexter squinted into the nearly dark street. He thought he saw Grover shake his head. Is he drunk? What was he doing with Marty? Suddenly, Grover started the engine again and turned left, off toward Speer Boulevard. Dexter quickly started his engine and moved out to follow him. Something was wrong with the big man.

It wasn't easy, but Grover negotiated his Mustang into the

traffic on Speer. Have to make it home, he kept telling himself as he rolled over the Valley Highway on the Speer viaduct. About every fifteen seconds he'd swipe at his eyes with his left hand as blood from a deep cut on the top of his head swept over his face. He could taste it in his mouth, see it in his eyes, and feel it all on his shirtfront. Blinking to concentrate, he tromped on the accelerator. Once over the bridge, he glanced at his rearview mirror. The pickup truck following him about two car lengths back looked familiar but he couldn't quite place it. Damn, the driver looked familiar, too, he thought as he wiped once more at the blood.

As he approached the first intersection on the other side of the bridge, he was looking into the rearview mirror more than he was looking out the windshield. He kept wiping the blood from his eyes and frowning at the mirror. What the hell was Dexter Calley doing following him? Grover shook his head in rage and pressed harder on the accelerator. Had to get home. Get away from Calley. By the time Grover got to the intersection, between the blood in his eyes and his fixation on Dexter, he didn't even see the red light he was facing. Entering the intersection, Grover's speedometer registered sixty. And climbing. He ran his hand over his face one more time. No way he saw the bus coming from the right. But later, when the police inspected the Mustang and pulled his crushed body off the steering wheel, the speedometer was stuck on sixty-eight. At that speed, Grover probably didn't feel a thing when he rammed the bus.

Dexter couldn't believe how fast Grover was pulling away from him and flying into the intersection against the light. Jesus, he thought. Damned steering wheel must have gone all the way through the big man. Dexter slammed on his brakes, watched until both the Mustang and the bus had stopped, then made a quick U-turn over the safety island. He was absolutely stunned as he headed up Speer Boulevard and back toward downtown.

Tina called 911 and the medics came and got both Marty and Streeter to St. Joseph's Hospital. Denver General Hospital was much closer, but too many people came out of that place in worse condition than when they went in. Streeter had a heavy, dull ache in his left arm and his head was pounding from Grover's punches. But the ER doctor quickly set his broken ulna—which wasn't as badly damaged as he originally feared—and gave him some painkillers for his headache. Within an hour, he started feeling almost human again.

That didn't last long.

Two uniformed officers—an elderly white man and a Hispanic who looked like Jimmy Smits—arrived at the hospital while Streeter was being looked at. They took Tina's statement and, just before the bounty hunter was done in the ER, they got a call from downtown. When Streeter came out, the Hispanic officer nodded for him to sit. Then he pulled out his notepad.

"How you feeling?" he asked, glancing at the cast that took up most of Streeter's forearm and wrist.

"I've been better. There must be an easier way to get Percodans."

No one laughed. For the next fifteen minutes, Streeter walked them through his recollection of what happened at the store. As he and Tina had agreed while waiting for the medics, he didn't mention why they were meeting Marty other than a vague "We had some business papers he wanted to see." They'd deal with the rest of it the next day with Bill McLean present.

When he finished, the older cop kept his eyes welded to him. "And you say Grover was hit only once with the crowbar? By the woman?"

"That's right."

The Hispanic cop jumped back in: "And he left under his own power?"

Streeter nodded. "I think I heard him drive out of the alley, but I didn't see him. I've got his home address if you want to get someone over there to talk to him."

"That won't be necessary," the white cop said. "Grover was killed in a car accident on Speer just north of Mile Hi Stadium about an hour or so ago. From what I heard there's no way to tell how many of his injuries were due to you two and how many to an RTD bus."

Streeter couldn't just go right back to the church. He needed a few stiff hoists with bar people, so he had Tina drop him off at Gabor's on 13th. Now that Grover was dead and she was out of danger, Tina could stay at her own place. And because they'd both had their fill of the entire mess, neither one of them wanted to wait around and talk to Marty. They made sure he was all right and then left. Before walking to Tina's car, Streeter called Frank and gave him a quick summary of what had happened that night. He said he was going out for a few drinks at Gabor's and not to wait up for him. He'd catch a cab later. Streeter was in a mood so foul he didn't even care to talk to Frank for long. All he wanted to do was get loaded in a bar packed with people he didn't know and didn't want to know. Gabor's was a decent choice. He seldom socialized in that part of Capitol Hill and the crowd was young enough to leave him alone. It was dark, smoky, and the CD jukebox was turned up to a level that didn't allow any quiet contemplation.

For nearly two hours he sipped Scotch with beer chasers, ate an occasional painkiller, and debated whether to have a cigarette, something he hadn't done in years. The go-for-it side was about to carry the day when she walked up to him. Wearing bleached-out blue jeans and a black turtleneck sweater, Connie stood across his table looking down at him. He squinted through the smoke and couldn't place her at first.

She smiled broadly. "Rough night, huh?" Her voice was gentle and he struggled to hear it above the jukebox.

"Connie?" He frowned and squinted harder. "That you?"

She nodded once.

"What are you doing here?" Streeter shifted his shoulders quickly as a small wave of pain shot up from his broken arm.

"I thought maybe you'd like to see a friendly face."

He looked off, nodding and considering that. Then he glanced back up at her. "How'd you know I was here?"

"I called your place a little while ago to see about our big date and your partner Frank and I had a nice conversation. He told me a little of what happened." She took a step closer to his table. "I guess you'd just talked to him and he was pretty upset. He said you'd been in a fight and would probably be down here licking your wounds." She nodded to the cast on his arm. "How does it feel?"

He glanced down at the cast as well. "Terrible, probably. I should know more tomorrow. Tonight I'm in a self-medicating mode."

"You figure a lousy night's sleep and a horrendous hangover'll help, do you?"

Streeter shrugged. "I haven't thought things through that far yet." He pointed to the chair next to him with his good arm. "Care to join me?"

Her nose crinkled up slightly and she shook her head. "Not really. I was thinking maybe we could get out of here. My apartment's less than three blocks away. A little walk might do you good. You can tell me how you beat up the bad guys or whatever happened. I'll give you an Alka-Seltzer and then you can crash out on my couch if you'd like. We'll get you home in the morning."

He studied her face for a long time. "That's very nice of you," he finally said. He glanced at his drink and then back up at her. "I accept."

Connie held out her hand. "Let's go."

Streeter got up and dropped a few bills on the table. Then he nodded toward the front door and they left without another word.

Connie's apartment was small, tidy, and in his confused state, seemed to him to contain a large guitar collection. There must have been two dozen of them, all different sizes, colors, and shapes. He was going to comment on them, but instead he just looked around. They hadn't talked much on the way over, and as she prepared his Alka-Seltzer in the kitchen, he knew he was too tired and groggy to explain what had happened that night. He was having a hard time remembering. She walked back into the living room, where he was standing, and handed him a glass that was still fizzing from the Alka-Seltzer. He studied it for a moment. Then he downed the whole thing in one shot.

"Good boy," she said, her voice friendly. He just nodded and handed the glass back to her. Then Connie made up the couch with a pillow, two sheets, and a plaid blanket. Neither of them spoke as she did. When she finished, she looked at him. "The bathroom is down at the end of the hall. Let me know if you need anything." She studied him for a second, her face soft and kind. "Do you want to talk about it?"

He shrugged, his upper body moving slightly. Then he shook his head.

"Will you be all right out here? Think you'll need anything else?"

Streeter felt embarrassed at being so messed up, but he also appreciated her kindness. Not lecturing him, either. He glanced at the couch and then back to her. "This should do it. Thanks."

She took a step closer and touched him gently on the cast. "You're welcome. If you do need anything, my bedroom's next to the bathroom. Just knock." With that, she reached up and planted a soft kiss on his cheek, the same as she had done the week before at the music school. "Goodnight, Streeter."

After she left, he stripped down to his boxer shorts and socks. Then he wrestled himself under the covers. But once down there, he couldn't fall asleep. His head was pounding and his bladder was full enough to catch his attention, but not to the point where he had to go to the bathroom. And he kept thinking about how good it was to see Connie at the bar. How good it was to get out of there. She was right: a hangover wouldn't help. After about half an hour, he finally got up and went to the bathroom. When he'd finished, he walked back into the hall. He stopped in front of her door, staring at it for a minute. Soft light came out from underneath it. He reached over and knocked on it gently, not sure what he would say.

"Streeter"—her voice came from inside the bedroom—"are you all right? Come in."

He opened the door slowly and squinted into the light. Connie was leaning up against a stack of pillows and reading a book. She was wearing what looked to him like a silk nightshirt, but he could see only the top part. He frowned. "What time is it?"

"Almost midnight." She put the book in her lap. "Can't you sleep, either?"

He shook his head.

She looked down at his shorts and smiled. "Nice outfit."

Streeter, too, glanced down and remembered that he had only his boxers and socks on. Instinctively, his hands moved to cover himself. Connie shook her head, still smiling. "It's okay. After all those Calvin Klein ads, that doesn't shock me." She looked at the empty side of the bed next to her and patted it. "You can sleep in here if that'll help. Just don't get frisky. The socks have to go, but the shorts stay on."

"Thanks." He walked the few feet to the bed and, sitting at the side, laboriously removed his socks with his good hand. When he turned to face her, she had put the book down and was settling in. She had pulled a pillow from behind her and placed it in his spot. Without another word, he slid under the sheet and light-blue blanket. He could feel her warmth next to him and he smelled what he imagined to be the moisturizer she used. Streeter closed his eyes for a moment and tried to think of something appropriate to say. But he fell asleep so fast, he didn't even see her turn the light off.

When he woke up just before seven the next morning, it took him a few minutes to realize where he was. Then the dull throb from his left arm and the soreness around his mouth brought everything back. He was alone but he could hear Connie moving around in the bathroom next door. The faint smell of fresh coffee came all the way from the kitchen. When he tried sitting, his equilibrium took another half a minute to catch up. Grover was dead, his arm was broken, but his hangover was barely noticeable. He'd slept in Connie's bed without either of them touching the other. As he sifted through all of it, he heard her out in the hallway.

"Are you awake yet? I'll make us some breakfast." The bedroom door opened and Connie appeared. She was wearing a tan skirt and white blouse. Ready for work, looking as fresh and friendly as he'd ever seen her.

"That sounds great," he said. "But I'll just get myself home. No need to bother with breakfast."

She smiled and shook her still-wet hair. "I guess if I looked as bad as you do, I'd want to hide out, too. Go wash up and I'll have the juice and coffee ready when you're done. There's a clean toothbrush on the sink. Aspirin, too. I'll still have time to give you a ride home before work."

He walked past her into the bathroom. Cold water, clean teeth, mouthwash, and aspirin helped put him back in the game. Standing over the toilet taking a leak, he saw something that might explain Connie's strange behavior toward him initially. There was a framed color photograph hanging on the wall in front of him. It was Connie and a man hugging. They were in the mountains and both of them were smiling, he more than she. The man's face startled him. With the exception of longer sideburns, he looked exactly like Streeter. This had to be the someone she'd said he reminded her of. Was he the one who'd ended up with her best friend? Why would she keep him hanging there? Streeter washed his hands and went to the kitchen.

He felt grubby and uncomfortable during breakfast. Sensing that, Connie was quiet, too. Streeter told her only that his injuries were related to a case he was working on that appeared to be almost completed. He'd fill her in over dinner.

"It shouldn't take long to wrap up the loose ends," he said when they'd finished breakfast. "But I think last night and this morning makes us even for my finding Lomeli. Dinner at Alfresco's is my treat."

"No way, Streeter," Connie came back. "You're not done with Mr. Lomeli and a deal's a deal. I pay but you have to serve him the papers." She glanced at his arm. "You don't need two good arms for that."

When she pulled up to the church, they said a quick goodbye. Before he got out of her car, Streeter was tempted to ask her about the man in the bathroom photo. But he was so anxious to get cleaned up as best he could with the new cast that all he said was he'd call her later.

24

Marty Moats had one tough skull, you had to give him that. The crease laced into his forehead from Grover barely registered with the old man once he came around. He was treated for a mild concussion and released from the hospital within an hour. By the time Marlene came to take him home, he was already second-guessing the doctors. First thing the next morning he was on the phone to Streeter.

"Marty called about twenty minutes ago," Frank said as his partner walked into his office just before nine. He studied the bounty hunter, cast on his left forearm, his shirt rumpled and torn, and his slacks sporting bloodstains. The left side of his face was bruised and swollen, and there were bags under his eyes. "I suppose I should get a look at the other guy before I comment on how bad you look."

Streeter stood in front of Frank's desk, not amused. "The other guy's dead."

Slowly, the bondsman nodded. "So I hear. It was in the morning papers, too, but you weren't even mentioned. They said he had a car accident. Ran flat into a bus over on Speer."

"I have no idea how that happened. When he left Marty's store he was bleeding pretty badly from where Tina cracked him with a crowbar. The cops told us about the accident over at St. Joe's later."

"Marty just said you had some problems last night but he didn't go into any details," Frank said, shaking his head. "He didn't mention that either of you were hurt and he definitely didn't say nothing about Royals. But he did say he's coming by here this afternoon to have a powwow with us. Can you be here at three?"

Streeter nodded. "I better call Bill McLean and see if he still wants to talk to the police today." He sat down and reached across the desk for Frank's phone.

McLean's secretary said he was on the other line and he'd call back as soon as he was available.

"I don't know how much Grover's dying will affect things," Streeter said after he hung up, "but I'd almost like to put off meeting with the cops. Maybe clean up and feel a little better first. But being in the position I am here, it's best that I get it over with fast." He stood and was turning to head upstairs when the phone rang.

"Bail Bonds," Frank said when he picked up the receiver. "Yeah, he's right here." He held up his hand for Streeter to wait. Then he reached out with the phone. "It's Tina Gillis."

Streeter frowned and grabbed the phone. " 'Morning. I hope you're doing better than I am." He took a shot at a smile, but couldn't make it.

"Good morning, Mr. Streeter." Tina sounded rested. "How's the arm?"

"Still broken. Have you seen Richie yet?"

"I'm heading down to the hospital now." She paused. "I just got a very strange call from Rudy Fontana. Actually, any call from Rudy tends to be strange, but this one was more so than usual. He wants to meet me for lunch. Rudy isn't usually the kind to do lunch. As a matter of fact, he doesn't do much of anything before dark. But he said he wants to talk about where we go from here, meaning how can he get his money and drugs and everything from the lockers."

"Are you going?"

"I'm meeting him at The Cherokee Grill at about noon. I picked that place because it's usually full of cops, being so close to the police station. I'll be safe there."

"Do you want me to come along?"

"I thought about it, but Rudy was insistent that we meet alone. I'll be all right. The Cherokee is too public and crowded for him to try anything. Besides, Rudy Fontana may try to talk like a hard guy and hang out with maniacs like Grover, but he's nothing more than an oversexed slacker with a big mouth. He's not the violent type. What I'd like to do is get together with you this afternoon when I'm done with him. He'll give me his conditions about how he wants to handle the transaction, I'll tell him I need time to think about it, and then we can discuss it later."

Streeter glanced around with the receiver against his head. "Sounds good. I'm meeting with Marty and Frank here at the church at three. We can all kick it around then."

"This changes things. Now that it's just Rudy's money we've got, I'm half tempted to keep it. What's *he* going to do?"

"Say you're joking. You've got to make this right and get out."

"I know. It's just that Rudy'll be a lot easier to handle." There was a pause. "I never thought I'd be glad to see someone die, but I can't say I lost any sleep last night."

Streeter knew how she felt. Royals's death did make the world a slightly better place. "Find out what Fontana wants and we'll take it from there. See you at three."

Frank took the phone back and hung it up. "I take it she'll be joining us later."

"Right. She's meeting her old boss for lunch and he'll be laying down his terms for getting his money back."

Once again Streeter turned to leave, and once again the phone rang and he stopped. Frank picked it up. "Bail Bonds." A pause. "Hey, Billy. How you doing?" Another pause. "That's good. Sure. He's right here. He looks like dogshit. Feels like it too, but he's still standing."

Streeter again took the phone from his partner. " 'Morning, William."

"Good morning, Street. I can't imagine why you'd feel bad on such a wonderful morning. The sky is blue, spring is here, the birds are singing, and Grover Royals is dead. Don't you read the papers?"

"I don't have to. I was about the last person to see him alive. That was right after he busted my arm." Streeter went on to tell McLean what had happened the night before.

"Man, that's quite a story," Bill said when Streeter'd finished. "But life is for the living and your living should go easier from now on. I just got off the phone with a Sergeant Haney of the Denver PD. He was working with the Englewood police on that shooting last week when Richie Moats was ambushed. Haney's also been into Grover's face for some time now about prostitution, drug running—you name it. Anyhow, now that Grover's dead, Haney's lost a lot of interest in the matter. It also seems that most of that big exposé the TV stations were running lately about Richie and Grover being hooked up together isn't checking out very well. The whole story's unraveling, for obvious reasons. Where the hell do those reporters get their material? So the bottom line is that about ninety-five percent of Haney's interest died with Royals. He was the one they were all after.

"One other thing. That Sid What's-his-name—the one who shot himself when they ambushed Moats—well, he's worse off than they thought. He's still in a coma and it looks like he may die soon. The Englewood cops are still looking into that whole mess, but I think we should lie low for a while and see how they make out. There's nothing pointing to you, and if Wahl dies, there never will be. I say we just ride it out for the time being. Maybe I'll give Englewood a call in a couple of days."

"That's fine with me. Give me a holler if you hear anything, okay?"

"Will do. And take a rest, Street. Keep a low profile. Promise me?"

"I'll do the best I can."

Rudy sat at a table near the Cherokee's bar thinking that this probably was the best day of his life. Grover gone forever. That was a hell of a way to start out. Now meeting Tina and being this close to getting the money and all those Quaaludes. And the file copies would soon be his again, too. Life was definitely good. He didn't even have to cut Dexter in on a penny of it. Not that anyone had seen him in days. No sir, nothing would ever come back to haunt Rudy and he was now positioned to take over Grover's business interests. Damned near everything had his name on it and he didn't notice anyone lining up to claim even part of it. There still was the matter of Grover's alleged silent partner. Rudy had never seen any hard evidence of who it was. Maybe when he got the files back he could look into that some more. But for now he was in such a good mood that he didn't want to think about it. He even figured he'd make it easy on Tina. Maybe offer her her old job back. Lord knows he could use her now more than ever.

Speaking of which, he looked through the crowded room and saw Ms. Gillis herself walking toward him. She was wearing a black skirt and a white sweater. Rudy had forgotten what a knockout she was. Even in the bulky sweater, he could see her breasts move like a pair of playful bobcats. And that red hair framing that drop-dead face. No wonder every man in the place shot her a glance. She'd be a hell of a piece in Fontana's eyes if it weren't for two things. One, she was only about ten times smarter than him. And, two, she'd made it clear in a thousand ways over the years that she'd rather live out her days in a Turkish prison than spend even one night in bed with Rudy.

"Tina, you look lovely as ever," he said, standing when she got to his table.

She studied him before sitting down. Same dopey slicked-over hair, same shit-eating grin about as sincere as aluminum siding. Same old Rudy. "You, too," was all she said, her face showing him nothing.

"Would you care for a drink?"

"Just iced tea."

He nodded and waved at a nearby waitress, who didn't seem to notice him. Then, turning his attention back to Tina, he said, "Terrible news about Grover."

"I can see where you'd be pretty upset. You and Royals were like brothers." She rolled her eyes. "Cut the crap, Rudy. At the very least you won't have to take his guff anymore. You probably didn't sleep last night, you were celebrating so hard."

She always did know the score with him. "Give me some credit, Tina. The man *was* my business partner for all these years."

"I read those files line by line." She leaned into the table, pulling a cigarette from her purse. "You were his front man, nothing more. You're probably in line to take over a few of his properties, but my read is that Grover had a backer. And whoever the hell that is, they'll be coming forward any day now."

Rudy took a long pull from his Jack Daniel's as the waitress finally arrived. "I'll have another one of these," he told her. "And the lady here will have an iced tea." Turning back to his guest, he felt like saying, You let me worry about that. I'm the only one who knows how everything works. I'm the only one who can keep it together. Hell, I've been keeping my own books at home for years. I even called the hospital this morning and they told me little Sid is getting worse. This is all mine now, bitch. But what he actually said was "You might be right about that. I'll just have to deal with whatever comes up."

"Look, Rudy. I'm not hungry and I have a million things to do today. Just tell me how you want to handle this and we'll take it from there."

"Fair enough." He stopped to light a cigarette. "Get me those locker keys and we're square. That gives me the money you took and the drugs. I should be able to turn a nice profit on those ludes." He paused for a moment. "How much cash are we talking about in the lockers?"

Tina returned his look. She had been thinking about this number all morning. They'd already skimmed forty thousand from the pickup money and she planned on scaring Rudy out of another piece of it. But with Grover dead, she had no leverage with Rudy. But she still needed more of the money to help her father. She planned on getting the keys from Streeter and going into the money locker one more time. Then she'd pull another thirty thousand out and adjust the ledgers accordingly. All that before turning the keys over to Rudy.

"I'm not sure I remember the exact amount anymore," she finally answered. "Something around three hundred thousand."

Rudy frowned. "That's a small load. We've done closer to four in the past."

Tina sat back and exhaled a thick plume of smoke. "We've also done closer to two in the past. Look, Rudy, all of Sid's accounting is in there. If you don't think it's right, take it up with him." She didn't speak for a moment. "You know I'm going to keep the original files. Just to cover my butt."

"Fine by me." He squinted slightly for sincerity. "We go back a long way and we know each other pretty well. I assume that little stunt you pulled with Richie was a fluke. Hell, I'm half tempted to hire you back. We're a good team. But I doubt that I could ever trust you again."

"Whatever." She glanced slowly around the room. The Cherokee was a large restaurant with big windows on the east and south. Lunch crowds were its main business and there was the usual waiting line at the front door and at the bar. Tina settled her gaze back on Rudy. "That bounty hunter Marty hired still has the keys to the locker. I'll get them today. When did you want me to hand them over?"

"The sooner the better."

"I'll call you later and we can meet at the bus station tonight." She stared at him and added, "Answer me one thing. Was that you who called Streeter and tipped him off about what Grover had in mind for me and Richie last week?"

Rudy was startled and he blushed like he always did when he was rattled. "Of course not. Grover and I were a team. Did someone actually do that?"

Tina shook her head and grinned. "I thought it was you. Thanks, Rudy."

Everyone arrived at the church closer to two-thirty than three. Their big meeting lasted all of ten minutes. Streeter and Frank sat at the desk with Marty, while Tina leaned against the credenza. The mood in the room was light if slightly strained.

"Well, son, it looks like this should about take care of things," Marty told Streeter after Tina filled them in on her meeting with Rudy. "Miss Gillis here gives that little pissant a call and meets him at the bus station tonight. You're out of it as of now."

Streeter looked at Tina. "It doesn't bother you to do this yourself?"

"No." She shook her head. "Grover was one thing, but Rudy I can handle. No point in you going down there. I'll call him when I leave here and it should only take a few minutes tonight. We'll probably be done by seven or seven-thirty. If he gives me any trouble, I'll let you know."

"How about if I meet you down there a little ahead of time? I could keep an eye on you until everything's over and he leaves."

She thought about that. Her plan was to go to the station from the church, take the extra money and fix the ledgers, then go home and call Rudy to set up a time. Having Streeter there tonight wouldn't interfere with that. "If you'd like." Tina stood up. She held out her hand and Streeter gave her the three keys. "I'll call you in a couple of hours and let you know where and when to meet me."

"So be it," Marty said as he stood up. "I wish you both luck." Then he pulled a white envelope from his back pocket and handed it to Streeter. "There's a final payment for what you've done for us, son. I put a nice bonus in there seeing as how you got your arm all broken. Thanks for a job well done. And tonight, stick around long enough to make sure this character gets the lockers open. Then your work is finished."

"That sounds about right," Streeter said as he ran a hand gently along the swollen side of his face.

"Maybe when Richie gets out of the hospital, we can all get together and have a little dinner," Marty added. "On me. I spoke to the boy on the phone today and it seems he wants to come to work for me."

Tina perked up at that one. "He did? What else did he say?"

Marty winked at her. "Seems he's interested in starting a family."

"And what did you tell him?" she pressed.

"I said I can manage to find him a place to get started in the business and earn a living wage for three. At least for now. Who knows where he could go from there?"

Tina broke into a wide grin. "I'll walk you to your car, Martin." They moved toward the door and suddenly she stopped and turned around. "Talk to you later, Mr. Streeter."

When they left, Streeter turned to Frank. "Richie and Tina heading down the aisle and him working for old Marty. It's a world gone mad."

25

Rudy was torn in half as he drove to the bus station that night. His perfect day and his perfect mood had both taken a swift kick in the teeth a couple of hours earlier. The man behind the man had called him. At least he said he was the man behind Grover. And he knew enough about everything, including Richie taking Royals's money that night in the alley, to convince Rudy that Grover's deep partner was on the line. Silent no more and looking to make things right for himself.

"If you think I'm going to let a clown like you keep everything in those lockers all by yourself, why hell, you're even dumber than everyone says you are," the man had told him. "And that don't hardly seem possible."

He then went on to dictate a meeting that night at nine o'clock. Just the two of them at a truck stop north of town. Rudy thought he remembered being at the place a few years ago but he wasn't sure. Damn, the man sounded pissed off and serious on the phone. Actually, he sounded vaguely familiar, too, although Rudy had no idea from where.

Now, as he walked up 19th toward the bus station, his thoughts turned to the business at hand. This should take only a few minutes. Tina gives him the keys and he puts the stuff from the lockers into his car. Mr. Silent Partner might know about the cash, but Rudy couldn't believe he'd have a clue about the Quaaludes. Rudy'd still make out fine on all this, and whoever was behind the voice on the phone, well, no way he could be half as bad as Grover Royals. A mean peckerhead like Grover only came along about once every fifty years or so. Rudy was certain of that. The man on the phone sounded heavy, but at least he was human.

From across the street, the bounty hunter watched Rudy walk up to the south door, stop, and glance around. Slowly, Rudy looked up and down the block, his mouth open slightly, one hand casually reaching back to scratch his butt. This has to be the guy, Streeter thought. Look at that hair. Like a flat helmet or something. At the same time, Tina approached the door from the other direction. When she got there, she and Rudy talked.

"Tina," Rudy said as he extended his hand to be shaken, "good to see you again."

She ignored the hand and reached into her purse for the keys. Glancing at Rudy's wide-flap lapels, à la *Soul Train*, and the twitchy way he carried himself, she said, "This should be the last time." Then she handed over the keys, adding, "We're being watched by a good friend of mine and we both want to go home fast. I'll keep an eye on you to make sure you get everything and then I'm out of here." She nodded to the station door. "Let's get a move on. Just go open the lockers. If it all checks out, you glance back out here and give me a wave. It'll probably take you more than one trip back to your car."

"You wanna give me a hand?"

"If you waste any more of my time with your stupid questions, Rudy, I'll call my friend over and he'll give you the back of his hand."

Rudy could see she was serious, so he just nodded and headed toward the door. Once inside the station he walked through the main lobby, which was about half full of people, and made his way to locker 112-R on the opposite wall. He spotted the two locker numbers next to it that were on the other keys. He opened 112-R. The door moved slowly like the hinges needed oiling. At first he had to squint to see what was inside. The top of a large red Igloo cooler took up most of the space.

He opened the locker to the right and saw a small stack of manila file folders along with two fat accordion folders, presumably with the money taken off Sid and Dexter. That brought a quick smile to his face.

Before he opened the third locker, he wiped away a fringe of sweat from his forehead with the back of one hand. Then he pulled at the handle to the final locker and his smile widened. It contained a cooler identical to the one in 112-R. He reached out and gingerly touched the top. He turned around and saw Tina standing where he'd left her. Rudy waved quickly, his grin still in place. Spinning around slightly to face the lockers again, he groaned. This was a lot to carry three blocks to his car. So he turned his glance back to the door to wave for Tina to come in. He'd ask her again to help him carry the stuff. But when he looked, she was gone.

Streeter took a long, hot shower the next morning. He'd slept like a dead man the night before and he wasn't quite sure if that was Connie he had dreamed about somewhere along the line. As he made his morning coffee he decided to call the music store later and set up their date. He didn't want to wait until his lesson that night and risk missing her. By the time his coffee was ready and he was walking downstairs, cup in hand, he was in a very good mood. No more dealing with Marty and his troubles. Get back to his usual business. And, finally, to Connie. As he walked into Frank's office, he was ready to devote his attention to whichever bail jumpers his partner had for him.

Frank Dazzler looked up from the morning newspaper as Streeter approached his desk. "Hey, Street. Good to see you up and around. It's not like you, sleeping past nine-thirty."

"I know. I think wrapping up that business last night left me completely relaxed and drained. I haven't slept that soundly in a long time."

Frank nodded but he seemed worried. His forehead was lined with concern and his mouth was puckered-up sour.

"Speaking of last night, what was the name of that goof you and Tina delivered the keys to downtown?"

"Rudy Fontana. A real winner, by the way. Why?"

"The Commerce City police found a guy name of Rudy Fontana shot to death in a vacant lot behind some abandoned doughnut shop up there last night. I don't suppose there could be two men by that name in a town this size."

Streeter reached out for the paper. "You're kidding! What time?"

"Paper says they found him about eleven-thirty or thereabouts. They think he'd been out there a couple of hours. Shot twice in the head." Frank handed over the *Rocky Mountain News.*

Streeter studied the article on page five. There were no photographs of Rudy or the lot in which he had been found, but the police sergeant described the slaying as "execution-style." Two slugs from a .44 Magnum in the back of the head, both at close range. The story was short and the details sketchy, and the police had no motive or suspects.

"It says here that it looked like Fontana was shot while kneeling down. His hands were tied behind him and a handkerchief was stuffed in his mouth. They don't have anything about Rudy's business connection to Grover Royals," Streeter said as he put the paper on Frank's desk. "It'll probably take a few days for them to figure that one out."

"What time did you last see him?" Dazzler asked.

"A little after seven."

"Tina mention anything to you about where he was headed from there?"

"No. And I didn't ask. We just said goodbye and that was it."

"You've got a habit lately of being around guys just before they end up dead."

"Tell me about it." Streeter sat down. "I better get together with Bill McLean one of these days and talk about that."

"Might be a good idea, although I can't see how the police

can tie you to this one in any way." Frank was rocking slightly in his big swivel chair. "And they already know about you and Grover having a run-in."

"I know that, but they still might be sniffing into it."

"Marty Moats called a while ago, all upset about the story."

Streeter looked at his partner. "He doesn't seem to me to be the type to get too sentimental over something like this."

"I know. I think he just wanted to find out what happened at the bus station. Marty was thinking how the shooting must be tied into the drugs and money Fontana was hauling around after he met you."

"Probably a fair assumption."

"Well, give Marty a call when you get a minute." Frank studied his partner. "You know, Street, no matter what happened to this guy, it's none of your business anymore. If the cops come nosing around, just tell them the truth. If not, this is all ancient history to you."

Streeter didn't seem to hear him. Instead, he picked up the paper again and reread the article. Once he'd finished, he looked back at Frank. "What did you say?"

"I *said*, this is none of your concern anymore."

"I suppose," Streeter muttered absently. "But I still might make a few calls later and see if I can find out what happened out in that field."

"I was afraid you might."

Dexter was in one hell of a mood that morning. First, Grover Royals kills himself driving home on Tuesday night. Then, the next afternoon, old Marty calls him with a job. Twenty-five thousand dollars, cash money. All he had to do was squeeze a couple into Rudy Fontana's head. It took place out in some field north of town. No hassles, and Rudy even drove himself there. Man, Dexter thought. He'd never seen anyone as shocked as Rudy was when he got out of his car and spotted Dexter and Marty coming at him. He didn't know who Rudy was more surprised to see. 'Course, when Dexter hauled out his .44 and they marched him out by the trees, he was more than surprised. Just like Rudy: crying and begging the whole time until they bound him up. Wet his pants for sure.

Whole thing took about four minutes and Dexter came away with more money than he'd seen in a long time. More to come, too. The old man said he wanted to get Dexter involved in running things from now on. He'd even let him have part ownership in some club. 'Course there still could be some more grunt work like Rudy in the next day or so, but Dexter was ready for that. Yes sir, from now on, no more hustling for nickels. Old Marty would see to that.

26

Tina wasn't sure how she felt about Rudy's murder. With Grover, it was easy to sort out. He was totally bad news and he'd killed more than once himself. That was pretty much common knowledge. Hell, he would have killed her and Streeter if the bounty hunter hadn't fought him off that night at Marty's, and he'd set up her and Richie before that. But painfully hapless and sleazy as he was, Rudy was fairly harmless. Sure, he dealt in practically every vice a person could yield to, but he never sold anything customers didn't want or couldn't get from a hundred other sources. Tina didn't make value judgments like that. And Rudy had been a more-than-all-right boss. Paid her well, never came on to her, and always respected her opinion.

Sitting at a window table in a coffee shop on West 38th, not far from her apartment, Tina thought about him as she waited for Streeter. Whoever killed him would have had to know about what he'd picked up at the bus station earlier that night. She stared into her coffee cup, frowning. With Sid and Grover out of the picture, she couldn't imagine who had the knowledge and the motive—not to mention the temperament—to kill her ex-boss. She glanced out the window and watched the late-afternoon rush of traffic picking up. It had been a nice day and the sun was still bright and warm. Just then, she was shaken from her thoughts by a voice from behind her.

"Hey Tina."

She looked up and saw the bounty hunter standing next to her table. "Hello, Mr. Streeter."

"Actually, you don't have to bother with the 'mister' part anymore."

"Okay." She studied him for a moment. His face was still swollen on the left side and he looked very troubled. "You've had a pretty rough time lately," she added, glancing at his cast.

He sat down and nodded at her. "You might say. Although not as bad as Grover and your friend Rudy. I tell you, that was about the last thing I expected to hear this morning. Him being taken out like that."

"You and me both. I've been practically paralyzed thinking about it."

"I didn't realize you two were that close."

Tina shook her head. "We weren't. He was pretty worthless and I wouldn't trust him as far as I could throw him. But I did work for the man for a lot of years. Despite all his tough talk, I never saw him hurt anyone and he treated me okay."

Streeter glanced over at the file folders on the table next to her coffee. "Are those the files? The originals?"

She nodded and, reaching out, put her right hand on top of the stack. "These are them. The one and only set, other than the copies Rudy took last night. God only knows where they are now." She paused. "When you called and asked to meet me, you weren't very clear about why you wanted these."

Streeter stirred his coffee and frowned. "Because I doubt if this thing is over yet. It seems to me that whoever killed Rudy had a lot of inside information. Fontana had other employees and normally they would be my first hunch as to who killed him. But Rudy wouldn't have any reason to fill them in on that pickup at the bus station, and there may have been another motive for killing him besides just getting the cash and those ludes." He looked at her. "You told me once that you thought the files might have referred to another partner. To a silent partner who was behind Grover and Rudy. If that's the case, that partner just might have whacked Rudy to protect himself."

Tina was frowning when he finished. "So maybe this was

about their business arrangement and Rudy having the other stuff was just part of it?"

"That's possible. Or the partner may have killed Rudy to get him out of the operation."

"But why would the partner choose to kill him now? If Rudy was a good front man for Grover, why wouldn't he be a good front man for the silent partner?"

"I haven't quite figured that one out yet." Streeter leaned back in his chair and looked out the window for a moment. When he glanced back at Tina, he seemed troubled. "But Rudy made a good front man partly because he was under the hammer all the time. Grover was around enough to keep him in line. Maybe the silent partner doesn't want to get too close to the business and he just didn't trust Rudy enough on his own without Grover around. Or maybe he tried to work out an arrangement with Rudy and they couldn't come to terms. Or the silent partner had his own ideas about who he wanted as the front man. Who knows? But the first thing I want to find out is who the hell that silent partner is."

"You're hoping that's in here?" Tina patted the files again.

"I'm hoping there's something in there I can use. Some hint as to who this guy is. What was it that got you suspicious about a partner?"

"Well, mainly, Grover's notes explaining certain things. Procedures, places. It's almost like he's filling someone in on how he worked. I can see why he was so anxious to get his hands on the originals. There's a lot of damaging information in there that leads right to Grover. But if it was just for his own information and for Rudy, why would he explain things? Supposedly both of them knew how everything worked. Hell, why would they even need ledgers at all? Theirs was a cash business almost exclusively. Sure, they'd have to put something together for the IRS. You know, to account for the money from the bars and all. But these ledgers detail drug money, the sex parties in the mountains, prostitution at the massage parlors. Everything.

There's no need for that to be down on paper unless he was reporting to someone."

Streeter thought about that. "Well, I'm going to go over all of it with Frank and see what we turn up. You never know." He paused. "If we're right about this and there was another partner, whoever it is might come after you to get these files. We should think about going to the police with them."

"I know. That's why I want you to hang on to them for safekeeping. I was going to leave them with Marty, but you'll be just as good."

"Sure. Speaking of which, he called me early this morning and now I can't find him. I've left messages with his secretary at work and with Marlene. Have you talked to him lately?"

"No. I was down at the hospital most of the morning and he wasn't there."

"I thought Richie was supposed to get out soon."

"He was. But I guess they're still afraid of an infection, so they're keeping him through the weekend."

Streeter smiled. "Listen, I have to get going. I've got a piano lesson in a while, if you can believe that." He slid the files toward himself and stood up. "I might call you later if I have any questions. If not, we can talk again in the morning. Be careful, Tina. Everything's still up in the air. And if you have an attorney, you better talk to him. I have a feeling we'll be going to the police soon."

Streeter almost ran into Connie in the parking lot in front of the music store that evening. Literally. She was leaving for the day and he was just arriving for his lesson. She started to pull out of her slot near the middle toward the front and he was thinking about Rudy's murder, not paying much attention to where he was going. He slammed on his brakes and pulled up with his front bumper just inches from her left rear quarter panel. They looked at each other for a moment in surprise. Then he backed up and she continued to pull out and swung around alongside him so their front doors on the driver's side were next to each other and about a foot apart.

"I wanted to catch you before you left," he said.

Connie nodded. She looked tired, having been at the store for the past ten hours. But she still seemed upbeat. "It's been a long day. I was headed home to take a bath and go to bed and finish my book. The one from the other night." She flashed him a smile. "How are you feeling? Is your arm hurting you?"

"Not too bad." He ran his left hand over his swollen cheek. "This feels worse, actually." He enjoyed the way the laugh lines around her eyes looked as she squinted slightly into the setting sun. And those almond eyes looked sensational. "Thanks again for Tuesday. It's good to be taken care of like that once in a while, and you came and got me at just the right time." He paused. "Look, I was going to call you today and set up our big dinner. But then something came up and I'm not sure about my schedule for the next few days."

"Now there's a shocker." Her voice stayed upbeat. "You lead a pretty crazy life, Mr. Streeter."

He shook his head. "Believe me, it's not usually anything like this. It's just that right now I'm dealing with the case that won't go away. Every time I think it's over, something weird happens and we move on to the next round. I'm not trying to put you off, Connie. Really. I'm looking forward to seeing you again, but you'll have to be patient. Is that okay?"

Her smiled eased up slightly but she nodded. "Call me when things settle down. Maybe you can tell me all about if and when we finally go out."

"When this thing finally ends, you'll be the first to know. Enjoy your book, Connie." He thought for a moment. "And when we get together, maybe you can tell me about that picture in your bathroom. The one with the good-looking guy holding you. He reminds me of someone."

She nodded but didn't say anything at first. Then, "I was afraid you'd notice the resemblance." Her voice was softer. "I keep that up there to remind me to be careful around men. Of course, with someone like you, I don't need any reminders. You've got 'stay away' written all over you." She shook her head and neither of them spoke for a long time. "Nolan," she finally said as she put her car into gear and looked ahead.

"What?" He leaned toward her out his window.

"My last name is Nolan. Seeing as how we've already slept together, I think you should know that. Just in case anyone asks." She gave him a quick wink and pulled away.

He watched her leave the lot. Streeter was in a much better mood as he walked to another session with Chopin.

When Streeter got back to the church at about eight-thirty, Frank brought them beers and they cleared off his desk. Then they emptied the files on top and placed them in three piles. One was for the accounting ledgers, which was the bulk of the material. Crude and for the most part perplexing, they consisted mostly of columns of dollar amounts for income and expenses under the headings of the businesses Grover owned. They looked loose and in some kind of code, which would substantiate Tina's theory that they were meant for someone other than Grover's accountant.

The second pile, much smaller, consisted of legal paper covered with handwritten notes from Grover, many apparently to himself. To-do lists, notes on who owed him for what. Things like that. The third pile was almost exclusively photographs of very perverse partying by mostly middle-aged white men and young women of all types. They were clearly candid shots, undoubtedly taken without the participants' knowledge or permission. Judging by the trees and open spaces seen through the windows, the setting seemed to be a large house in the mountains. Also in that third pile were several pages of notes that had been clipped to some of the photos. Those notes contained the men's names, dates, and dollar amounts. They included fairly heavy hitters in the local business and political arena. Frank and Streeter organized the three piles chronologically as best they could.

"You have any idea what we got here?" Frank asked, standing in front of the desk and looking down.

"A lot of something, I guess. Let's see if we can make any sense out of the ledgers first." Streeter picked up the top page and squinted at it. "Tina said almost everything is in Grover's handwriting. She said she had never seen most of this before she studied it down in Florida. She thought she was taking documents that Rudy had either prepared for his accountant or just things he needed for his own use. Some of them are Rudy's, but mostly it's Grover's work. It's like he needed to track every penny the businesses took in. But only some of them." He looked back at Frank. "There's nothing in here about a couple of the massage parlors he and Rudy owned. That could be for a reason or maybe he just kept those papers in another file that Tina overlooked."

It took them only about an hour to go through the ledgers. Mostly they just found numbers, with short notes in the margins. Things like "bad weather that week" or "big convention in town," apparently to explain wild fluctuations in the amounts taken in. One thing that caught Streeter's eye was a ledger with "11048 Club" written on the top. All of the other documents were for stores or parlors or bars, the names of which he recognized. But 11048 Club meant nothing to him, so he set it aside.

The second pile took a little longer, even though there were fewer documents. It consisted primarily of notes Grover had written to himself regarding personnel moves, suppliers he was dealing with for everything from towels to porno magazines to cocktail napkins, and names and addresses of customers. There were also several references to the 11048 Club. Streeter thought he was finally getting somewhere. The name "Tired" also popped up several times. "Let Tired know . . ." or "Keep Tired out . . ."

"This could be a nickname or code word for the partner," he told Frank.

"Possibly. It's a person's name, all right. Look there. What do you make of this 'MoCo'? I see it three, four times. Once it's on the same note with Tired."

Streeter straightened up and stretched his back. "It looks almost like a company name. Or a corporation. Remember what they used to call the Ford Motor Company—FoMoCo? Maybe they still do. MoCo has that same feel to it. I'll check with the Secretary of State's office in the morning and see if a MoCo is registered with them."

In the third stack they thought they found out what 11048 Club meant. It seemed to be referring to the house in the mountains where the sex parties were held. The notes attached to some of the photos had lines like "go to 11048 Club before eight on Saturday" and "get house cleaners to 11048 this week." There was a receipt for a pool service in Conifer, a small mountain town about thirty-five miles southwest of Denver.

"So they called their house the 11048 Club and it seems to be located around Conifer," Streeter said when they'd finished at a little before midnight. "My hunch is that 11048 is a street address."

"How do you track that down?" Frank drained the last of his beer and studied his partner.

"Who knows? My first move is to find out if MoCo is registered as a corporation. If it is, that should give us some names to go on. We might see if any of those names own property in Jefferson County. Conifer. I'll also check to see if Grover or Fontana owned anything up there. If we find the place, we can maybe sit on it and see if Tired shows up."

"That could be a long chore, Street. And it's not like we're getting paid for any of this."

"I know, Frank. You don't have to keep going with me here. But I've got to find out who's behind all this."

The next morning, Streeter went downtown to the office of the Secretary of State. His hunch was right. There was indeed a MoCo, a corporation that first filed its articles of incorporation in February 1983. When he pulled the microfiche for the papers, the first name he came across hit him like his piano had just landed on his head. Streeter stood there at the machine staring at the name in utter disbelief. Martin Moats: President. MoCo: Moats Company. There was no reference to Grover Royals or any of his businesses. MoCo was the corporation name that Marty used for his waterbed business and Streeter gathered that Grover used it as a reference for convenience in his notes. The bounty hunter was numb as he wrote down the names and addresses of the other company officers. This opened up a world of possibilities that left him stunned and shaken with rage. As he walked out of the building toward his car, his thoughts were in a jumble. On the one hand he couldn't believe the old man was involved with Grover in any way. The implications were too astounding and sick. On the other hand, documents don't lie and MoCo was Marty's company.

When he got back to the church he went right to Frank's office. The bondsman wasn't in, so Streeter went behind the desk and looked up the number for the Jefferson County tax assessor's office, real property department. He asked the clerk if any residential properties were listed under the ownership of a Martin Moats. Nothing. Then he asked if there was any property listed to a MoCo. As the clerk was checking, Streeter was pretty sure what he would hear.

The clerk's voice came back after about two minutes. "There is one under that name. It's located on Wagon Wheel Road. The address is 11048 Wagon Wheel. Purchased in August of 1984. Do you want the sale price?"

Streeter's mouth went completely dry. "Sure," he answered weakly. But he didn't bother to write that information down.

When he hung up he spent a long time just staring at the

wall across from him. If Marty was behind Grover and all that had happened since the robbery, could Richie have known about it? Not likely. That would mean that he was in on the attack at the warehouse where he was shot. Richie. Streeter thought of him and his relationship to his uncle. He looked down at the phone, picked it up, and called Littleton Hospital. The receptionist switched him through to Richie's room.

"Hello." The voice at the other end sounded hoarse but strong.

"Richie?"

"Yeah. Who is this?"

"Streeter. Have you seen your uncle lately?"

"No. But he called a while ago. For some reason he's still after those files. Tina told me she gave them to you yesterday. Are you about finished with them?"

Streeter ignored the question. "I understand you're going to work for Marty."

"Just as soon as I'm feeling better. They're saying now that I should be out by Monday." He paused. "That was pretty bad. Rudy getting killed. Tina and I were just talking about it."

Streeter frowned. "Have you ever heard of something called MoCo?"

There was no response at first. Then, "No. Why?"

"Can I talk to Tina?"

"Sure." There was a muffled sound as he handed the receiver to Tina.

"Hello." Her voice indicated she was in a good mood.

"Can you come over to the church?"

"When?"

"Now would be good."

"You found something, didn't you?"

"Can you come over?"

"Give me half an hour."

When he hung up, Streeter went to his loft to make coffee. He was too dazed to eat lunch, although it was almost noon.

When his cup was filled he went downstairs and was glad to see that Frank had returned.

"Hey, Street. Any luck this morning?"

"I think so. Tina Gillis is stopping by in a minute. Let's wait until she gets here and then I'll fill you both in at once." He paused. "Do you trust Marty Moats?"

Frank looked puzzled. Finally he answered, "I don't know. He'll shave the corners with the best of them and I doubt if he's ever filed an honest tax return in his life. But other than that, I suppose I'd trust him okay." He shrugged. "I never gave it much thought. Why?"

"Nothing."

Tina arrived at quarter past twelve and came back to the office. "What's up?" she asked Streeter after everyone was sitting down.

He looked at both of them. "I found out who was behind Grover, pulling most of the strings." He looked hard at Frank. "I know what and who MoCo is. Martin Moats is the man we're after. He's the president of MoCo. I figure MoCo stands for Moats Company. 'Tired' must have been Grover's snide way of referring to him."

Frank's mouth dropped and he looked down frowning. Tina just about jumped out of her chair. "I remember seeing MoCo on some of the papers."

"I took a flier with the Secretary of State this morning," Streeter explained. "It's all there in black and white in the company's articles of incorporation. Then I called the Jefferson County assessor's office and found out that MoCo owns a big house near Conifer. It's valued at almost half a million. The address is 11048 Wagon Wheel Road. Does 11048 Club ring any bells?"

She nodded but before she could speak Frank jumped in. "This can't be right. I know Marty's got a lot of scam in him, but if he's the guy behind Grover that means he set up his own nephew to be killed."

"That he did. Either he set him up or Grover was acting on his own." Streeter stood up. "But that's not likely. How would Grover even know where Richie and she"—he nodded toward Tina—"were staying? Marty was working with him all along."

"Which explains why he's been so hot to get his hands on the files," Tina said. "You know, he's still after them."

"That's what Richie told me on the phone." Streeter paused. "He wants them when I'm done."

"But what about all that other stuff," Frank said. He looked pale. "Didn't Grover burn up his trucks? And what about Marty's getting knocked out the other night."

"The trucks were nothing," Streeter answered. "Marty was bragging to me how he made out with the insurance on those. And as far as that bump on the head goes, it was just window dressing for the police if Grover had killed us. Plus, how would Grover even have known about that meeting. Tina and I sure didn't tell him."

"But Jesus, Street," Frank continued. "Killing his own nephew? The guy'd have to be some kind of monster to do that."

"True. But he tried to talk Tina and Richie out of the files first and when they wouldn't play ball he probably figured they had it coming. Marty's a bottom-line kind of a guy and even if killing them wasn't his original plan, it was his fall-back position. Keep in mind he didn't know everything that was in them but Grover must have told Marty that they could lead to him. No way he was going to take any chance of that happening."

Tina crushed her cigarette in the ashtray and leaned forward. "He never cared much for Richie, anyhow. And as far as me, Martin always thought I was trash. I wouldn't put killing us past him. But I wonder why he killed Rudy."

"Maybe he gave Marty a hard time," Streeter responded. "More likely, Marty just wanted his money and the drugs and he didn't want anyone else knowing about his involvement."

Tina stood up. "How can he run things without coming out in the open?"

"I'm not sure. He probably has someone in line to take over. Maybe he just didn't trust or like Rudy Fontana."

"There's always that long shot," Tina deadpanned.

"Makes me sick just to think about it," Frank said. "I always liked old Marty."

"He's a charmer, all right," Streeter said. "Hell, he's the Waterbed King of Colorado. But he's also a killer and he still doesn't have the files." He glanced at Tina. "He might come after you to get them. We have to figure out a way to keep him off guard and get the police on his ass. And we better do it now." Streeter paused for a moment. "I think I know someone who can help us."

27

Marty Moats tried to settle back on the recliner in his central Denver office. He sipped his bourbon, swirling the thick brown fluid in the glass in one hand as he straightened the front of his silk robe with the other. The last few weeks had been more of a strain on him than he'd realized. All that wheeling and dealing and killing had screwed up his sleep most nights lately. And now this. It had been a long time since Marty had been so preoccupied that he couldn't perform up to snuff in the bedroom. Sure, he'd been hit-and-miss with Marlene for years, but that didn't rightly count in his mind. Sex in marriage is a whole different breed of cat, he reasoned. A man's not supposed to stay hungry for the same woman after all those years. But this afternoon actually bothered him.

He glanced at the door to the bedroom. On the other side, Cheryl was getting dressed. He wondered what she made of his failure. Seventy years old or no, coming up short like that was horseshit and Marty would never get used to it. Relax, he told himself. Get those files back and he'd hit his former stride, sexwise that is. And that would happen soon, one way or another. Marty didn't care what had to be done. If Richie and Tina needed to be shot, consider it done. Whoever had the files had to be dealt with. Killed, bought off, or scared off. No problem there. Those files could still sink him, and old Marty had come too far to let that happen. Hell, he'd even let Grover smash him in the head so it would look like he was out cold for the cops that night at his store. And that turned out to be unnecessary, as the big goof botched up the hit on Streeter and Tina. But now he had Dexter on standby, waiting to do what it took to get the files back. Whatever it took.

Cheryl coughed from beyond the door and Marty glanced back in that direction. Hell, the main reason he got into business with Royals in the first place was to have access to women like Cheryl. Not much different than Rudy Fontana on that score. Just then, the bedroom door swung open and he winced as the latest *Baywatch* type appeared, damned near popping out of clothes at least one size too small. Cheryl shot Marty a grin and then studied herself in the wall mirror behind his desk.

"We'll give it another try real soon, Marty," she said, still looking at herself. "Just don't worry about it. If I had a dollar for every time that happened to a man, hell, I'd be as rich as you." Then she turned around to face him, throwing a smile. "A man like you's worth waiting for."

She walked over to him, bent down, and kissed him lightly on the cheek. "I just know you're a real animal once you get her cranked up." She winked. "Call me anytime for a rematch." Then she turned and walked toward the front door.

When she was gone, Marty again swirled his drink. First thing when Dexter starts managing the 11048, he told himself, I'll tell him to fire that bitch. No way Marty Moats would have Cheryl running telling his friends what happened just now. Or, rather, what didn't happen. Not on Marty's payroll time, thank you. Cheryl was history. Marty knew there were a thousand others to take her place.

28

Detective Bob Carey held a can of Budweiser in one hand and several photographs of the Conifer parties in the other. "Jesus, Streeter," he said, looking at the bounty hunter and Tina Gillis, both of whom were sitting on his couch. "These are pretty disgusting. All of them." He glanced back at the photos.

"What's the matter, Bob?" Streeter responded. Carey was a friend and poker-playing buddy, as well as his best contact in the Denver PD. "Haven't you ever seen five people in love before?"

Carey's frown deepened. "What the hell are these idiots thinking about? I hope that was chocolate sauce on that one broad."

He shook his head incredulously once more and then tossed the photos on the cocktail table in front of him. After taking a long pull from his beer, he looked back to his two guests. Streeter had called him shortly after lunch and they had agreed to meet at Carey's house after work at six. His eyes kept wandering over to Tina, who was looking particularly good in a short black skirt that fit her like nylons. Carey even waived his usually ironclad no-smoking rule for her and let Tina light up all she wanted to in his basement rec room.

"I tell you guys what," Carey said. He nodded to the material from Tina's files that were scattered over the table. "You've got some interesting stuff here. No doubt about that. But is it enough to get a warrant to arrest Marty Moats?" He shook his head. "No way. I mean, what do we got? Some dirty pictures. Dirty as hell, I'll grant you that. We've got Moats owning a big house up near Conifer where these pictures may or may not have been taken. We've got the word "MoCo" written on some ledgers that may or may not be connected to some alleged illegal activities done by one recently deceased piece of shit. There's nothing here, really."

Tina took a quick drag from her cigarette. "But if you could get a search warrant for Martin's office or maybe his house, you'd likely have all that cash we delivered and probably a ton of Quaaludes."

Carey shrugged. He was a big man, standing maybe three inches taller than Streeter. And he'd been with the Denver Police Department for almost twenty-five years. "Maybe, but I'd need probable cause to get a search warrant. I doubt if you have that here."

"Don't you think it's at least worth a shot?" Streeter asked. "Get it to a judge and let him decide if you have PC."

Carey looked at him long and hard. "Normally, I'd say yeah, let's roll the dice. I mean, everyone knew what a asshole Grover was and if we got a shot at who was behind him, hell, let's go get the guy. Not to mention that whoever it is might have killed that little pervert Fontana. But this is Marty Moats. This guy has juice everywhere. He contributes to every police benefit and I even know for a fact he golfs with the chief. I'm not saying Moats's got him on the payroll or anything, but let's just say there'd be a much higher standard of evidence for old Marty. Now, maybe if we take some time and build on this and dig into it for a while . . ."

"We may not have time," Streeter said. "What if he thinks Tina's holding out on him? He could come after her right now."

Carey raised his eyebrows for a second. "I see what you mean. Have you talked to the nephew about all this? What's the kid's name?"

"Richard," Tina answered. "No. He doesn't have a clue about it and I want it to stay that way. If I told him he'd confront Martin with it."

"Which might not be a bad idea," Streeter interjected. "I don't mean the part about telling Richie, but maybe we could rattle his uncle if we confronted him."

Tina and Carey both looked at him. "What are you talking about?" the detective asked.

"Maybe I can get Marty to cop to some of it if I meet with him and throw this in his face. I could rig up a wire and get something on tape. I think he half trusts me and if I make it sound like I'm shaking him down for hush money he might say something we could use against him."

"That sure wouldn't hurt," Carey said. "You'd be willing to do that?"

Streeter nodded. "This guy's been using me all along to get to Richie and Tina for the files. I wouldn't mind giving him a taste of his own medicine. Plus, if it helps put him on the hot seat for what he's done, sure I'll do it. We could set it up so he couldn't come after me right away. Somewhere in public. I could tell him that Tina gave the only copy to me and if he wants it back it'll cost him. That way, he'd lay off of you," he added, looking at Tina. "If I do it right, he might say something damaging."

"What if he doesn't bite and instead comes after you later?" she asked. "Martin is no fool. He might pretend he has no idea what you're talking about and then hit you when you're not expecting it."

"The lady's got a point, Street," Carey said. "This could get dangerous."

The bounty hunter glanced at his broken wrist. "Could get dangerous? What's it been up until now? We've got two people dead and two in the hospital, with Sid Wahl not looking at all well. Tina and I have been attacked and I got this little memento. It can't get much worse. Besides, if I press him hard for a quick answer, he'll bite. Marty's almost got all he's after. Being this close, he'll want to end it fast. My hunch is he'll fall for it if I approach him the right way."

"Where would you do it?" Carey asked.

Streeter thought for a moment. "Well, the hospital Richie's at might work. It's too public for Marty to make a move on me. Not in Richie's room, though. Maybe in one of the waiting rooms or in the cafeteria downstairs. I'll walk him through what I found out about the Conifer place and MoCo." He nodded at Carey. "You could be there as a backup, Bob. He doesn't know what you look like, does he?"

"I doubt it. We've never met and I'm not what you'd call a public figure."

"Will you do it?" Streeter asked and then took a long drink from his beer.

"Why not?" Deep down, Carey had his reservations, but he didn't want to look reluctant in front of the gorgeous redhead. "It might not hurt to have a little firepower there just in case. If I can help shut down Grover's operation, it wouldn't hurt my career none, either. 'Course, if we're wrong about all this . . ." He just shook his head. "Like I said, the man has a lot of friends."

"Have you talked to Martin lately?" Tina asked Streeter.

"Not for a couple of days. But I spoke to Marlene before and she swore she'd have him call me at the church tonight."

"I want to be there when you confront him." Tina focused hard on Streeter as she spoke.

His face soured and he shook his head. "No way. There's no need for it—plus, how can I tell him that you and Richie are out of the way if you're standing right there. He has to think this is strictly between me and him or it defeats the whole purpose."

"He's right, Tina." Carey finished his beer. "No point taking any chances on you getting hurt. Streeter has to do this on his own or Moats won't bite." Turning to his friend, he added, "Get yourself home now and wait for him. When he calls set it up for real soon. Tomorrow would work best. The hospital has a lot of visitors on Saturdays. Plus, that way there'll be less chance that I come to my senses and call it off."

Frank wasn't home when Streeter got back to the church, so he waited in the first-floor office by himself. It was almost ten when Marty called. He sounded tired but in a good mood.

"Marlene here says you wanted to talk to me, Streeter. What's up?"

"Nothing, really." His voice was calm but firm. "What do you make of our friend Rudy Fontana getting killed like that?"

"Can't say that I think much about it one way or another." His voice hardened slightly.

"Listen, Marty. I went over those files from Rudy's office. There were a couple of things in them that I'd like to discuss with you a little further. No big deal. I just had a quick question or two."

"Richie told me that you were going to give the originals back to him and then he'd give them to me for a glance of my own."

"So I understand. But like I said, I had a couple of questions before I give them back."

"Not much I can help you with there, son. I haven't even seen them."

"I know. It'll just take few minutes and then they're all yours. I did a little digging into something called MoCo. Found out all about it. Seems we might have an issue over money to discuss, too."

Marty was silent for a long moment. "You learned about MoCo, huh? And you have the originals? Tina doesn't have any other copies?"

"No. Tina and Richie are out of this. She gave me the originals and I know she doesn't have any questions about them. As far as Tina and Richie are concerned, this is all ancient history."

"When did you figure on getting together?"

"How about tomorrow? Are you going over to the hospital?"

"I was planning on it. About noon or thereabouts."

"Good. Do they have a visitors' lounge on his floor?"

"They do. Third floor, south."

"Meet me there at eleven-thirty," Streeter said. "Just you and just me."

"I don't know what all this secretive horseshit is, son, and I can't think of a thing I can help you with." Marty paused again. "But I don't suppose it'll hurt to talk about it. Just make sure to bring the files."

"I'll do that, Marty. You can count on it. You'll have them in your hand by noon."

When Streeter hung up, he sat at Frank's desk, nursing a Johnnie Walker Red. Then he picked up the phone and called Bob Carey. "It's on for tomorrow, Robert. Third floor south at Littleton Hospital. Eleven-thirty. You okay with that?"

"We're there."

Streeter could tell his friend had had a few more beers after he and Tina had left. "I'll call you in the morning but plan on meeting me in the third-floor visitors' lounge. South. And take it easy on the brews, okay? I want you sharp in the morning."

"Not to worry. We'll nail 'em."

Streeter finished his drink and headed up to his loft. A little piano practice would calm him down and help him concentrate on what he'd have to do the next morning. But once he got to his loft, he couldn't focus on music. He thought about the next day and old Marty Moats. Streeter was just starting to like the guy and now this. Frank was right. Setting up his own nephew like that was beyond bad. All that cornpone folksy charm he used in his waterbed commercials made it seem even worse. And what about Marlene? She was supposed to be a good woman. Did she know the kind of man she was married to? Nothing about this case surprised Streeter anymore.

Then his thoughts turned to Connie. Bad timing there, so far. Ever since he'd really started talking to her, he'd been bogged down in this Moats fiasco. Couldn't concentrate on her. He remembered how lonely he'd felt that first night in Mazatlán. What would it be like to take her there for a vacation? The moon, the beach, the soft night air. And Connie in his room. This time he wouldn't just fall asleep. He had to grin at the thought of their "night" together. She'd looked so warm and friendly reading her book. She'd smelled vaguely of coconut, probably from her facial oil. But Scotch, beer, and painkillers kept him from exploring that. Of course, he probably wouldn't have been invited into her room if he hadn't been such a mess.

What did she mean when she said he had "stay away" written all over him? Maybe that was what Frank was talking about when he said that Streeter panicked every time a woman wanted to get close. But wasn't that what he wanted most of all? A woman like Connie close to him? Streeter looked at the keyboard and shook his head. Too much to think about for tonight. Just get some sleep and deal with one thing at a time. First, Marty Moats. Then Connie Nolan.

Dexter Calley leaned into the open refrigerator looking for the last beer. He spotted it next to an old pizza box on the bottom shelf and reached down to grab it. Closing the door with his left knee, he simultaneously opened the twist-off top to the bottle of Miller Genuine Draft. He was thinking about the conversation he'd just had with Marty Moats. The guy calls him at ten-thirty on Friday night and says to be at Littleton Hospital by eleven in the morning.

"And you better bring along some hardware, son," Moats had told him. "You won't be shooting anyone but there's this one young man we might have to show how serious we are. Streeter doesn't seem like the type to cause real trouble and he says he just wants to ask me a few questions before he hands over the files. But I got a feeling he's going to ask for something, and if push comes to shove, we might just have to persuade the big dumb fucker to our way of thinking. You know, like we agreed on when we started all this."

Dexter had told the old man that he more than likely wouldn't be doing any shooting on a busy weekend morning in a crowded suburban hospital. Not a wise policy. And he had asked why the the gun-toting part always ended up being his job. Moats didn't care much for the nature of that question. "Because," he'd answered, obviously pissed, "I say it is. You pulled the trigger on Mr. Fontana by yourself, which means you're in deep trouble if anyone ever finds out. Hell, you Indians are good at all this tracking-and-hunting nonsense. Everyone knows that. Just do what comes natural and don't be giving me any more shit about it."

Dexter was going to keep after him on the subject but he wanted a beer. So all he said was "I'll be there. Out front at eleven. You know my truck."

Standing in the kitchen now, nailing his beer, Dexter thought about how he'd hooked up with Marty when the old man called him a few weeks earlier. It seems that Moats had heard about Calley from Grover. All of it unflattering. But with relations between Royals and Moats deteriorating almost daily, Marty liked the idea of signing on someone who hated Grover. At first, Calley didn't believe that the waterbed salesman was in business with Royals. But once they got together and Marty told him a few insider secrets, he was convinced. It took less persuasion to get him to blow Rudy away. Dexter never could stand that weird asshole. Not to mention that getting half of the ludes and twenty-five large for his trouble—well, that was one sweet night. Plus, the old man was dangling one hell of an offer in front of him. Sure, the massage parlors and the porno shops were history. All that reverted to Grover and Rudy's beneficiaries. And no more drugs: the old man was a complete tight-ass on the subject. But that club he ran up near Conifer would be turned over to Dexter to operate as he saw fit. That is, provided, as Marty had put it, "You run it at a profit and keep the skimming at a tolerable level. It's a mostly cash business and I don't hire no saints. But just don't think you can screw me blind, son."

So he'd meet him at the hospital and do whatever "persuading" the old man had in mind. Hell, he'd even pull the trigger again if the situation called for that. But it wouldn't.

Suddenly, a whiny female voice called out, "Dex? You coming back to bed or am I going another round with my vibrator?"

Calley rolled his eyes and glanced toward the rear of his apartment. "Damned white people," he muttered. "They always want something."

29

When he picked up the phone at a little after nine that next morning, Detective Robert Carey was so hungover that Streeter almost called off the meeting with Marty. But Carey assured him that he'd be positioned in the third-floor lounge, in plain sight, reasonably clearheaded and armed, by no later than ten minutes after eleven. Eleven-fifteen at the absolute latest.

When Streeter walked into the room at eleven-twenty, Carey wasn't within two miles of the place.

Some fifteen minutes earlier, in the parking lot along the west side of Littleton Hospital, Dexter Calley had shown Marty Moats his .38 short-nose. Then he'd stuck it into his front pants pocket and smoothed over the bulge with his hand.

It was that kind of a morning.

Marty had taken Dexter by both shoulders as they stood next to the driver's door of the pickup. He'd stared deep into the man's eyes and spoken in his best closer's voice. "Here's the situation, son. I'm meeting this Streeter fella on the third floor in the south lounge. He should have a stack of three or four files for me. He also should be handing them over with a minimum amount of crap. Now I expect he'll try to squeeze me for a few thousand. I don't necessarily mind that. Hell, the man went through the damned things and found out about me. I don't mind rewarding enterprise like that. God knows, Richie couldn't do it if I spotted him my corporation papers.

"But here's what I need you for. First off, I want to make sure the price isn't too steep. I'd say twenty's about my ceiling.

Secondly, I want to impress upon the man that this is a one-time payment. Third, I want to know that he hasn't let anyone else in on what he found. I don't want my old friend Frank Dazzler squeezing me next week himself. Let's show Streeter that gun of yours and put it upside his head. I want the man to know we're not just fucking around here. That sound like something you can handle?"

Dexter slowly glanced at Marty's hand on his right shoulder, and over to his left shoulder, and then back at the man. Moats's breath, at this close range, smelled like stale coffee. Slowly, the Indian reached up and took the hands off his shoulders while keeping even eye contact. Then he simply nodded. "No problem." His tone of voice let Marty know he meant it. "What if he's not alone? What if he told someone already?"

"Well now, I suppose that's always a possibility, son." Marty took a step back. "You see any police, it's all off. Just give me a sign and get out of there. I'll deal with him later."

Streeter glanced at the clock on the wall above the television set. Eleven-twenty-eight. Still no Carey in sight. The visitors' lounge was small and quiet. On the couch in one corner sat an elderly man in his bathrobe and pajamas talking softly to a middle-aged woman and a boy who looked to be about fourteen. A young couple, not talking, stood near the large entryway. They seemed to waiting for someone. There was a baseball game on the TV but the sound was turned off. Streeter held the files in his left hand and scratched idly around his cast on that arm. Down the hall he saw a large, dark man with a thick ponytail, wearing dress slacks and a white T-shirt, approaching. His shirt was packed so tight with muscles that Streeter pegged him for an athlete. The man walked into the room without even noticing Streeter and sat in a chair facing the television, his eyes glued immediately to the ballgame.

Streeter looked up at the clock again. Eleven-thirty-two and no Carey or Marty Moats. He walked out into the hall and looked both ways. Then he moved back into the lounge. He wore a loose plaid lumberjack shirt, unbuttoned, with a black T-shirt underneath. There was a small tape recorder in his back pocket with the mike line running up his left side against his skin and out the T-shirt arm, down his left arm and under the cast. The tiny microphone itself was sticking out the top of the cast, no more than a quarter of an inch, and resting in his palm. It would pick up anything said within five to eight feet. He shifted the files to his right hand and glanced at the baseball game. One more look at the clock. Eleven-thirty-five.

Suddenly there was a tap on his right shoulder. Streeter spun around to see Marty Moats standing off to his side and slightly behind him, smiling calmly.

"You seem a little spooked, son," Marty said quietly. "It's just me."

"I was wondering if you were going to show up," Streeter said. He glanced around the room and noticed that the young couple had left and that the three people from the couch were now standing. And still, no Carey.

Marty nodded toward Streeter's right hand. "I see you brought the package. You want to give it over now?"

Streeter studied Marty's face, which was frozen in a tiny smile. The man who had probably had Rudy Fontana murdered and was willing to kill his own nephew and Tina. Here he was within inches of the files. Calm and charming as if he were peddling a bedroom set. "In a minute," Streeter said. "I think we should discuss the terms first. You know, I was pretty surprised when I found out about you and Grover."

Marty frowned. "We're not here to discuss that, Streeter. We're here to get those papers into my hands and to make you go away." He glanced toward the door to the stairwell and then back. "I tell you what. Why don't you and me step outside where it's a mite more private and take care of everything?"

Streeter shot a quick look at the door. "We're okay right out here." He scanned the room and saw that the three people on the couch were leaving. The muscle man was now watching him and Marty. "This is private enough."

"And I say this here conversation doesn't go any further unless we have some privacy." Marty nodded toward Dexter, who stood up and walked casually their way. When he got to them, Marty added, "This here's a friend of mine. I think he'd like to join us out there in the stairwell."

With that, Dexter raised his eyebrows for a second and pulled the top of his .38 from his pocket. Streeter glanced down at it and then looked at Marty. "I thought I said you should come alone."

"That's what you said, but I brought Dexter here to help me emphasize my bargaining position." He nodded toward the side door again. "Let's step out there quietly and talk. Given what's happened in the last few days, Rudy's accident and all that, I think you know we mean business." There wasn't a trace of charm in his voice.

Streeter knew that without Carey in sight, he didn't have much choice in the matter. Finally, he nodded and all three men moved toward the side door. When they got there, Dexter opened the door and let the other two walk out into the stairwell. He took one more quick look around the lounge and then followed them.

As Robert Carey got into the elevator on the first floor, his head felt like it was filled with burning charcoal. Damn, why did I stay up and drink so much after Streeter and Tina left last night? Carey hadn't gotten that drunk in a long time. Just sitting there in his rec room, thinking about Tina Gillis and Marty Moats and pounding Budweisers. Barely watching the movie in his VCR. His wife, Cookie, had called down once about ten-thirty, saying she was going to bed. But Carey kept drinking and ended up sleeping on the couch right were he sat. Now he looked at his wristwatch. Almost quarter to twelve. Streeter's going to be furious. Carey wasn't paying much attention to what he was doing, so when he reached to hit the third-floor button and pushed the one for four instead, he didn't even notice.

Riding up, he moved his hand back to make sure that his service revolver was in the holster in the small of his back, under his jacket. Like he'd really need it. What was Marty going to pull in the hospital? Carey shook his head and wished Streeter had not called him the day before. The elevator stopped and he got out without checking the floor light on the panel. Once in the hallway, he asked a nurse for directions to the south waiting area. She pointed to the end of the hall to her left and he nodded, then started in that direction. As he approached the room, he could see it was empty. Streeter'd come and gone without him. Or maybe he wasn't there yet. The way his forehead was pounding, Carey didn't much care. Then he noticed that the small wooden sign on the side of the entrance read FOUR—SOUTH. His stomach did a turn as he realized his mistake. He glanced back toward the elevators way down the hall and then he looked around the room. Off to the left of the television was an open door. He squinted toward it and saw that it led to a back stairway.

Carey walked to the open door and moved through it without looking back.

Eddy Spangler walked fast as he left Richie's room. He hated hospitals. Always had. Not that he had ever been a patient in one himself, but the other times he had visited them it was to watch someone dying. Two uncles, his grandparents on both sides. His mother. His aversion was so strong that he'd waited over a week to visit Richie. He kept thinking his friend would be released soon. But when he'd called the day before, Richie had said he had to spend the weekend there for observation after his leg became infected. Eddy could put off the visit no longer. Even at that, he stayed less than half an hour.

He took a wrong turn, so he ended up approaching the south lounge rather than the elevators. As he got closer to the area, he saw Marty Moats just leaving through the side door to the stairwell. This puzzled Eddy. Where was Marty going? And who were the men with him? The big guy with the cast he could only see from behind, but the dude with the ponytail looked like a prison bully in nice slacks. At first, Eddy was tempted to let it slide and just get the hell out of there. He had enough on his mind with his recent D.U.I. and drug charges. But he had nowhere to go just then and he wanted to say howdy to the rich uncle. After all, if he had a decent spot on the payroll for Richie, maybe Marty could come up with something to get him out of that ridiculous résumé business.

The door the ponytail guy closed behind as Eddy entered the room. On the television, the Rockies were playing a day game against what appeared to be the Reds in Cincinnati. Not that Eddy cared about baseball. He stared at the screen for a moment, considering what he'd say to Marty. They'd only met a couple of times and that was over a year before. Richie had told him later that his uncle blamed Eddy for them going down the tubes on the telemarketing scheme. Maybe he should just turn around and head for the elevators. Naw, he thought. This is as good a time as any to press the old guy for a job. He took a deep breath and walked toward the side door.

Streeter went into the stairwell without looking back. The place was done up in a dull beige: the cinder-block walls, the concrete floor, even the metal-pipe guardrails. It smelled vaguely of some kind of disinfectant. When he got into the middle of the third-floor landing he turned around just in time to see the door closing behind Dexter, who pulled the short-nose pistol from his pants.

"What the hell is he going to do?" Streeter asked Marty. "Shoot me right out here?"

Marty smiled and raised his eyebrows slightly. "If you're not reasonable with us, that's exactly what he'll do. And then I'll have him go over and shoot Frank just for good measure." He nodded toward Streeter's right hand. "I'll take those now."

"I was going to give them to you anyhow," Streeter said as he reached out with the files and handed them to Marty. He looked at Dexter. "Put that away."

"Don't be stupid," Dexter answered. "Marty wasn't joking. A hospital's as good as anywhere to get shot."

"Actually, Streeter, there shouldn't be any need for violence," Marty interjected, moving farther off to the side to allow Dexter to get directly in front of the bounty hunter. "I just wanted him to come along to make a point."

"What point is that?"

"That I'm a serious man," Marty said. "That I have a very serious side to me."

Streeter lifted his cast arm slightly so the microphone would be closer to the two men in front of him. "So I gathered. Like that side of you that set up those parties at the 11048 Club in Conifer? The ones in the pictures? And I really like the side of you that arranged to have your own nephew killed by Grover's guys."

Marty nodded slightly but said nothing. Not good enough, Streeter thought. "I take it that was you who had Rudy Fontana killed the other night, too."

"We're not here to discuss your theories about that," Marty responded. "Just what will it cost me to make sure that I've heard the last of all this nonsense from you? Forever. That means you and Frank. I assume you've spoken to him."

"I didn't tell him a thing. This is just between you and me."

"And Miss Gillis? Have you told her about MoCo and the rest?"

Streeter shook his head. "Like I just said, this is strictly between you and me. By the way, how are you going to keep Grover's businesses going without coming out in the open?"

Marty ignored the question. "How much do you want, Streeter?"

"Fifty thousand. Hell, you probably took ten times that off of Rudy when you killed him."

"I have no idea what you're talking about, but I'm prepared to give you twenty. That's a one-time payment. If you try to open the negotiations again down the road, son, you'll be dealing directly with Dexter here and there won't be any money involved. Take it or leave it."

Streeter realized that Marty was too smart to admit to anything. He felt ridiculous now, standing in the stairwell, getting nothing on tape and having a gun pointed at him. No Carey and no confessions. He just wanted to leave. "You've got a deal."

"I'll have the money delivered to the church later today. This should—"

His sentence was interrupted by the loud clang of a door slamming shut above them. All three men looked up simultaneously. Then they heard what sounded like footsteps coming down the stairwell. Dexter winced and turned quickly to Marty. "Let's get the fuck out of here." He pulled his pistol toward his waist but still kept it pointed at Streeter. Marty held up his left hand for silence and listened closely.

As Carey negotiated the stairs, he looked down and saw part of Streeter below him. He stopped and strained to see if he could make out anything else. Then he noticed what appeared to be the right half of a man standing in front of Streeter, along with the lower portion of a third man, including his arm and hand. Seeing what appeared to be a pistol in the hand, Carey instinctively reached back and grabbed his service revolver.

"Streeter!" he yelled. "That you, Streeter?" He started down the stairs two steps at a time.

"Shit!" Calley rolled his eyes and stepped toward Streeter, his gun hand coming up again to where it was just inches from his face. "Shut up."

It took Carey only about half a minute to make the final turn on the half-floor landing and get a good view of what was going on below him. Directly in front of him and eight steps down stood Streeter, cast on arm, with a big Indian-looking guy holding a gun on him at close range. A step or so behind the Indian and off to his right stood Marty Moats. Carey had never seen him in person, but he thought Marty looked bigger than on television.

"Hold it right there!" Carey yelled. He squatted down slightly, his knees bending a tad, and held his revolver with both hands in the firing position. He was aiming at the Indian's head. "Denver police! Drop it!"

Everyone froze, with the three men on the landing staring up at Carey, who, in turn, had his eyes riveted on Dexter's head. No one spoke. Suddenly the door to the visitors' lounge swung open and a smiling Eddy Spangler strolled out onto the landing. The door clanked shut behind him with the noise echoing throughout the stark stairwell.

"Hey, Uncle Marty," he said cheerfully. "How are ya?" But he dropped his smile when he noticed the big muscle man who had followed Moats into the stairwell standing with the bounty hunter. That Streeter prick who had come to his office way back. The muscle man was holding a gun and Eddy felt like he was about to cry. If that wasn't confusing enough, he heard a voice from above and off to his right.

"Hold it right there!"

Eddy looked up toward the voice and saw the bottom half of a man holding yet another gun. The man squatted more and part of his face and shoulders came into view. It was a large white guy, pale as hell and sweating. He moved the gun quickly between Eddy and the big Indian. "Freeze! Everyone!"

There was another pause. Dexter was the first one to react this time. He took three quick steps back in Eddy's direction and spun around, grabbing the stunned newcomer by the back of his neck and pulling him in close. Then he shoved Eddy in front of him, between himself and the stairs where Carey was now moving slowly down. Dexter ended up with Eddy's back against his own front, the small .38 tight against Eddy's right ear.

"Hold it or I'll shoot him!" Dexter yelled at Carey.

The detective stopped, now in plain view of everyone. Streeter had instinctively taken a step forward whereas Marty had moved over slightly to the side. Poor Eddy didn't know what to make of it all. Marty was on his right. Streeter was in front of him, looking alert, and a fat cop was pointing a gun either at his head or at the head of the man behind him.

"Wha . . ." came weakly from Eddy's mouth and then he fell silent. His expression was beyond fear, sort of an exasperated resignation.

"Looks like you've got a habit of being in the wrong place at the wrong time, son," Marty said, remarkably calm given the circumstances.

"No shit," Eddy said softly.

"Drop the gun and no one has to get hurt," Carey ordered from the stairs, although his voice sounded less sure than before.

"You drop it or I'll blow this fucker's head off," Dexter responded steady and low.

"Let's all of us just calm down," Streeter said, taking another half step forward.

Dexter noticed that. "Hold it right there! The next move I see, I start shooting."

A gurgling noise came from Eddy's throat but he said nothing. He was so pale by now, he looked like he would pass out any second.

No one moved and the stairwell was dead-still. Suddenly Dexter's nose wrinkled up in disgust. He began sniffing wildly and pulled his head back several inches from Eddy. Streeter didn't get it, although he did catch the faint whiff of what smelled like a backed-up toilet. Then Dexter glanced down at where the horrible odor seemed to be originating. There was a dark, wet spot on the seat of Eddy's pants that dripped several inches down his right leg.

"Jesus Christ!" Dexter yelled, looking at the back of Eddy's head. "You did it right here?" With that he let go of his grip on the man's neck. That release allowed Eddy, who by now had passed out from fright, to drop straight down to the floor like a sack of rocks.

Dexter stared down at him in utter revulsion. In that moment, Carey took a couple of quick steps on the stairs and hollered, "Drop it now!"

Dexter recovered from his shock and looked up at Carey. Without thinking, he squeezed off a round in the detective's general direction. The slug caught Carey in the meat of his right thigh, causing him to stumble the remaining steps and land in a heap at the bottom of the stairs. Dexter again looked down at Eddy, so Streeter took the opportunity to step forward and reach over Spangler with a hard right cross to Dexter's chin. His head shot back. Streeter's fist broke the man's jaw and badly dazed him. Without hesitating, Streeter reached out with his left arm, cast and all, and grabbed at Calley's gun hand. Dexter shook his head to focus, but before he could, Streeter drove his right fist into the middle of his face, this time flattening his nose and sending a surge of blood out one side. Streeter kept coming, holding the gun hand down. Calley squeezed off another round, but it ricocheted harmlessly off the floor. The bounty hunter shoved him hard against the door behind him, bringing his knee up deep into Dexter's crotch. That was the final blow. Dexter crumpled downward, curling up in pain as he did.

The gun dropped from his hand as he hit the ground. Streeter quickly picked it up. Then he spun around and looked at Carey. "You okay?"

Carey nodded, studying his leg. "Call for help."

Before he could do that, Streeter saw Marty turn around and move toward the stairs leading down to the second floor. Streeter followed him and caught him by the back of the neck before he got halfway down the flight. He was surprised at how thick it felt. If Marty had been fifteen or twenty years younger he would have been able to put up a hell of a fight. But he was seventy and he stopped the minute Streeter grabbed him.

"Take it easy, son," he said as they headed back up the stairs together. "Might be we can still work something out here."

Streeter ignored him. Once they returned to the landing where the others were, he opened the door to the lounge. The gunfire had drawn a crowd, including two perplexed-looking doctors in surgical scrubs.

"There's a man been shot out here," Streeter told them. Then he paused and let a smile work across his mouth. "And there's been an accident. Better bring a bedpan and some towels. Lots of towels."

As the doctors walked past them he let go of Marty's neck. The old man turned to face him and Streeter shook his head. "You were going to kill your own nephew."

"I never cared much for the boy, myself." Marty shrugged. "Richie was always Marlene's favorite. You know how women are."

30

When he was finally finished with the police that afternoon, Streeter tried several times to get hold of Connie. He didn't get back to the church until almost five, when he called her and left a message. Then he went upstairs and washed himself before calling again later. Again, no answer. He tried once more after another half an hour. Still no Connie. The incident at the hospital was the lead story on the local TV news, although no one had any notion of how Marty figured in with Grover. The police would be sorting that one out for days, but for openers, Marty faced conspiracy to commit murder, obstructing justice, and assault on a police officer.

Detective Robert Carey came off looking like a hero, although when Streeter left him at the hospital he wasn't sure which hurt more, his hangover or his leg. Dexter Calley was facing attempted murder right out of the blocks for shooting Carey, with more to come later.

As for Streeter, the story the media got from the police department made Carey sound more pivotal in the arrests. Streeter came off as a victim who got caught in the middle, with his old poker-playing buddy from the DPD pulling him out of a jam. It sounded as though Streeter just held Dexter Calley down until the authorities stepped in and made the arrests.

At about nine, after an hour of wrestling with Chopin, he debated whether to call Connie again, but decided against it. Three messages, two with him leaving his number, were enough. He briefly wondered why she hadn't called back, but he was so tired he just crawled into bed shortly before ten and dropped off immediately.

Both papers the next morning contained several stories on Marty Moats and what had happened at the hospital. There was little new in terms of police developments, but they each carried large features on the downfall of the Waterbed King of Colorado, with long stories profiling Marty. Streeter felt bad for Marlene and he knew Richie was going through some serious pain over what his uncle had planned for him. But to Streeter, that was already yesterday's news and he'd be glad when the media attention disappeared. When he finished his breakfast and the morning papers, he heard Frank yell up the stairs to the loft. There was a phone call for him on the office line, so he grabbed his coffee cup and headed downstairs. It was Tina Gillis.

"How are you doing today, Streeter?" she asked. "I called Detective Carey before to thank him for his help and it seems you did more than you got credit for in the news."

"About all I did was punch a guy a couple of times."

"Carey said you saved his life."

"Maybe. Of course, if I hadn't asked him to be there in the first place, it wouldn't have been necessary." He paused. "How are Richie and Marlene holding up?"

"Richard's okay but Marlene took it hard. Martin might be a shit, but he was her shit and I gather that he treated her pretty well. This probably means the end of the Moats family's waterbed business. Marlene's too old to work at it and she has no interest in it, anyhow. And Richie doesn't want to keep it going, either. The plan is that he'll help her sell off everything, get a slice of the profits, and then we're leaving Colorado."

"Really? Where to?"

"Back to Florida. Richie liked it there, except for the trailer-park part. We're going to do what we planned all along. My father owns a little business down there and we're going to help him out with it." She paused. "Near the water, but not the waterbeds. Tell me one thing. What did Eddy Spangler have to do with all that yesterday? It said in the papers that he was there, but they weren't too clear on exactly what he did."

"Eddy was instrumental in ending the standoff." He smiled at the thought. "Somehow he stumbled into the middle of everything and thanks to his quick action, we were able to break up the stalemate."

"Eddy? Quick action? Will wonders never cease?"

"Well, it wasn't exactly a voluntary action, but it moved the negotiations along."

"Whatever that means. Anyhow, thanks for everything. I'd hate to think of what might have happened if you hadn't found out about Marty's involvement in Grover's business. Take care, Streeter. And if you ever get down to Naples, give us a call."

"I'll do that. Goodbye, Tina."

Frank was watching him when he hung up. "I still can't get over Marty," he said sadly. "If he'd gotten you killed, he'd a had to answer to me."

"That's very comforting, Frank." Streeter was about to say something else when the phone rang. He picked up the receiver and immediately recognized Connie's voice.

"Well, well, Mr. Streeter. I got back from Vail this morning and what do I see in the papers? You punching the bad guys out. Just another day at the office?"

"Not really. Finding the Ernie Lomelis of the world is more my usual speed."

She didn't say anything at first and when she did talk again, her voice was more serious. "Are you all right? It sounds like that must have been pretty intense."

"Guns always make me nervous, but it was over in a second. I didn't have time to get scared and no one shot at me, anyhow. In fact, I slept like a rock last night and I feel great today."

"I take it this was that case you were working on that wouldn't end."

"That it was. But now it's really, really all over."

Her voice perked up again. "Does that mean we finally get to have our dinner together? I have work for you. Mr. Lomeli still has to be served."

"Dinner and dessert if you're going to throw Lomeli at me again," he said.

"Fair enough. Alfresco's tonight at seven?"

"Sounds good."

"And for your information, Streeter, I finally took down that old picture on my bathroom wall. The one with the guy who reminds you of someone."

He thought about that for a moment. "Good. And I'll try to leave my 'stay away' sign at home."

"Now *that* I'd like to see. You're more guarded than you probably realize."

"So I've been told. You live long enough, you get your share of scars. Believe me, this broken arm's nothing compared to what I've felt from women."

"We all have some scars, Mr. Streeter." Her voice was upbeat but thoughtful. "That goes with the territory."

Streeter nodded, the phone propped under his ear, but said nothing.

"I bet that you're real good at the hearts-and-flowers side of a relationship, but when the heat starts to drop, you don't know what to do. That's when you panic. It's part of your appeal. Women see you as a challenge, like they'll be the one who finally changes all that." She paused. "Am I right about any of this?"

"You're not completely wrong," he answered.

"You have this way of looking at a woman that says you really like her but you're afraid of her at the same time. That's what I felt from you that day at Alfalfa's. It's very compelling but very confusing."

"You got all of this just from our couple of meetings and from the look in my eyes?"

Connie laughed lightly. "That, and I took Frank out for a couple of drinks Friday night. He told me all about you. That's one very terrific partner you've got there. He cares a lot about you, too."

"You took Frank for drinks to find out about me?" He shot his partner a glance and then said back into the phone, "Aren't you a clever little thing."

"That's right. I like to know about the men I've slept with, Streeter." She let out another short laugh. "Now I just have to figure out why I'm so interested. Maybe you can help me with that one at dinner. See you at seven."

When he hung up, Streeter again looked over at Frank, who was reading the Sunday paper across the desk from him. "You went out for drinks with Connie Nolan on Friday night?"

Frank looked up, his eyes wide with a fake "who, me?" innocence. "So?"

"And you told her about my ridiculous history with women?"

"It may have come up. That's a very persistent young lady. My hunch is if you two hit it off, she'll be around for a while."

Streeter didn't know what to think. "You feel okay about that? Talking behind my back? You gave her a hell of an advantage, you know."

"So what? I get a nice feeling from this woman. She might be good for you. I won't be around forever to take care of you, and look how you've been complaining lately about not having a lady in your life. Lord knows if I wait for you to get off your ass you'll be in a walker by the time you find one. A couple of dates with this Connie, you'll be thanking me for the help. Trust me on that."

Streeter tried to keep a stern expression but he couldn't. He was flattered that Connie had taken the time to work Frank and that his partner had cared enough to respond. "You could be right about that. Just do me one favor, okay? Never tell a woman I'm afraid of her again. Even if it's true."